THE BEST AUSTRALIAN

STORIES

20

THE BEST AUSTRALIAN STORIES

2016

EDITED BY CHARLOTTE WOOD

Published by Black Inc.,
an imprint of Schwartz Publishing Pty Ltd
Level 1, 221 Drummond Street
Carlton VIC 3053, Australia
enquiries@blackincbooks.com
www.blackincbooks.com

ISBN 9781863958868 (paperback)
ISBN 9781925435337 (ebook)

Cover design by Peter Long
Typesetting by Duncan Blachford

Printed in Australia by McPherson's Printing Group.

Contents

Introduction

Charlotte Wood

Like many writers, I keep a collection of talismanic, consoling or provocative quotations from other artists close to hand. Lately these seem to be coming from painters more than writers – like the American abstractionist Laurie Fendrich, who says the notion that abstraction is always about self-expression is both romantic and narcissistic. Abstraction can also be about ideas, she says: 'The complex struggle between order and chaos, for example, or how the flux of the organic world modifies the rigor of geometry.'

Something else Fendrich wrote struck me with great force: 'Ever since the invention of painting on canvas, paint itself has been part of the meaning of a painting.' She was lamenting the pressure on young painters to offer explanations about the intentions behind their work, sometimes even before they had made it. But meaning comes, Fendrich asserts, not just from the artist's internal process, but from the actual application of the *paint.*

For me, this concept may also offer the best explanation for what gives life to a piece of writing: meaning is generated in the application of language itself, rather than purely from the writer's desires or intentions.

While I believe this truth is present in any writing that pulses with brightness and energy, no matter how inexperienced the writer, perhaps the mature artist is best placed to articulate it.

The novelist Lloyd Jones, for example, has often quoted Samuel Beckett saying of James Joyce that the latter's writing 'is not about something, it is that something itself'. When I asked Jones to elaborate in a *Writer's Room* interview, he said:

> Yes. He's not writing *about* something – 'about' suggests an object. In other words, it thrusts you into the task of describing something that's already there. But the something is emerging from the actual writing. So it's not starting with any objective in mind, but an objective actually results from the act of writing. It's a subtle distinction.

Michelle Orange also expresses this distinction in the *New Yorker* when she says, in relation to Vivian Gornick's *The Odd Woman and the City*, 'Gornick's voice ... does not just tell the story, it *is* the story.'

The paint itself is part of the painting's meaning; the words do not merely tell, but are the story.

I think an acceptance of this might result in what novelist Amanda Lohrey says she demands of any book: the presence of 'messages from another realm'.

'There's the literal surface of life,' Lohrey told me, 'and then there's that oceanic meaning underneath ... any narrative that doesn't have a few messages from that realm is, for me, deficient. Too mastered, too known, too literal.'

I've slowly come to realise that, for me, this sense of meaning arising from the words as they are placed, this 'message from another realm' that arrives in the act of writing, is what distinguishes art from mere storytelling. And at the end of the selection process for this anthology, I can see that it's this sense more than anything else that has guided my choice of stories. (The title of this collection, by the way, must surely be a headache for every editor. The idea that one could choose the 'best' twenty from the hundreds of submitted stories – or even that there's such a thing as 'best' in the first place – feels nonsensical to me.)

If anything unifies the stories in this collection, it might be my own preoccupation, which emerged as I read, with what I came to think of as the trio of ghosts, monsters and visitations.

The presence of these in some stories will be clear from the outset, as in Paddy O'Reilly's magnificent 'Monster Diary'. Or they might be buried a little deeper, rising up, say, from the ominous line of graffiti in Kate Ryan's 'Where Her Sisters Live', or from the sudden clarifying mirror-glimpse of the narrator and her friends offered in Tegan Bennett Daylight's 'Animals of the Savannah'. Other visitations – perhaps benign, perhaps monstrous – come from the natural world, in stories by Gregory Day, Ellen van Neerven, Michelle Wright and Fiona McFarlane.

Sometimes they come from the inner self, such as the hovering spectre of suicide for Elizabeth Harrower's protagonist, or death's aftermath in the stories by Trevor Shearston, Georgia Blain and David Brooks. In these – and Nasrin Mahoutchi's 'Standing in the Cold' – the space between the living and the dead is never straightforward, and never quite breached.

Some threats are delivered from the realist realm of looming economic and class despair, as in the stories of Jack Latimore and Jennifer Down, or they might come from the future, as they do in the 'glimpse [of] the possibility of other lives, as yet unknown' in James Bradley's and Elizabeth Tan's poetic speculative visions.

Another aura, or sense of mystery, is created by formal experimentation and semantic playfulness – the paint itself being part of the meaning – in the pieces from Brian Castro, Julie Koh and Michael McGirr. Finally, there is the simple, yet hard-won, joy of acceptance in Abigail Ulman's story, when a mother learns that attachment to one child can only come from allowing another to become a ghost.

Every editor of this collection has faced the inevitable agony of choice and omission, and I was sorry not to be able to include at least another five, if not ten, stories I very much admired. I hope you enjoy the pieces I have chosen, and the ways they continue to echo within and speak to one another.

Monster Diary

Paddy O'Reilly

A monster is something too big or too small, too dark or too light, too much of one thing or not enough of another. It is ugly and its ugliness makes people turn away. A monster is unable to speak like us. A monster cannot fit comfortably into a chair. It thinks about flesh and eating and pain and misery and ecstasy. It cannot articulate these needs but must enact them. Sometimes the monster does not know it is a monster. It lurches towards you expecting you to open your arms and embrace its desires, its needs, its drive.

Near my flat is a block of housing commission units. Five fibro-cement units on raised stumps with a mean three steps to the front door cluster under a copse of undersized sunburnt she-oaks whose dry needles collect in drifts around the rubbish bin enclosure. A monster lives in Unit 5. I see the lights go on in the evening behind the yellowed net curtain and the blind is pulled down immediately. No cooking smells issue from the unit. When I walk past I hear no television or radio noise. The monster is in bed by nine.

Even people who pity the monster shy away when it approaches. Do they know the monster's DNA is identical to ours? There are people in government departments whose job is to deal with the monster. In my research I've heard those people sigh and complain about the difficulty of working with monsters, the impossibility of teaching the monster and of bringing the monster into the community. They shrug, eventually, and say that their best is all they can do.

When monsters come together they recognise the other as a monster, but not themselves. This inability or unwillingness to recognise their ilk leaves them solitary. No one knows where they come from. A child monster has never been identified.

I want to befriend the monster, if that can be done. I have questions to ask, even though the monster probably cannot answer, either through inability to speak or inability to explain its own monstrousness. But surely asking the questions is important. I understand that I can never truly know the monster, but if I can only acknowledge it, perhaps touch it, offer it a peppermint sweet or lay out a bed for it, then something will change in me, I am certain.

*

The monster sits on a picnic bench under the she-oaks. She is docile. Her hair is fluffy and her nails filed. I can never predict what kind of a day she will be having, so I approach warily. Today she humps her arm over my shoulders and I lean into her warmth. Tentatively. Remembering the time she bit my ear savagely and the other time she tried to wrench my arm from my torso.

The stink from her armpit is less meaty than I had first expected. She exudes an odour of freshly sawn timber mixed with coffee grounds and fermented grain. I have thought about this odour a great deal. Is it from what she eats, or from the metabolic processes of her body? Occasionally I bring gifts of food and she has consumed everything I have brought, although it is difficult to tell whether she enjoys the food or simply consumes it because it *is* food. Her vocabulary of grunts, hawking, wheezy high-pitched gibbering and growls is as yet unintelligible to me.

My visits take place in the early morning or the evening. During the day she is employed to clear the stormwater rubbish that washes into the river and collects with branches and leaf matter at the trap on the south side of the city. Summer and winter she wades back and forth across the river, dragging out the sodden mats of plastic bottles and wet paper and woody material and scooping up cigarette butts and condoms into a net that she empties into the council skip on the bank.

On a warm day, the heat the monster generates is intense, and I cannot nestle under her comforting arm for long. I ease my way out, after which I make sure to face her and look into her eyes as soon as I am free. I want her to know that I am not repelled or disgusted but simply hot. She stares back at me, her muddy yellow eyes revealing nothing of her inner life. We hold each other's gaze for a few moments, then I feel I can look away. There have been days when, the moment I let my gaze drop, she has swatted me in a gesture that may have been playful or may have been tinged with anger. I can't tell. I am so far off reading her that I'm beginning to think my attempts at communication might be hopeless.

I stand before her ready to take my leave. She is magnificent, frightening, pitiful.

*

It is said that you cannot make a pact with a monster because the monster has no ethics, morals or apprehension of contractual law. This hasn't stopped me trying. I told her that I would bring freshly baked meat pies every Thursday if she would teach me her language. I thought she understood my meaning but we immediately came to an impasse. She cannot speak English (although I honestly believe she comprehends everything I say) and she cannot read or write, so how is she to explain anything to me?

Last week I pointed at the pie and said, 'Pie.' I waited for her, in turn, to point at the pie and make a sound in her own language, but she snatched the pie from the wooden picnic table and crammed it into her mouth, issuing gluey squeals of pain because the filling was very hot. I should have warned her.

Obviously, pointing at food and speaking its name had been a failure because the monster assumed I was offering her the food. So I printed off photos from the internet to show her. A pie. A cat. A plate. An orange.

I thought I should track down pictures online of some things she would be familiar with. I found a plastic bottle. A cigarette butt. Dirty supermarket bags. An icy-pole stick. The more images I collected of the things the monster encounters in her daily life, the more dispirited I became. Where is the beauty in her life? Wading day after day through polluted water, handling the detritus of our civilisation. When I found a photo of a used condom I began to cry. How can we treat our monsters like this? What does she think of us?

*

The population of monsters has never been measured, as monsters are reclusive and unlikely to participate in any kind of census. Is my monster one of hundreds? Thousands? I think of her as *my* monster now. My Thursday monster, something like my Monday grief or my Sunday melancholy. I can't say our communication has improved, although I am better at recognising the moment she is about to lash out. Most of my wounds have closed and healed to scars. My monster carries on with her work, her eating, her mysterious thoughts. Each Thursday I bring a pie and new pictures, which she seems to take some pleasure in ripping up and chewing into spitballs to expectorate in my direction. I know you're thinking this is a bad thing, but me, I'm not so sure. Spitting, after all, is an important element in the lexicon of llamas. Monsters and spitting? Perhaps I will be the first to know.

*

Three months on and my monster remains inscrutable. She has picked up a hat, I imagine from her work, a wide-brimmed straw hat with a once-blue nylon bow that has been battered through the river grime for who knows how many miles and now is torn and blackened and feathered where the straw has ripped. And it smells like blood and bone. When she pushes the hat towards me I imagine it is a gift. I almost weep. At last, a gesture of goodwill.

I hold the hat for some moments, trying to block the smell by breathing through my mouth, and smile at the monster. Then I put the hat on my head. She reacts by leaping at me, snarling, and punching my face before she knocks the hat off me and stomps on it until the straw is pulp and the indestructible ribbon stretched thin and translucent. I sit still and silent with my head bowed, my hand nursing my cheek where the punch landed. For ten minutes I am afraid to move. When I lift my head she is gone. The light is on in her unit. The blind is drawn. The shoulders of the she-oaks droop with their usual despondency.

Animals of the Savannah

Tegan Bennett Daylight

Raffaello's face had grown in the years between fifteen and seventeen, forming a kind of clod, as though the new face was a growth over the first, finer one. He was going out with Katie Goldsworthy now. They were our Romeo and Juliet. You might wonder how I knew this as I had, now that Judy was gone, absolutely no friends. But it was the news, which is democratic in its reach. Even I was included when Katie told the story of the secret party on her father's moored yacht, falling asleep in the cabin, being reported as missing, the police called, Katie and Raffaello dragged, beautiful with sleep, out of their berth and onto the deck. I hated myself for being interested, but the other girls made space for me in the circle around Katie, and I gratefully moved into it.

I could have had a boyfriend. Jonathan Schultz from Year 11 was flouting everything and everyone by declaring that he loved me. I don't know what started it. Perhaps a dream. That was how I had first fallen in love with Raffaello. If Jonathan saw me on the oval or in the concrete streets of our school he would grin and wave, or squash the palm of his hand to his mouth and kiss it furiously, to show me what he would do if he could just get hold of me. He was skinny, with brown hair in a curly corona around his head. A big smile, tanned skin, very white teeth.

'I have to study,' I said when he walked up the hill with me, giving the thumbs up to his friends as they passed in the bus. He tried to take my hand but I snatched it behind me. Instead he walked beside me, shortening his stride to mine. He grinned and laughed, he tried to tickle me, insisted on carrying my bag.

'Come on. Come back to my house. My parents aren't home.'

'I have to study,' I said again.

'Study at my house.'

'Go *away*.'

'Look, I got you something.' He made me stop while he fumbled in his backpack, and brought out a pink teddy bear with a red heart stitched on to its chest. He held it out to me. 'It's for you.'

I took it.

'Lov*ers*!' shouted some boys from the windows of the second bus. The exhaust from the bus, clear and hot, made the air ripple.

'Thank you,' I said, and gave it back to him to carry for me.

'Hopelessly devoted, too-oo yooo,' he sang.

*

Sometimes you'd see Andrew Johnson walking ahead of Katie and Raffaello, clearing a path for the royal couple, shoving younger kids out of the way. Andrew's face had remained small and pinched, like a sultana. One day I stopped after the entourage had gone past, to buckle my sandal, and heard someone call my name. When I turned to look I saw Andrew, also stopped, Katie and Raffaello receding in the distance. He stood amidst the flow of people, watching me. And then Jonathan was beside me; he'd memorised my timetable and had come to carry my books, if I would let him.

One lunchtime Katie and her friends came over to where I was sitting alone under the windows of the History rooms, in the loose shade of a eucalyptus. I was reading, or pretending to, as the group of girls grew closer, larger. It was only four weeks until our formal, and then the exams two weeks after that. There was a feeling of permissiveness, a relaxing of boundaries, the air already sick with heat and cicadas.

'Jonathan likes you,' said Katie. The girls fanned out behind her as though she had spread wings.

'I know,' I said.

Jonathan and Katie had something to do with each other. I thought perhaps they were cousins. You saw them walking home together sometimes, or dropped off in the same car. They had the same look of privilege, clear of skin and bright of eye.

'Come to my house this afternoon,' said Katie.

'What for?'

'Have to tell you something.' Not for a second did it occur to her that I might say no. It didn't occur to me either.

*

Katie led me down her driveway, which was so steep it would have been suicide to run, though the angle made it nearly impossible not to. The house was sandstone, two storeys, with ivy growing across it. There was a keypad at the door; she pressed in four numbers and the door unclicked. Katie pushed it open and showed me where to take off my shoes, which was something I had never had to do in any other house. The air was perfumed. We walked into an enormous kitchen with wide white benches and a TV, which was switched on with the sound down. At the bench, sitting on a stool and reading the newspaper, was Katie's father.

He was a TV newsreader. I had not thought to see him here, when all the other fathers were at work. He looked up at us and smiled. He was older than all the other fathers too, with his new hair stitched neatly across his forehead, and those square glasses. He was wearing a richly patterned dressing-gown made of silk, tied around his waist, a few hairs from his chest sprouting from the opening. He looked like his own ailing twin: face and body a little smaller, more withered than those of the man on TV. His white-toothed smile was knowing, as though he had seen many people reading him the way I was.

Katie did not introduce me, but took a carton of chocolate milk from the fridge. I followed her down the stairs to her bedroom, which was big and light, and which also had a television and a record player. I had been here once before, at the party when Judy had drunk half a bottle of tequila, and I had disgraced myself with Raffaello. Back then I hadn't noticed how big the room was; in fact, it had seemed small, hot and oppressive, with all the girls standing at the door and Judy weeping and moaning on the bed. There were tall windows looking onto the river, and there was the swimming pool and the jetty and the yacht.

'Jonathan wants you to ask him to the formal,' said Katie. She put the carton of chocolate milk down on the dressing table, which had a mirror and little crowds of lipsticks and nail polish bottles, like tiny people at a party.

'He can't come. He's not in Year 12.' I looked around for somewhere to sit and chose the bed, which was bigger than last time, and which shifted and gurgled.

'He can if someone in Year 12 asks him.' Katie leaned in to look at herself. She was wearing her long hair in a side ponytail. She fixed her fingers around the elastic that held it in place and drew it out in one long movement, shaking the thick caramel waves around her shoulders. There were pale, creamy hairs among the caramel, repeated in the lovely arches of her eyebrows. It did seem somehow moral. As though she deserved to look this way.

I had once thought I might ask Judy to our formal, which was not generally done, but would be understood in the context of me being an outcast, practically a lesbian, and Judy being exiled from our school. Nobody liked Judy, with her big fat bosoms and big fat bum and her way of blushing so hard that she was hot to the touch, but she was a part of the bigger story of our year, and if she had come as my partner to the formal it might have made sense.

'As long as I don't have to go out with him,' I said, and Katie shrugged. 'That's up to you. I didn't promise him that.'

There was the sound of someone at the door – church bells through the house – and, I realised, a shower running somewhere. Katie stood still, listening. '*I'm not getting it!*' she bawled suddenly. And then the sound of her father shouting something from the shower.

'Fuck.' She left the room and ran up the stairs, thumping on each step. After a second I got up, the waterbed rocking behind me, and followed her. She pulled the front door open to a blonde woman who I thought must be her mother, but this woman kept her handbag over her shoulder instead of putting it on the hall table, and gave Katie a smile that seemed to want to placate.

She smiled at me, too, as she passed me on the stairs. She had a Lady Di haircut and a pale blue suit with padded shoulders. It looked right and even enviable at the time, but now, in my mind's eye, it is as though every woman over eighteen was dressing for a meeting, a meeting in which she was the soft-voiced but iron-willed head of a baby powder company. My father's wife dressed like this, or had the last time I'd seen her.

And then the rushing of the shower as the downstairs bathroom door was pulled open, the voice of Katie's father, the sound muffled as the door was closed on them both.

I stood there at the top of the stairs, waiting. I hoped that Katie might explain what was happening. If she told me something secret I would immediately be stronger. She knew this, and pointed at my bag and my shoes where they lay in the hall.

'Jonathan's waiting for you,' she said. 'He'll walk you back across the bridge.'

She opened the door again and there was Jonathan, grinning expectantly.

I didn't need anyone to 'walk me across the bridge'. When we reached it, down the long sandstone steps that ran through the bush past Katie's house, I told Jonathan I would go with him to the formal and he clapped his hands together for joy, and then shook his fists at the sky. Then he folded me into his long arms and kissed me all over my face, and then he let me walk away, on my own, with a little push on my behind. He appeared to be playing a part, although it swung between the triumphant young lover and the much older man, experienced in the ways of women. I turned back to see him watching me, and he shook his fist again, as though cheering me on. I turned away, face into the salty river breeze.

When I looked again he had gone, back up the stone steps. I leaned on the rails and stared down at the water. It was high tide. You could have jumped from the girders safely. The boys from the big Catholic school were rowing. From this distance I could not make their faces out. Now I would not have to go to the formal with Andrew Johnson.

*

I still loved Raffaello for himself. But I also loved him for what Katie had made him. She was not meant to be at our school; it was a mistake. She should have been with other girls who looked like her, wearing the knee-length tunic of one of the eastern suburbs private schools, and a hat with a ribbon. Instead she was stuck with the ugly variety of us. She wore our uniform just below the line of her underpants, like all the other tough girls, but her velvety skin and silver necklace made her privilege clear. When you stood close to her you could see those fine pearly hairs on her brown arms, and each eyelash as black as ink against her cornflower eyes.

Next to her Raffaello looked like something grand, or ancient, despite or perhaps because of the acne and the new thickness in his face and body. The things they did together, like going to restaurants, even the theatre, were beyond anything I could imagine. The things they did *to* each other were the same. It seems odd now that we all knew Raffaello had lost his virginity to Katie, and odder still that he was not teased or harassed for it. There was a sort of reverence around his goodness, his pure Italianness. His mother loved him, it was easy to see. I heard that now he'd started he could not stop. It was said they had sex in the toilets, behind the weathersheds, in one of the science labs. I would have made do with lying privately in the grass somewhere with the sky sailing above us, faces close together, hands entwined. I knew everything I needed to know about sex except how it happened, how you came to be close enough, and willing enough, to make that absurd next move.

*

I wasn't able to get away with just the formal, as it turned out. Jonathan wanted me to go to his house the following Saturday. My mother accepted his invitation for me because I would not come to the phone when she called.

It seemed impossible that I had to go there on the weekend, the only time that belonged to me, which usually I would spend on my bed reading, or sometimes studying. We were doing *Hamlet* for our exams. I wish I could say I liked it but I did not. It didn't seem true – just a dreary assemblage of motives for Shakespeare to hang his language on like mad brocade curtains. I did not believe that Hamlet would not be able to kill his uncle. I had blood in me and would willingly have killed, if given the weapon. I liked this: *There is a special providence in the fall of a sparrow.* I could see the sparrow when I read this: the sparrow and its flight arrested, its tumble through the air. My father was dead too, but that did not seem true either, more like a thing that had happened and was obscurely my fault. The fault glowed darkly at the edge of my consciousness, like a bad dream not properly forgotten. I did not approach it.

My mother loved Shakespeare and had all of *Hamlet* in her head. It was because of Laurence Olivier, who had been Hamlet and Richard III and Henry V when she was young. She was in love with Laurence Olivier and imagined him coming to Australia, and then to her suburb in a black car, seeing her as she walked home from school, inviting her to climb into the car and come to the 'studio' with him. She told me that once she had been at the city library and, running her eyes along a shelf, had come to a book about Olivier and Shakespeare, with photographs; plates of Olivier in noble poses. Her knees went weak, she said; she had to sink down right there on the carpet, pulling the book with her.

This capacity for fantasy would be the reason she married my father, who was also tall and handsome and dark-haired, but was always thrusting her behind him or snatching her away from parties when he realised that one of his other lovers would be present. She believed that only she had his heart, only she could change him or rescue him from his profligacy. This is what she told me. Once they were crossing the Gladesville Bridge in his car and he told her that he was also engaged to someone else, but that it would be fine, he just needed to break it off and could do so by letter, and my mother threw herself out of the moving car. This was the old Gladesville Bridge, which was flat and straight, and it was past midnight, and the car was not going very fast. She rolled a few times and my father stopped and rushed back to her. He picked her up and bundled her into the back seat and took her home.

It was, she thought, a decisive moment, when her passion had obliterated his deceit. Even though she had been proved wrong, I still believed in the essential truth of this.

I had been back to my father's grave in the weeks following his funeral, not knowing that it took some time for a grave to be finished, to become like the other graves. Of course a cemetery is really just a paddock waiting to be filled, and my father's grave was on the outskirts of this paddock, as he was among the most recently buried. It took me some time walking up and down the rows of the established graves before I found him out in the empty spaces. The orange earth was still in a hard heap above him, like an ant hill. Three other Catholics had been buried since he had. Two had no marker, his and the one next to him had small white wooden crosses: name, date.

Now, two years later, all the space around him was populated. He was a resident, with neighbours, with his little concrete headstone and its stainless steel plaque.

*

Jonathan's father was tall and wolfish with sleek grey hair. He greeted me at the front door with a wicked smile, with pleasure, like a procurer.

'I'll get Jonathan,' he said, his eyes dancing. And then, 'I'll leave you two alone,' after bringing us a bowl of chips and a glass each of lemonade. We sat in their living room, which looked onto the water and across to our school. Jonathan moved closer to me on the white leather couch. He put an arm over my shoulders. I heard a flurry of feet behind us and turned round to see his twin sisters, who were still in primary school, blonde and skinny and shrieking and ducking into the hall when they saw me looking.

Jonathan shooed away his sisters and nudged his hip and then his shoulder closer to mine. I felt weary at the thought of the formal to come, which would be more of this, only fuelled by booze and thus harder to fend off. I let him kiss me, which was cool and spitty. His mouth seemed too spacious; I could feel his small teeth. It did not matter. I think he had as little desire as I did. But he was enjoying being in the play about love. Today he was the masterful older man, a little tired of passion, but always courteous. He stroked my spiked, sticky hair and sighed.

In the hall behind us the front door opened. It was his mother, and she came in to say hello. She was the same woman I had seen at Katie Goldsworthy's, the woman who went downstairs and disappeared into the bathroom with Katie's father. She was wearing a pink dress this time, also with padded shoulders. She did not seem to recognise me. She gave us the same treatment that Jonathan's father had, the devilish pleasure in our youthful love. 'I don't want to *disturb* you,' she said, a low thrill in her voice. She stepped back and pulled the French doors closed, dividing us from the hall and the rest of the house.

*

My mother made me a dress, understanding my need for something that swirled from the waist, with petticoats underneath. She had taken me to choose the material and we had seen the same bright stuff at the same moment, both of us reaching for it. She had found black net to make the petticoats from. She seemed to know what she was doing, but at the first fitting I found she had decided to make the dress not sleeveless and scooped at the neck, but short-sleeved and round-necked, like a T-shirt. I said nothing, hoping that she was planning to change it somehow, that this was a first draft, in a sense. The image of the dress had burned so vividly in my head; it was a great surprise to find that it had not been transmitted correctly. Once I had understood that this was so it was too late to stop her.

We were invited to a drinks party that would be held before the formal. It was to be at Katie's house. It was a chance for the grown-ups to be together, to celebrate our final year at school, to send us out into the world of adulthood, pushed off from shore like pretty boats. The invitation came on a piece of parchment in a falsely aged envelope.

'Let's not go,' I said to my mother, aghast.

'Drinks and hors d'oeuvres,' she said, reading the calligraphy.

'Argh,' I said, clutching my throat, watching her through half-closed eyes.

'We really should,' she said. 'I haven't seen the Goldsworthys in years.'

I didn't know she had ever seen the Goldsworthys. She had never mentioned them.

'Besides, your formal partner will be there and it's the right thing to do,' she went on, reaching for the phone.

Every so often these rules surfaced, and it would be as though I lived in the 1950s, in my mother's young adulthood, instead of the 1980s. 'You must say yes to the first boy who asks you,' she had said when the idea of the formal was introduced. This had led me to accept the invitation from Andrew Johnson. But then Katie had commanded me to invite Jonathan to the formal. I hadn't told Andrew I was going with someone else. I'd hidden from him at school and hoped he would get the message.

'I don't want to,' I said frantically, but she was speaking now, in her telephone voice, and there was no going back.

*

Frances was Katie Goldsworthy's mother. She was taller than Keith, her newsreader husband. They both seemed to be wearing make-up. She looked like a gaunt older sister of Katie's, with bony legs and more caramel hair in waves around her tanned shoulders. If you saw her from behind you might think she was quite young, and get a surprise when she turned round and gave you her lined smile.

We were not asked to take our shoes off, which I was sorry about, as mine had begun to hurt me on the steep run down the driveway. Frances and Keith both kissed my mother – so wonderful to see you, what a long time it's been – and ushered us in.

I wondered if Frances knew about Keith and Mrs Schultz. They had not seemed especially careful with their secret. I had not said anything to my mother about what I had seen at the Goldsworthys', because I couldn't think of a way to introduce the subject without being asked questions myself. When my mother was interested in something she would ask forensic questions that reduced every story to a pointless heap of facts. She would want to know why I had been at the Goldsworthys' and why I had let myself be talked into taking Jonathan to the formal with me. She would think that I had been bullied, and would have to bully me herself in order to feel better. Explaining about Andrew would only have made things worse.

When I had understood that my father had maintained two marriages, two families, I'd wondered why his secret wife was not blonder, more buxom, sexier than my mother. In fact, Anne was small and thin with a nose like a Stone Age flint and slightly bulging eyes. Hyperthyroid, said my mother once, which also explained the dry skin and crackling hair. Anne was mean and tight and conservative, not the sort of woman you run away to, or that was what I thought. My mother looked a little older than she should have, because of the drinking, and her cheeks, if you looked closely, were filigreed with tiny broken capillaries. But she looked interesting: Spanish or Irish with her black hair and blue eyes. She was bosomy, like me, and wore her blouses with a button undone so you could see the freckled bags of her breasts. Tonight she was dressed like Linda Ronstadt: the bosom, and the drawstring top.

Katie was in the kitchen with Jonathan's two sisters, who had been got up in silver and pink for the occasion. She was opening a bag of chips for them.

'You can watch TV in my bedroom,' she said to them, and then looked up at me. The sisters dodged past me, giggling, scattering chips.

'You look nice,' Katie said, without trying to take the sarcasm out of her voice. Her hair had been caught into French plaits, pearly strands floating around her face, catching the evening sunlight. She looked as though she should be sitting in a casement window in Florence, with Raffaello on his knees beside her. I could not tell if she was wearing make-up, although her blue eyes looked smoky and her lips were the colour of plums. I was wearing make-up that I had applied myself, white and thick like a Noh mask. The kitchen was full of light – good for Katie, bad for me.

'Come on then,' said Katie. I stood out of the way so she could pass in front of me. She smelt like flowers.

There were three young couples – Katie and Raffaello, Jonathan and me, and Katie's best friend, Erin, and Matt Willmott, whose tallness and skinniness had shot out of control, and now looked like it hurt. Jonathan's parents were there, and Erin's parents, and Matt's too, his father also towering painfully above us. There was champagne and a waiter. Raffaello's parents were not there. Raffaello wore a pale blue tuxedo, buttoned across his thick chest in a way that made me think of a baby in a cardigan.

There was fresh acne on his cheeks. The evening sun was vast, white, in the huge upper rooms of Katie's house, and the smell of the river filled the place, sweet and briny. Katie's father handed me a flute of champagne. My mother was replacing her first on the waiter's tray and taking a second.

Jonathan appeared beside me. He was decently dressed in a black tuxedo. He was clearly younger than Matt or Raffaello, his features still fine and light, his shoulders slight and his skin clear. The tuxedo was boxy over his slender body. He took my hand and led me aside to the big windows, and when we were at a distance from the others he said quietly, 'You look beautiful.' He had clearly established his persona now. I wouldn't be seeing the youthful lover again.

I'd had a need, an unignorable need, to dye my hair that morning. I'd suddenly known that without it I was not adequate. I cannot quite explain why it seemed to me that my short spiked hair needed to be purple, but my mother was sympathetic, and when we could not find purple hair dye at the chemist, we'd bought gentian violet. I can tell you that gentian violet will dye your hair purple – and the colour will last – but it has a sheen, an iridescent green, when you turn your head towards the light. Shampoo will not remove this sheen. Do not allow the gentian violet to drip onto your face. Wear gloves.

Jonathan kissed my purple fingers. 'The most beautiful girl in the world.'

I jerked my hand away and stared out at the water, at the masts of yachts, swinging like metronomes as a ferry went past. I could not say to him that these chivalries felt like insults. It was more humiliating than being ignored or scorned; this pretence that in my T-shirt dress, with my shining green hair and my blistered feet, that I was anything like a real girl, the kind you might say was beautiful.

'Get me more champagne,' I said, handing him my glass.

'We're only allowed one,' he said.

'I never could see the point of an open marriage,' my mother was saying in a loud voice. 'I was in one without knowing, of course.'

*

The stretch limousine arrived and the boys handed us in. The parents had come to the top of the drive, my mother with her glass. She was sweating a little.

'We'll see you later!' Frances stood waving. She'd had a little cry as we gathered ourselves to leave, as we stood in the hall shifting about and sighting ourselves in the enormous mirror by the door. The mirror was like a cage, trapping the six of us, animals of the savannah. Matt was the giraffe.

'We'll be on board if you need us,' shouted Keith.

Frances and Keith were hosting the afterparty, too, and were planning to sleep on the yacht in order to be out of the way. The waiter would still be here when we got back from the golf club. I'd seen that the fridge was full of West Coast Coolers.

*

Jonathan fell asleep in the attic bedroom, where he'd dragged me so that we could be like the other couples. I'd pretended I needed another drink and left him sitting expectantly on the sofa bed. When I came back in, having stood on the stairs for several minutes, counting and looking at the ceiling, he had slumped sideways, eyes closed. I stared at him for a minute. I would probably never see him again. He still looked light and fresh and clean, despite the champagne and the Brandivino and my hipflask of Southern Comfort.

I had no money and my mother would be dead asleep, unable to hear the phone. I would have to walk home. My feet hurt, even without my shoes. I would soak them in the pool to cool them down.

I made my way down the sets of stairs, shoes in hand. Katie and Raffaello were in her bedroom, with a sentinel at the door. I came to the pool, which in the dark was like an underground cave of blue light. It was cooler out here, by the river. The yacht was a quiet black shape on the water. Girls sat on the lawn in groups, some weeping drunkenly. I sat down on the pebbled edge, lifted my petticoats and slid my feet into the silky water.

A group of people sat on the other side of the pool, passing a bong around. One was Andrew Johnson, out of whose way I had carefully kept, all night.

'Hey, it's Tasha,' someone said.

'Look, Andrew, it's Tasha.'

Andrew lifted his head and stared at me. He was so stoned that his head kept dropping forward, but he focused on me. 'Ooh, Tasha.'

I looked down at my feet, which were at strange angles in the lighted blue water.

'I love you, Tasha,' said Andrew, and the boys around him laughed. 'You're so beaudiful. So sexy.'

I kept staring down.

'I want you Tasha. With honey all over ya cunt.'

Now I stood up, although I knew this would draw more attention to what he was saying. People near us began to stare as he said, 'But you wouldn't fuck just anyone. Only Raff.'

In the distance the yacht was rocking, and a figure, a shape emerged from it, and came to stand at the end of the jetty. It was Mrs Schultz, although when she saw me looking she stepped back into the shadows. I had my shoes. I turned away, my feet feeling as soft as if I had just been born, feeling each pebble, the points of the grass, and Andrew shouted after me, 'Didja get lucky, Tash?'

I went in through the open French doors, up the stairs and through the house. I was aware of my reflected self, escaping the big mirror as I ran out the open front door.

*

When I got home my mother was not asleep but sitting up in bed, reading *The Great Gatsby* and drinking a glass of wine. She looked relaxed and happy and sleepy, so I took a risk and told her about the Goldsworthys, about Katie's father and Jonathan's mother. She smiled in a dreamy sort of way and said, 'They're still doing that, are they?'

I looked at her.

'They all do it,' she said.

I'd known my father had *done it*; there was the living proof, his other wife and my half-siblings.

'There's always been the question of that boy,' she said, gazing into the distance. 'Is he Keith's, do you think?'

I stared at her.

'We'll never know,' she said.

I thought I'd understood why Katie had made me go to the formal with Jonathan. I'd thought they were not cousins after all, but *related* because of Keith and Mrs Schultz. Forced into a kind of family by their parents' sex lives. Jonathan had even talked about holidays together.

But perhaps it was more. Perhaps they were brother and sister.

Or perhaps Katie had just been trying to keep me away from Raffaello. He was the only person I cared about. I'd had one kiss from him at the height of his drunkenness, under the trees behind the golf club. I'd put my face into the hot wall of his chest; I'd smelt him, kissed him, been ready to put my hands where they'd never been, down into his pants, to drag the hard weight of him on top of me, into me. I had not been able to persuade him to leave with me.

It was so lonely, all this hunting, never catching anything.

Moth Sea Fog

Gregory Day

I talk to the moth caught in the car. Driving past heat-mottled dams whiskered with reeds. I tell him about the fog of the day before. It was not just any fog, but a time-fluxing sea fog outrolling the waves, creeping over neap-tide ledges, tickling the glossy anemones with its smoky edges. It made silhouettes of the gods.

The sunlight was a recent memory, I tell him. The physical became metaphysical. He bats the patterns on his wings, letting them whirr against the windscreen.

You know in your guts when you've made a friend. And so I tell him more, watching the way his blackwire legs work adhesive, like a dancer in a heavy carpet cape except for the fact that his wings have made a shuffling pact with the light-sheafs of the air.

It rolled in moved in hefted in, a light-changer seeking the convex of the coves. It greybrushed the ocean, narrowing the spectrum from blue green and gold to heron-grey and tint of ash. Yet this was not a creaturely dirge, this wasn't death or aftermath, this was *le temps*.

The moth doesn't speak French and nor do I. But when I'm with the moth all languages, like all the cars on the road, could potentially be ours: those bonnets of steel, we could be in any of those glary glass and steel chariots, they come from the same marketplace, just as the words are all restored to sounds with long histories, joint histories, like the *tempest* in *le temps*, the weather in time.

And the fog, I told the moth, was a new moment cast, made visible, a *momento* that rolled in and would roll out again, or uplift, streak and stretch, or disappear, or dissolve like honey in the teacup of the world, leaving us savouring, remembering, re-imaging.

Every late October I wait for the moths, who come in numbers to thrum on the ocean windows. How many springs is it that I've been vigilant? Relative to the time it took to paint those carpet wings, or to the time it took to create those honeyed cliffs which the fog greyscales into, it's only a few. I tell him that. How the grey sea fog painted the ocean cliffs ... and how we were down below on the sand of the cove. The Horseshoe Rock had been veiled, the great tower-stack of Eagle Rock was one of the silhouetted gods. The day had been too hot but now it was antechambered, as the great meteorological shift came in.

As I began to drive out of the farms onto the edge of new suburbs the moth flew in close. And still. It had probably slept between dash and steel armature but was now accustomed to the light. Awake in the daylight. Displaying his totem mirror-wings.

Perhaps the sound of those wings is the musical equivalent of the way the fog crept. My boys and I were going to cool down with a swim until we'd noticed the tumbled uneven tendril-edges of the fog moving silently over the cliffs. We decided to go anyway. For the excitement of new phenomena rather than the cooling down. The invisible air was suddenly visible, as if a billion atoms had clenched into an optical fact, into visible existence.

Things, big things, come unannounced. Like the moths in spring. This little forerunner, companion in the cabin of my ute, did not phone ahead. And before we knew it we were on the path down, the fog's damp hem tingling our bare skin. We stepped down the steep winding path, moving further under cover, towards the sea-sound, further into the secret.

Another thing I tell the moth is that it was a midweek sea fog. No other human stick-figures materialising out of the spectral air, just us three: me, the eldest, the youngest. We got down to the bottom of the steps, onto the sand of the cove, thrilled to be besieged, so gently besieged by something so much bigger than we are. It too was both old and young. An ancient character freshly, wetly, minted. So it felt like strange kin, a spectacle we were part of, an unannounced visitation both ghost-ish and real, like the moth's cloud thrumming through each spring. I told him that, as we drove over a bridge: how he reminded me of the fog, how they seem connected.

It's like someone you meet who you know loves travelling. You talk destinations. Or someone who loves to cook. You talk food, or kitchenware. To a friend of the stars you talk astronomy, myth, astrology. To a friend of the river you talk birds who've roosted in the river-trees. So it was with the moth and the fog. Sometimes we have a hunch, a secret message comes travelling through the air between us, and we feel we know. And so we raise a subject however unlikely, as if on a whim. But it's not a whim. It's a windlassed knowledge so deep and fast, so multi-sensed, that even the word 'intuition', which after all is a nicely sinuous word, doesn't come close. *Feeling* is better. As in *sensing* and *seeking* at the same time. The fog and the moth would be interested in each other, that's what I felt, they were like family members. Like we three on the beach.

The water was calm, with small silky blue-grey waves unpeeling under the blue-grey creature. The world was birdless for an hour. The clifftop bristlebirds did not make their quirky twee-wit calls, the gannets did not glide or dive, the cormorants did not bob up or stand as if sermonising on the rocks. We did not ask where they were though, we did not picture them huddled up, holding breath, or overawed. We took this vast mysterious ethereal birdless cove at face value.

The eldest wanted to swim, I told the moth. The youngest wasn't so sure. He clung to me, as if the fog clung to him. Sometimes in a dream we see the world like this, seldom in reality. Sometimes in a dream we can cross over, as if into other worlds. Perhaps that's what it reminded the youngest one of. He obviously needed, in this waking hour, for the world, and my presence in it, to be real. Like the moth.

I had life on my dash, one dry stalk of slender velvet-bush, one wizened stalk of lavender. Still with a faint perfume. To be inside the cabin of my ute, its plastic and steel, could have also seemed like a dream to the moth, like the fog could seem. The world as you know it changed. A different, unfamiliar hall. But I'd wound the window down to let the moth out if he so desired. I'd let the window open, both when the car was still and moving. But no, the moth was staying. There was something in those dried stalks, those clefts and crannies of the car, that dam-mottled windscreen, that kept him there. Still, or tiptoeing across the glass, or thrumming his wings like a thinking thought. Something kept him there. So I told him the story.

Once upon a time, on an otherwise ordinary day, insofar as a too-hot day can be ordinary these days, a sea fog rolled in from the endlessness of ocean and gently covered the reefs, the coves, the cliffs and downsloped shoulders and valleys of our town. Every pond was lightly brushed. Every road sign shrouded. One boy went for a swim in the fog, another boy stayed back on the beach with his father. The two on the beach peered through the dimmed light, through a wispy world, at the swimming boy. Until he was gone. Diving obliquely through the ocean's skin and swimming like a star pulsing under the water. He swam and swam, until he could breathe no more and came to the surface. His hair was plastered wet, he felt that he shone, but they could not see him. He had gone into the fog.

The father yelled, suddenly frightened. The younger boy's face screwed up in fear. But the water lay still, the impervious waves peeling in with what seemed now like stealth, an awful regularity and silence. The father broke clear of the grip of little hands, moving towards the water. He yelled again, but there was only absence now, erasure, an awful clarity on the sea.

The moth thrummed and whirred before standing still at an angle on the dash. Staring at me, as if accusing. No, I said. No, it wasn't like that. But that was my fear as the eldest went in. Like a seal in his black wetsuit, but for the short sleeves and leggings. His pale young limbs outstretched. As he slipped under the skin of the water my fear went imagining. Like the CFA alarm used to go sounding over the hills. One day a boy swam into the sea fog and when the fog had passed over he was not there anymore. The sea and sky had merged then unmerged and he was not there anymore. Nowhere to be seen. As if he'd been abducted by the fog. As if the world had warped for half an hour, as if fate had held the boy's life between its forefinger and thumb, held it suspended, before dropping it again from its great height. And changing everything.

But this is not how it had gone, I told the moth. It was not like a fable or fairytale. Though it had such an atmosphere. No, he was there, standing there in perfect form, in the water still, in his short wetsuit, overjoyed to be encompassed by this ocean shroud, this magical blue-grey cape, this smoky secret . . . and me calling.

'Come in, come in,' I called, 'we'll walk around the point a way.' Thus forestalling any possibility of what might then be written by the strangeness of the world. Let's write something else, old moth, I say, young moth, moth both old and young. Let's write simply of encompassing moments, how small we are in the large world, yet always kindred. Let's walk the cove – moth, father, eldest, youngest – to the dribble of rocks at the point, over the dribble of rocks, pushing our way through the mystery as if through a blue-grey curtain.

And so we went, the moth and I. Along the ordinary roadway. The boys and I too, around the rocky point to the seaweedy beach on the other side.

I seek the seasons, I told the moth then. I seek your arrival as the last of the wattle has faded, I seek the coming of the snakes. I seek the mutton-birds darkening the sky with a texta smudge, the gum's lurid flowering, the coming and going of *le temps.* I seek the new chapter of the budding plums, the wide grassy cast of field freesias, just like I seek new light in the morning and the shading of dusk towards dark. I seek the seasons, the season of rainbows, mushroom seasons, seasons of the nesting kites. *Thara.* What the men and women like me, the boys and girls like my own, called those nesting kites. Before the white men came like bad weather that would never leave. A fog outside of time. *Thara,* they said. The black-shouldered kites, we say. *Thara,* they said. And they knew the seasons, coming on the unbroken loom of *le temps.*

So the fog is like spun air, like wool too, wool unravelling. Unravelling from the giant loom at the end of the sea. It unrolls in. Unrolls in. Like a memory, a freshly remembered thing. And yes, we go seeking through it, through the clammy wet stench of the seaweed beneath the marbled cliffs. Seeking to reassemble the broken parts of the loom, dear moth. The loom that wove your wings, the turning wheel releasing the fog-skeins, the sound of your whirring. In this deep and secret shroud the truth of seeking is made real. Aren't we always pushing through a fog we can't see? Except here, in the veiling unveiling coves, we can see it. *Feel* it. Our seeking made real. The feeling we have that the world hides and reveals, that the loom spun those patterns on your wings.

So this then, in this season, is our moth country. Not so much car country or road country or radio country or traffic-light country but mothy-foggy country. An ephemeral routine. And in the fog, as I say to the moth, we sense the truth of the deeper season. Season of invisible things. Things not so easily grasped and held. Season of a billion atoms, season of risk, of our disappearing. Our coming and going. *Le temps.* Your season, dear moth. Season of swimming in the fog. Season of driving with the moths.

I'm here to record, as a father must, that the younger one eventually loosened. We rounded the next point all smiles. We looked back. The cliff was not a prop. Nor were the gods. They had almost disappeared, like the past. Into the future.

A Few Days in the Country

Elizabeth Harrower

'Heavens!' Sophie put her suitcase down on the concrete path and watched the cat flatten itself under a daphne bush and disappear.

'I don't know why she does that,' Caroline said, looking after it abstractedly.

'I don't usually terrify cats.'

'No, it isn't you.' Caroline led the way up the broad steps to her house. 'She always acts as if she thinks someone's going to murder her.'

Knocking Sophie's bag against the wall as she went ahead in a nervous rush, Caroline stopped at the entrance to a bedroom with two big windows and a view of eucalypt-covered hillside. She looked anxiously about. 'Is this all right? Perhaps I should have given you the other room?'

'Caroline, *no.* This is lovely. It was so kind of you to let me come.' And Sophie, who thought she never blushed, blushed from waist to forehead, and turned to give the oblongs of countryside her polite attention.

'I *asked* you.'

Drawing a dubious breath, Sophie saw imposed on the wooded slope another landscape of such complexity that she could think of no one thing to say.

Caroline straightened the Indian rug, then eyed her guest, and went on laboriously, 'How are you, anyway? Now that we're established.'

'Oh, extremely healthy, as always.' Sophie heard the sudden liveliness in her own voice, felt herself brim, for Caroline's benefit, with something resembling animation and high spirits. Apart from the fact that none of this was true, she could see it must seem a little odd that someone as fine as all that should have taken up in so urgent a fashion – involving trunk calls and telegrams – an invitation given warmly, but on the spur of the moment, months before in Sydney. They had friends in common. Caroline was a widow, a doctor, and lived alone in this small country town. She was grey-haired, sturdy and, Sophie felt, mildly fantastic. Sophie herself was a pianist. This was almost all they knew about each other.

By way of explanation, Sophie now repeated, as she blindly snapped open the locks of her case, what she had said in yesterday's calls. 'Suddenly the city just – got me down. A few free days turned up and I thought, if you don't mind ...'

This was so far from being a characteristic impulse that she hardly knew how to account for herself. The universe was hostile. The sun rose in the west. She was in danger. Only strangers might not be malevolent. Something like all this was wrong.

'Mind!' Caroline clapped her hands to her head, then fixed her springy hair behind her ears. 'If you knew how we like to be visited! Now, come and have lunch. Then we'll produce some of this famous country air for you. Scoot around in the car. There were mushrooms out the other day.'

'Really?'

They both smiled and relaxed slightly.

*

Sophie was not surprised to find that the mushrooms had been claimed by hungrier souls since Caroline first noticed them, but there was a wonderful cloud-streaked sky, a river, and waves of little hills to the horizon. Completing Caroline's circular tour, they returned to the house, took rugs onto the grass, and lay in the shade of a pear tree drinking iced coffee and losing control of the Sunday papers.

'You won't see much of me. I'm missing all day and sometimes half the night, so you'll have the place to yourself. Mrs Barratt comes in to tidy up. Oh, and I forgot to show you the piano. Mr Crump tuned it yesterday as a special favour. Came out of retirement!'

'Caroline.' Sophie looked at her in dismay. 'All this trouble you've gone to. So kind. It makes me feel—'

'What?'

'Terrible. False colours, false pretences.'

'I'll expect to hear of hours of practice when I get back every night,' Caroline continued firmly.

'But I wasn't going to practise. I don't practise much any more. I'm – getting lazy,' she improvised.

Caroline glanced at her quickly, then thumped at a party of scavenging ants with a folded newspaper. 'Of course you'll practise.'

Sophie shook her head. 'Truly. It doesn't matter. Music's not the most important thing in the world.' She gazed down the grassy slope and up to the hills in the distance.

'The most important thing in the world!' Scornful, roused, Caroline asked, 'What is?'

'Ah, well . . .' Sophie's voice had no expression. She did know.

But such a statement struck Caroline as merely silly. Quite apart from medicine, the world was full of causes, calls to effort. The list in her mind was endless. Even the imminent perfecting of man through education was not a thing she had doubts about.

The women eyed each other with goodwill and an awareness that they were natural strangers. The views of persons like that could not be taken seriously. It was almost a relief. They talked about politics and local controversies, and it scarcely mattered at all what anyone said.

'You see!' Caroline stopped herself in mid-flight. 'There's no one here to argue with except a few old cronies. So I rush back to Sydney every month, go round the galleries, and see some plays. Try to keep up . . .'

Sophie realised that she was at least partly in earnest, and felt a pang of appalled compassion as she habitually did now at what interested people, at the trouble they took to act in the world, move. If only they knew!

'I'm going to leave you in peace now while I do some weeding. It's the Sunday ritual.' Caroline stood up, looking resolutely about the big garden.

How courageous! What fortitude! Pity moved in Sophie and she got to her knees, ready to stand. 'Let me help. I can weed, or anything.' There was so much Caroline and everyone must never know.

'Stay there. You're on holiday. You can do some watering later.' Preoccupied already, Caroline disappeared round the corner of the house, and Sophie sank back horizontal on the rug, and the light went out of her. Tears came to her eyes and she wiped them away and sat up again.

*

Her instruction resumed at full volume. Phrases that were by now only symbols indicating the devastation caused by grief transfixed her attention. The instruction had been going on for several months now. When she was in company or asleep, the volume was reduced, but the question and answer, the statements below the level of thought, never really stopped. A massive shock. A surprise of great magnitude. 'A great surprise,' she repeated obediently.

In its way, the instruction was trying to save her, Sophie supposed. It wanted her to live. She humoured this innocent desire, attending to its words as though it were a kind, stupid teacher.

To be or not to be. Her lips half-smiled. Out in the world, when she lived out in the world, she had been stringently trained: nothing about herself, her life, her death, was worth taking seriously. Sophie smiled again. No wonder humankind could not bear much reality. The things that happened.

Caroline crossed the lawn, purposeful and silent, grasping secateurs. A long interval followed, during which only bees and shadows and leaves moved in the garden. The green tranquillity wavered and shifted in the currents of air. Sophie's heart jumped about in disorder as it often did now as the cat suddenly fled past her, out of a shady ambush. Patches of her forehead and head froze with fright. She took a deep breath and tried to stifle the bumping in her chest. Only the cat. Only Caroline's poor cat.

'Puss? Puss?' Her tone compelled the cat to acknowledge her presence. 'Don't be frightened. How nervous you are. Everything's all right.'

The stricken animal thawed and fled, leaving only a haunted path. Sophie mourned for it, mourned for its view of her as an object potentially powerful and evil, hardened. How wise are you, cat, to resist my blandishments, my tender voice, my endless – I would have you think – capacity for kindness. It *is* almost endless, too. I would never hurt you, except by accident, and hardly even then. But, oh, how sad I am, cat.

Her mouth smiled at 'sad'.

'You look very contented and peaceful there,' Caroline said, wandering over to her. 'That's good. Means you're settling in. Who volunteered to water the garden while I make some dinner?'

Syringa, woodbine, japonica, tangled cascades of roses hanging from old fences. Sophie wandered, trailing the hose, its silver spray hissing gently. Daylight was fading from moment to moment, the air cooling. Magpies held a dialogue as they flew, swooping low. Hearing them, Sophie told herself: I'm in the bush.

Then suicide thought of her. Unlike the instruction, which was of a labyrinthine complexity, suicide used simple words and images and, when it overcame the instruction and claimed her in a tug of war, it used them ceaselessly. Suicide was easy provided the balance of your mind was not disturbed. The essential point, neglected by faint hearts, was to commit the deed in a place where you would not soon be discovered. You would leave the city, taking with you a quantity of painkilling drugs or sleeping pills. You would post one or two letters before catching the train, because it would be cruel never to let yourself be found. And there were the reasons, the reasons you were dying for ... Which no one wanted to know and would prefer never to understand, anyway ... Then you would board a train going in a direction previously chosen, climb out at the selected station, walk to a secluded spot, lie down, and swallow the tablets. Having taken care, of course, to bring water.

Sophie sighed. A crude, peculiar, *material* way of dealing with extreme unhappiness. Like wars. Beside the point.

'What will you have to drink? Whisky? There's everything.' Caroline stood at the front door looking out remotely at the sky and the darkening garden.

'Thank you. Yes. I was watching the light on the hills there.'

'Lovely. You've brought good weather. Whisky, then. Don't stay out in the cold.'

'I'll just put the hose away.'

Light came on in the house. As Sophie went along the side path, she felt the consoling silence all about. Silence lay enormous behind the sound of her footsteps on grass, the dragging hose, late bird cries, insect scrapings.

Because, the argument resumed, being dead was not what she wanted most. It was the only alternative. Just as, presumably, generals did not want, first and foremost, dead bodies and buildings fallen down.

*

Over dinner Caroline, who had emerged as funny, generous, and Christian, asked about their Sydney friends and showed an inclination to dissect them as though they were interesting cadavers. Dismay ground Sophie to an almost total stop when this disloyalty displayed itself. Any betrayal, of whatever order, instantly related itself to the great calamities of the world. Which of these had not originated in one person? Her knife and fork grew heavy in her fingers, and it was an effort to breathe. Her dear friends! Unfitted to judge though she might be – no Christian – she knew she would judge Caroline later. Though even dear friends were now like faded frescoes. That response in their defence was only an outdated reflex. It was of no consequence that they would never meet again, so how should Caroline's mild malice disturb?

While Sophie drooped over her dinner, Caroline grew more and more inclined to ramble, and finally rambled right out of the field of friendship into small-town scandal – unfrocked ministers and cows that ate free-growing marijuana.

'Everyone drinks their milk. Can you wonder at the things that go on here?'

Sophie laughed with relief, a little too long.

*

In the morning Caroline left for the hospital at seven. Sophie showered, dressed, and brushed her hair, advancing jerkily from one operation to the next. No one and nothing could be relied on now. Nothing was automatic. The simplest habits had deserted.

Everything took thought, yet thought was what she had nothing to spare of. Because she had so much to think about and it was so important. And nobody realised.

Wandering through to the kitchen, she made some toast and coffee and set it out on the back verandah in the sun. The grey cat appeared at the door and saw her, coffee cup raised to lips, and after a moment's paralysis slunk off like a hunted thing. Sophie called after it in a beseeching voice, then rose and went to stand in the doorway. She spoke to the breathing garden, hoping the cat could hear, but there was no sign of it. When the dishes were washed, she trundled out the lawnmower and mowed some square yards of Caroline's dewy grass. The day was beautiful.

It was rather feeble to attempt suicide and fail. It definitely placed a person's good faith in doubt. It was worse to make an attempt with the conscious intention of not succeeding. Anyway. Anyway, she felt contempt for suicide. Butcher yourself ? Why should you? Fall into a decline because nothing was what it seemed? Some had ambitions perhaps to enter the higher reaches of blackmail. But Sophie had never thought of suicide. It was just that lately she could not stop thinking about it.

Little ridges of grass that had escaped her stood conspicuous. She pushed the mower to and fro, stopping once to throw off her sweater. Only a psychosis could make the deed anything but (Sophie pushed the mower so hard that it was airborne) pusillanimous. Pusillanimous. And had she any desire to be that?

Worn out by the violence of her repudiation, she stopped for an indignant breath. Then nervously ran the four fingers of her left hand across her forehead. It was just a fact that she wasn't safe, wasn't safe yet. And all you had to do was not be found too soon ...

Small black ants were swarming over her bare feet and ankles. She stamped about, brushing the tenacious ones away, dropping the handle of the mower. Bent right over, hair hanging, her glance slanted suddenly sideways: the cat sat under a bush some yards away, watching with round yellow eyes.

Cautiously, Sophie lowered herself to the ground, sat motionless on the grass, exchanging eyes with the cat. Then she began very gently to talk to it, and the cat listened, for the first time showing no fear.

Sophie looked vaguely into its green retreat, and rested her cheek on her knee. She closed her eyes. It was the tone of voice, she told herself. Cats must be susceptible to voices. And there was a slight, but temporary, amelioration of her suffering.

It was not a thing you could do, not in an immediate, noticeable way. It was not considerate to wreck other people's lives for no better reason than that you would prefer to be dead. Wreck? Well, perhaps that did overstate the case. Inconvenience, she amended.

'What a pity!' Sophie muttered. 'What a pity!' It was hard to understand, something she could never be reconciled to. Real love was not so common even in so large a place as the world.

Mortal wounds, the instruction said. The psychic knife went in; the psychic blood came out . . .

My own doing, Sophie reflected, while the instruction rattled on in the background monotonously. It was she who had done the empowering, delivered herself over. Nothing she had previously understood or learned had prepared her. Yet her life had never been sheltered. Again now, the magnitude of her surprise, of her mistake, bore down on her. Public violence, bombs, wars were this private passion to destroy made manifest on a large scale.

*

'That grass is wet, Sophie. I have to call on old Mr Crisp out past the church, so I came in to see if you were all right.'

As Caroline emerged from the tunnel of honeysuckle and may, Sophie scrambled up uncertainly, rubbing damp hands and cut grass on her damp slacks. 'Oh, Caroline . . . I was mowing the grass . . . I was talking to the cat.'

'Did she let you?'

'In a way. Almost.'

'I don't think there's time, or we could have a cup of tea together. Walk back up to the car with me, anyway. I only looked in. She was operated on once, poor Cat, and I'm convinced the vet was led astray by curiosity. He'd just qualified. She lost faith in the human race.'

Leaf mould lay thick beneath the trees.

'How awful,' Sophie said.

'Mmm.' Caroline frowned at the path for a few steps, then looked up briskly, glancing at her watch. 'You could try feeding her if you want to be friends. There's plenty of stuff in the fridge.'

'I don't think she's hungry.'

Her right hand on the gate, Caroline paused. Sophie looked at this small tough hand and waited obediently. She had the impression that she was expecting a message, and that perhaps Caroline was the person who was going to deliver it to her.

But Caroline just said absently, 'No, it isn't that. It's a bit demoralising to have her flitting about like the victim of a vivisectionist. Which she is. I really wondered if I'd find you practising. I was going to creep off. It isn't right, Sophie, that you should throw away your talents.'

Though once upon a time she herself had said this sort of thing to encourage other people, Sophie smiled with a sort of heartless gaiety. 'Did you really come back for that?'

'I did indeed. You practise, my girl, or we'll turn you into a medico and send you overseas to do good.' Her concern, which seemed real enough, disinterested, made Sophie feel ashamed of her own duplicity, though the concern was so misplaced and even preposterous that she laughed aloud.

'How can you think it matters, Caroline? Talent. Playing pianos. And even give it priority over doing good?' She felt tremendously amused, full of laughter.

'Just get on with it!' With a minatory nod, Caroline made for her little yellow car, and Sophie waited and waved through the familiar grating and humming of gears; then Caroline was gone, and so was the hilarity that had felt so permanent.

Alone again, Sophie conversed with herself about the weather as though to distract an invalid acquaintance. But, really, the light *was* dazzling, like the first morning of the world. Radiance pealed across Caroline's small valley from sky to dandelion. After staring into it for a time, Sophie continued back along the path to the uneven square of cut grass. Safely there, and gazing as if to count the blades, it seemed to her that something as mesmeric, as impersonal, and of the same dimensions as the sun was before her eyes. And this was the instruction.

*

'The Coopers and Stephen rang to say how much they enjoyed the other night.' Caroline looked up from the telephone directory.

'How punctilious! They were nice.' On her way to the kitchen with a large copper vase, Sophie paused.

'You were a great success.'

'I liked them, too.'

Caroline began to turn the pages distractedly. 'I'm looking for that new garage man who took Alec's place. The car's due for an oil change.' She sighed and let the book fall shut. 'I'll call in when I'm passing. It's a shame you have to go tomorrow. There's no reason to rush away.'

'I do work,' Sophie reminded her. 'Someone's going to notice I'm not there.' While she would almost certainly be nowhere, there was no reason to burden Caroline with that information.

'I daresay.'

'You've been marvellous.'

*

With Caroline gone, chains dropping from her, Sophie sank from the platform in space where it was laid on her to make conversation and act as if she believed in the great conspiracy. It was amazing what quantities of time could be passed out there when necessary, she reflected, filling the vase with fresh water. Some people spent the whole of their lives there without even knowing it. Like Ivan Ilyich and innumerable other characters who crowded to suggest themselves. Sophie clasped her hands round the cold vase and rushed through to the sitting room, leaning slightly backwards to avoid the spreading branches of japonica. Placing the vase carefully on the low table by the windows she escaped from the house to the open air, and stood bathed in surprise.

Here was the real world you could never remember inside houses: soft rounded hills and trees that had been there before history. Sophie looked at them and breathed. Help, her eyes said to the hills. Help, to the clouds, treetops, and grass. They bore her appeal like so many gods, with silence, no change of expression. She continued to look at them.

She continued to look at them, but addressed no more petitions. Words trivialised. Thought trivialised. Her unhappiness was so extraordinary that it was literally not to be thought of.

She stood motionless. But from a distance she was being stared at. After a time, her eyes were pulled to the cat's eyes, and she slowly roused herself and looked into them with some sense of obligation. Knowing it would come to her, Sophie drew a breath to summon the cat. Then she frowned and closed her mouth, repelled by her power over something more vulnerable than herself. She felt physically a nausea of the heart, and understood that 'heartsick' wasn't, after all, poetic rhetoric, but a description of a state of being. One which it would be preferable never to know.

Animals should beware of humans. How tempting, evidently, to play God and play games with little puppets for the sake of testing your skills ... Sophie shivered and shook her head. Some humans should beware of others. All should learn early the safety limits of love and trust. But what a pity! How could you? How could you? she thought. And how could I? Some other day, if there was another day, she would think about these rights and wrongs.

Glancing again at the cat, who was still awaiting command, Sophie said, 'Be independent,' and feeling itself without instruction the cat prowled in a circle, curled up, and slept.

Caroline had stolen a remarkable pink rock from a faraway beach, a golden-pink rock worn into a chaise longue by the Pacific. Now Sophie lay on its sea-washed curves, supported and warmed, grateful to the rock. She closed her eyes and a single line creased her forehead. Minutes passed, and she opened her eyes. In the whole sky there were only three small clouds, three of Dalí's small, premonitory clouds, looking as unreal as his. It was possible that this time tomorrow, this time tomorrow, she would be dead.

Of whom, Sophie debated with herself coldly, might that not be said?

She made no response. It was unanswerably true that she had placed herself in the hands of death; she was in the airy halls of death now, with all formalities complete except the last one. Everywhere there was the certainty, the expectation, that she would make the final move at any moment. And it was so clear that the alternative to death was something worse.

If she lived, sooner or later this sorrow would go, and then she would change and be a different person and a worse one, dead in truth. For the sorrow was all that was left of the best she had had it in her to be, the best she had been able to offer the world, the result of the experiment that she was. So it was bound to seem of some importance, just now, while she could still understand it.

She gave a shallow sigh and shifted her position on the rock. In its frame of leaves the cat dozed. Everything altered minutely. The small painted clouds had disappeared. And, of course, it was foolish to complain. In a way, she had been quite surpassingly lucky; and there was a great deal left. The only thing that seemed to have vanished entirely, now that she had time to search among the ruins, was hope.

'Hope ...' she said aloud, in a toneless voice. 'It's amazing what a difference it makes.'

*

The two women sat drinking coffee and glancing at their watches in the minutes to spare before leaving for the station and the Sydney train. For the twentieth time without success, Sophie sought to thank Caroline. 'Rubbish! I'm only sorry you're going so soon.' And they both smiled and rose from their chairs, glancing about to verify that Sophie's luggage was where she had placed it ten minutes earlier.

'Say goodbye to Cat,' Caroline ordered. 'You've made a friend there!' She swooped down on her pet and juggled it into Sophie's arms, before hurrying off to bring the car round to the front door.

For seconds Sophie held it against her chest, saying nothing whatever, feeling comforted by the weight, the warmth, the dumb communion, by the something like forbearance towards her of Caroline's cat. She let it leap down from the nest of her arms.

Lifting her bag, Sophie cast a final look at the silent room and its furnishings, and went to the door. As she turned the handle, with nothing in her mind but cars and trains and Caroline and, just beyond them all, the city looming, it occurred to her that, regardless of what was past, or what she now knew, she herself might still have the capacity to love. Need not, under some immutable compulsion, merely react. The idea presented itself in so many words. A telegram.

Like a soldier who, perhaps mortally wounded and lying in blood, hears a distant voice that means either death or survival, and unable to care, still half-lifts his head, Sophie listened.

Love ... That poor debased word. Poor love. Oh, poor love, she thought. It was the core and essence of her nature, and a force in her compared with which any other was slight indeed. Still alive? Even yet? Ever again? More illusions? Good feeling? The psychic knives had finished all that. Surely? It only remained for her to follow. Surely?

Yet in the car, while she and Caroline exchanged remarks, Sophie's mind considered her chances. Now and then it condensed its findings and threw her a monosyllabic report, like a simple computer. Her changes were exactly that – a chance. And the sorrow ... Only yesterday, the other day, she had believed that if she lived the sorrow would go and that she would then know a worse death than that of her body. But as it seemed *now* the sorrow would never go, could never leave her; like all else in life it had become an aspect of her person. As her love had. How strange, she thought, that nothing ever goes.

Nevertheless, detailing as they did the unconditional terms of her existence, these thoughts were in themselves a death. Had she been consulted, she would have chosen none of this, none of these steely thorns, inconceivable relinquishments. But no one had asked her; she had had no choice. One or two strengths and the love were what she had, and all she had, and what she would always have. And that was that.

Caroline said, 'Hear that clanking? I need a new car.'

Pedestrians cut through the tangle of traffic near the railway station. A dog pranced by looking for adventure. Sophie stared at shopping baskets, at boys on bikes, while debating the merits of this car over that with Caroline. 'Small ones are easier to park.'

Suicide produced just then, like a super-salesman, a picture of the very place. She knew it! Ideal, ideal. A hidden clearing off the track where you wouldn't be found too soon ...

And the instruction resumed its endless cries of surprise, trying to save her. How could you, how could you, it said. The psychic knife went in, it said. The psychic blood came out.

Yes, yes, Sophie agreed. She had heard this many times before, and could only suppose the reiteration had once served a useful purpose. But how like a human organisation! Even at the place of instruction, the right hand did not know what the left was doing. Someone down the line had not yet been informed that times had changed; the long-expected message had been received and was under the deepest consideration.

Walking up the station ramp with Caroline, Sophie took no notice, letting the two sides battle it out. They would learn, they would learn. She had learned.

Blueglass

Ellen van Neerven

A few years ago I noticed a bright blue smear running all the way across the beach. In the weeks that followed it got bigger, and wider, and soon the sand was a surface of blue glass shards, the whole beach glittered. Tiny little pieces.

We started making music out of it. I used my guitar and sometimes clapsticks and Michael stuffed his maracas with shards of glass. We played along the waterfront above the beach every Saturday. Singing songs like 'spat jewels of the sea', 'dirty sea blues' and 'crystal eye reflection'.

We were cross-cultural chemistry. We were brown and black. We were one half of Fleetwood Mac. People started buying our songs and soon there were other Blueglass bands starting up and playing on the same beach. There was a story in the *Courier-Mail*. And there was a story in *USA Today*. And people from other states and other countries came to see us. They talked about my 'mournful vocals' and how the lyrics reflected the 'hardscrabble existence' of living on this broken coast, this Blueglass region. They danced on the glass with their shoes on and when they walked back up after they kicked pieces of glass onto the path and grass and into the cafes and into their cars and into their homes.

*

There were festivals every month and always a new band. The first generation included the Waverly Brothers, The Liners (who also performed as Gerri and Jimmy) and Sea Dixie. Most of these guys we liked, but we always got the biggest loudest crowd.

After one gig I tried to pick up the shards that were brought up from the beach but there were too many. We stopped eating at the fish shop after we played because my battered snapper was a different sort of crunchy.

*

My Aunty's still around sticking the pieces together with old-time glue and selling bottles at the markets. One time when I visited her house, she took lemon cake out of the oven and knocked one of her bottles over with her elbow. I said some glass just wants to smash. Thought it'd be a good lyric when I said it. She made me look her way and said my father would have wanted me to do more and when we played our next show in front of 10,000 people all packed up on the beach, their arms out, I wondered how I could do more.

*

I used to take shells and other things off the beach and Dad would tell me to put them back in their place. Everything has a place to set in this land, if we take one shell it disturbs a landscape and we don't do that. I walked through the crowd of young people wearing Blueglass logo T-shirts and blue glass earrings. Dad said we need to keep our beaches clean otherwise we will become unclean, but he didn't get the hopelessness of it; the glass keeps coming back. It was part of the beach and now it is part of us. That was what I said in my interviews.

*

Nobody talked about the past except for Aunty. Singing these songs was the thing. Still going to the beach even with shoes on and forgetting the floods and how I saw young children with rock-salt coughs and blue teeth and nobody talked much at all. I wrote a song about those kids but that's not the sort of thing to sing about. Or about those pelicans I used to see and how the beach was like when Dad was around.

'Sa matter?' Michael said as we drank our blue glass beer in the beer garden. 'You look like you're dead.'

'Yeah, tough show.'

'Not just this show, is it?'

I looked over at Michael and admired his eyelashes, saw the times he had got me to come out of the water after a post-show swim. Wading towards me, reeling me in to the shore and pulling his jacket over my wet shirt and socks. He said he didn't want me to turn blue too.

*

Laughter behind us from the kids. Young enough to not know where the blue glass came from. They said the Blueglass movement was dying out and the subgenre Newglass was taking over. 'Progression' – electric, bigger bands, more than one singer. Some progression.

I thought it would happen slowly but Gerri and Jimmy are losing out and the Newglass bands, I don't even know their names, they're taking over with cheap lyrics and wrong sound. Dad was right. I hadn't learnt to keep things in their place.

'Haps we should stop while we're ahead,' I said.

'And what will we do?'

'Something different maybe. To get out of here.'

'Alright,' Michael said.

It's always been like that. Asked him for a kiss with my thickshake, told him we would sleep and live together, even asked him for marriage that day of the flood. He's gone on with it, especially when it's about the music, he follows my lead and I'm glad he's been with me all this time. We're the original Blueglass band and the connection between music ancient and modern. Nostalgia a trap but lyric gold. It was good, it was good.

*

We packed up next morning. I went to see Aunty. 'You know your father left some things for you.'

'Did he?'

'They're yours now.'

It was his old clothes. His old denim jacket from his band years. Big musky shirts that still smelt of him, sandy sleeves.

She wanted me to take some bottles with me.

'I'll wrap them up good for ya.'

'Still making those, Aunty?'

'It is not a trend,' she growled at me,

I think Dad thought I'd always live here. I did too. You know, it's easy to pack up a car and go, go. There's nothing hard about it. We put our instruments in the sensitive but not oversized baggage. We stood in the security line. We got through. No glass on us. Aunty's bottles left at the sandbags that marked my parents' graves. The level had come up years ago. At high tide the bottles floated into the sea.

*

Yesterday we played our last show. The old favourites, an extended version of 'crystal eye reflection', a new one untitled. Plenty of the Newglass scene were there. They were once our fans and they are now our witnesses but they still sing our lyrics as if it will save them, as if it will save all of us. It rained, and it seemed as if it was showers of glass.

Standing in the Cold

Nasrin Mahoutchi

One Thursday, when Mr Razi had emerged from the subway to walk to his home he saw that the snow had descended from the mountains and covered the streets. He tucked his head into his wool overcoat and his thick silver white hair ruffled out above his collar like a Shahin's open wings. He walked away from the main road and the sound of trains followed on the breath of the snow. He played with the corner of the metro ticket and then submerged his hands deep into his pockets and caressed his keys. On the way home he stopped at the corner shop to buy eggs and then he went to the local chemist to buy his new sleeping pills.

'I will give you the foreign brand, the imported one, the good one, not the generic one,' the chemist had promised.

Mr Razi watched those bony hands put the zaleplon into a plastic bag. 'It is hypnotic; *mesleh yek mordeh mekhabonatet, hichi nemifahmi.*'

Although Mr Razi had lived in the Meeremad area ever since he married Mrs Razi thirty-five years ago, he didn't have any friends in the neighbourhood. All the old neighbours moved out and the newcomers didn't show any interest in befriending an old man who wouldn't speak any more than a few words. Mr Razi felt he had nothing to talk about to these new neighbours. The only person Mr Razi knew in the area was Mrs Fars, an elderly woman who lived alone after all her family moved to America. Her eldest son demolished their home and made a five-storey building for his mother. Now Mrs Fars, who hardly could walk, sat in her first-floor kitchen and watched the neighbours.

*

When he turned into his street he saw the shadow of his house under the dim streetlight. He lived in a two-storey house built with cheap red-yellowish bricks. This house plus the one on the right-hand side were the only old buildings left from the '60s. The rest of the old houses in the street were demolished and rebuilt as four- or five-storey apartment buildings.

He took out his key. Then he remembered that he had forgotten to pick up Mrs Fars's kidney medicine from the chemist. *I will find an excuse to explain it to her,* he thought.

He entered the *hayat*, which was covered in snow. His footsteps crunched. The plastic bag he was carrying brushed against the bare rose bushes. He flicked at a branch with his key and snow fell from the branch. Then he reached the veranda, he cleaned his feet on a '*Khosh amedid*' doormat, opened the door and entered the hallway. He locked the door behind him and dropped the key into his pocket.

The living room was furnished with a two-seat sofa and three armchairs with a light-wood frame and a floral fabric. In the corner of a wall a picture of Van Gogh's 'Sunflowers' and 'Starry Night' were lost among numerous Gobelin tapestries, which covered all the walls. A large Gobelin of 'The Last Supper' was framed in green-golden Baroque style. Mrs Razi finished these tapestries four years ago. Her first heart attack had prevented her from going back to the *Pardokht* girls' high, where she had taught Year 12 ever since her marriage. She took art classes. These art classes were organised with their next-door neighbour's wife. Mr Razi loved his wife's artworks. He didn't care that all the other neighbours' living rooms were decorated with the same objects made by the neighbourhood wives at the art classes.

The coffee tables were light-coloured wood; the china cabinet was a bit darker. On all the coffee tables stood a tissue box with handmade lace tissue covers, all in light green to match the light green curtains. In the two years before a series of heart attacks killed her, she spent all her time on her art and craft.

In the evenings he had decided to learn how to use the internet and watch the news online on his new laptop, which his niece had encouraged him to buy.

'You have to send me an email every night and tell me what you watched online,' the niece said. 'It is a new world, uncle. You should be part of it. You can follow the news online. I know you don't watch news on TV since your TV was broken. Believe me, you don't need TV, you can watch everything on the internet now.'

He purchased the laptop by selling some of his wife's jewellery. To show his appreciation for helping him to buy and learn how to use the internet, he gave his niece one of his wife's favourite rings.

'She loved you.'

He watched the young hand wearing the golden ring. He kissed her face.

'You are like my own daughter.'

He kept his office the way Mrs Razi kept it. Above his working desk there were his Bachelor of Economics and diploma for chemical factory auditing framed in the same light green. Mrs Razi's diploma of teaching and certificate of tailoring were kept in the box of her sewing machine.

In the kitchen, he boiled two eggs and made a pot of jasmine tea, put it on a plastic tray and took it to his bedroom with the laptop. Sitting in bed, he watched the news on the internet. War, war, war, killing, killing everywhere, what a world is this? He talked loudly as if talking to someone. Then he opened his email and sent an email to his niece.

'My dear Homma, I watched the news online, as you showed me to do it. News all over the world is horrible; watching news online didn't leave any hope in me. I think I was happier when I didn't have TV to watch all the animosity human beings all around the world are facing these days. But sending an email to you every night is exciting. From your old uncle.'

Then he took two zaleplon and hoped to sleep as the chemist promised him. He slept at the left side of the bed. The right side of the bed remained untouched. He spent the next three days in bed. He left his room only once, to make tea, pour it into his flask and bring it to his bedside table.

*

On the next day, snow continued and he didn't go out. In the kitchen, he made scrambled eggs and while eating he walked to his living room. His courtyard was framed in tall glass windows; it was quiet and the snow obscured the skyline and the land, white flakes falling from unseen origins. Then he watched the weather news on his laptop. The next days would be cloudy with possible snow. He sent an email to his niece.

'I can't come out in this weather, tell your mum I won't come tonight. Love you both, goodbye.'

He turned off the laptop and in his mind he heard his niece's voice: *Dear uncle, take care of this computer and be careful not to spill water or tea. Just be careful, sometimes you can be like my mum, a bit forgetful.* He took another two sleeping pills from his bedside drawer and took them with his tea. Just before he turned the bedside light off, he heard the doorbell.

At first he imagined he was hearing echoes, as he did when he didn't sleep deeply. Then he thought it must have been a mistake and whoever was behind the door would go away. But the bell rang again. He looked at his silver bedside clock. It was five past eleven. The bell kept ringing. He pulled his wool robe and wool slippers on and when he reached his hallway he pulled a brown wool throw from the corner of the sofa and covered himself with it. He walked through the *hayat*, the thorns of the rose bushes clutching at his robe.

His fingers frosted to the iron handle of the *hayat*'s gate. The bell rang again. He couldn't remember the last time he had had a visitor.

'Who is there?' he said, still holding the doorknob.

'Hello. Sorry to bother you at this time, so late. It is late, isn't it?'

'Yes, it is. How can I help you?'

'Again, I am sorry to bother you this late; I am your next-door neighbour.'

He opened the door slowly. There was a young woman, standing on the other side of the gate.

Her gloved fingers pointed to an old building pressed between apartment blocks on the other side of the street.

'I know you don't know me. I am Lili. My internet is disconnected. You know I had to pay for my mother's medicine. So I thought if it is okay with you, I use your computer to talk to my sister. She lives in Australia. I have to ask her to send money.'

Ms Lili was pushing Mr Razi aside and was already in the *hayat.* Mr Razi was trying to process this conversation and at the same time was trying to remain calm and courteous. But he had heard that recently some robbery had happened in the neighbourhood, so he had to be careful. He was holding the door firmly; he was wondering that she might push the door open.

'But miss. Sorry, I am sorry, but I don't know you and it is very late. Can you call your sister tomorrow?'

Ms Lili was almost in the entrance to the hallway of the house. 'It is really cold here. Can we talk inside?'

Mr Razi's fingers, still cold, let the stranger enter his hallway. He locked the door and put the keys inside his nightgown pocket. In the hallway he took his throw off his head and took his shoes off.

The young woman followed him to the living room. 'Ah, it's so warm and nice here.'

Mr Razi turned the living room's lights on. Ms Lili bit off her blue wool gloves and removed her headscarf, overcoat and boots.

'Here, you can leave them here,' said Mr Razi, taking Ms Lili's snow-covered boots and leaving them inside the shoe cabinet. Ms Lili moved towards a sofa and sat there. Mr Razi was moving awkwardly around. 'Do you need anything? I mean, can I offer you something?'

'Yes, please – a cup of tea, if you don't mind.'

Mr Razi did mind. It was almost midnight. But he was obliged to make the tea for this stranger.

While boiling the water he looked through his kitchen window. The snow had stopped. He wiped the fog from the window. He realised that Mrs Fars's kitchen light was on. In fact, he saw that she was sitting there, watching him. *Has she seen this girl enter my house?*

When he entered the living room, Ms Lili was sitting on the sofa with her legs crossed and the throw on her legs. She had the Razis' wedding photo frame in her hand. 'Is this your daughter and her husband?' She stared at the photo.

'No, she is my wife.' He took the photo and put it on the table. 'She was my wife. She is dead. I don't have children. We don't have children.'

She stared at him. 'Is this you? No way!' the stranger girl almost shouted; her surprise annoyed Mr Razi. Then the girl realised that might be rude. 'I mean, you were so young when you married. And your wife, oh my god, she is pretty.' She stopped and corrected herself. 'I mean, she was a beautiful woman.'

'Yes, my wife,' he grunted, pushing the tea at her in exchange for the frame.

She noticed he was shaking. 'I am cold too. It seems that this winter never will come to the end.' Then she took the lid from a crystal bowl and scooped out two chocolates.

'I will bring my laptop and you can use the Skype for a moment only,' he said. He went to his office, and when he returned the stranger was walking around the living room, checking the objects on the entertainment unit, the photos, DVDs. She pressed the CD player's play button; 'Golden Dreams' by Javad Maroufi played; she turned it off. Then she took the wedding photo frame again. Mr Razi didn't know how to ask her politely not to touch it.

'You two look very nervous in this photo. Were you nervous on your wedding day?'

'Here, internet is connected. You can call your sister now.'

'Can I have another tea, please?' And then she took her cup and walked towards the kitchen. Mr Razi walked after her to take the cup from her, but she was already in the kitchen, pouring her tea and helping herself to biscuits, which he had placed on a china plate.

'This is nice.'

'Yes, yes. I buy them from the market at the Freedom Square.'

'Oh, no, not biscuits – they are nice too, but I was talking about your kitchen.' She finished her tea. Then she sat on the chair, her back towards the heater.

'Please, Ms? Sorry – what was your name again? It is very late. Maybe if you talk to your sister now – I, I have to go to bed.'

'Do you have to work in the morning?'

'No, I don't – I mean, I don't work outside anymore. I do some consulting work from home.' He was annoyed at himself for answering her question.

'When did you retire?' She took another biscuit from the plate. 'My father retired at age fifty. He was sick. We don't know what went wrong with him, but the doctors said it was something in his heart. My mother never worked. She is sick and is in a wheelchair. One reason we came to this house is because there are no steps.'

Mr Razi was feeling very dizzy and sleepy. He couldn't ask her directly to leave; he had never asked anybody to leave his home before. 'Sorry, Ms Lili. It is lovely to listen to you but it is very late and I have to go to bed. Can you please use the internet and go? I am so sorry, I hope you don't think I am rude, but I really have to go to bed.'

'Oh, I am so sorry to bother you. Certainly, I leave now. I come back tomorrow to talk to my sister because I think she will be out now. The time difference between here and Australia is a headache. When is night here, it is day there and my sister is at work. And when it is night there and day here, I can't leave my mother alone to come here to talk. I will come back tomorrow night.'

She put on her wool overcoat, scarf and gloves, then opened the shoe cabinet and pulled out her boots. 'Don't bother to let me out. I know the way out.'

The next day was Wednesday. When Mrs Razi was alive she used to have a cleaner on Wednesdays. Mr Razi kept this tradition but he knew because of the snow the cleaner would not turn up. So, after drinking his morning tea, he decided to clean the house himself. He found the dusting sponge, the carpet cleaner and the blind cleaner inside a small plastic blue basket in the kitchen cabinet under the sink. There was a bag of white nylon gloves too, but he didn't bother with them.

First he dusted the wooden cabinet. After dusting the CD player, he played 'Golden Dreams'. At lunchtime, he scrambled eggs and ate them with cucumber pickles while watching the street through the kitchen window. He couldn't see Mrs Fars anymore, but her kitchen light was still on. He wanted to check the news online but remembered some unbalanced mood that lingered around him last time when he watched the world news. He was feeling exhausted, so he decided to take his pills and go to bed. He didn't know how long he had slept when the bell rang. 'Oh my god, it is her again.'

He covered himself with wool and walked slowly through the snow in the *hayat*. The snow beneath his feet sounded as if someone was grinding something in their mouth. 'Who is it?'

'It's me, your next-door neighbour.'

'Sorry, miss, I am going to bed. As a matter of fact, I was in bed asleep, and you woke me up. Can you please leave?'

'Please, sir, open the door. It is freezing here.'

'Yes, it is freezing here too. Please, I beg you, young lady, go home.'

'Please open the door. Something happened to my mum today.'

The softness of her voice made him go back and get his keys to open the door. 'What happened to your mother?'

Mr Razi was rugged up, and covered in snow. It made her heart break. She put her arm around him and softly pulled him with herself. On the way, she flicked at a branch with her finger and snow fell from the branch. Mr Razi rushed to open the hallway door; a bare branch clogged to his wool shawl. He pulled the corner of the wool and freed himself.

Inside, she went to the kitchen, and Mr Razi followed her, still in shock from seeing this stranger in his home again. Lili made tea.

He watched Lili pull out the plastic step, which his wife had used to reach the higher cabinet. When she stood on her toes, Mr Razi saw the soft roundness of her bare heels.

*

After five days of deep sleep, Mr Razi decided to go out. There was nothing left to eat. He needed more eggs, toilet paper, toothpaste and some cleaning items. He also needed more sleeping pills. He checked his medical insurance booklet and made sure it was in his pocket. In the kitchen he checked the weather though the window. The sky had emerged, seemingly deeper, and darker, than before the coming of the mountain snows. Sparrows darted between the electricity lines, which had emerged from beneath a membrane of snow. He ground some dried bread in the palm of his hands and tossed it into the *hayat*. Still, the street was empty except for the bustle of the snow cleaners.

After he finished his morning tea, he took the shopping list and his medical insurance booklet and put them in his wool overcoat. He wrapped his neck with his shawl and took his key and left his hallway. The snow still dusted the footpath through the forecourt. He pushed some snow from a rose branch with his glove-covered finger and left his home. *She is very strange this new neighbour. Maybe it isn't such a bad idea if I just knock on the door and introduce myself to her mother. Poor crippled woman. I hope I never get put in a wheelchair. Awful.*

He walked only two or three steps, and stopped with a shock.

The neighbour's house had been demolished and was covered with snow. Corners of broken bricks and tiles and broken pieces of bathroom were strewn across the lot. He walked towards the rubble and called, 'Ms Lili! Ms Lili, where are you?'

An old peddler woman was walking past, selling handkerchiefs. She came closer to Mr Razi. He pulled out a few coins to offer her.

'Do you want to buy?'

'No, thanks.'

'Then I hope God makes your house worse than this.'

He knocked on Mrs Fars's door. No answer. Then he walked towards the chemist shop.

'There you are. I just knocked on your door, looking for you,' he said when he walked inside the chemist. Mrs Fars was sitting on a metal chair waiting for her prescription to be prepared. She was covered with her heavy wools. Her small wrinkly face looked like an old turtle's face covered in a wool shell. 'Mrs Fars, I am so sorry about not picking up your medicine last time.'

'Which medicine? When?'

'Mrs Fars, what has happened to our neighbour?'

'Which neighbour? The young couple upstairs? Oh, they are fighting again over their divorce. So you could hear them too? I told police. You know, I was the one who called the police. They came late, of course. So if you have heard them from the other side of the street, no doubt my other upstairs neighbour should have heard them too, but when police asked and questioned her she said she has heard nothing.'

Mrs Fars's prescription was ready. She walked toward the cashier but she was too short to reach the desk. Mr Razi took the money and her medical insurance booklet and handed it to the girl behind the desk. Then he helped her out, holding her arm.

'Mrs Fars, I am not talking about your neighbour in your building. I am asking about Ms Lili's family, my next-door neighbour.' Mrs Fars's arm in Mr Razi's hand felt light as a twig. The distance from the chemist to their homes was only a few streets but even that was too long for Mrs Fars, especially with this snow.

'Can we catch a taxi?' she asked, like a little girl asking for a doll.

Mr Razi stopped at the corner of the street to check for a taxi. 'There is no taxi. I don't think in this weather anyone comes out of their home. We better walk, otherwise we will freeze. Why did you come in this weather?' he asked.

'I didn't realise that I didn't have any painkiller. My rheumatism is unbearable. At my age, my children should be around me to help me. But as you know, these days, whoever can run away from this place, they will do it at any cost.' Then she pressed Mr Razi's arm even firmer, to stop herself from falling into the piled-up snow.

'Yes, I know, Mrs Fars, how you feel. I don't have children.'

Then his face moved towards Mrs Fars for confirmation. 'Since my wife passed away I feel so lonely in this world. I can't sleep at nights. That is why I came out in this weather, to buy more sleeping pills.'

They turned onto their street.

'Mrs Fars, where are Ms Lili's family? Where did they go? When did they demolish the building?'

Mrs Fars stopped. 'Mr Razi, what is the matter with you? Your next-door house has been empty for the last five years. Don't you remember? Don't you recall the day? It was your wife's funeral, the car stopped in front of the building, and the last resident asked you to move the car because of the removalist van? Don't you remember?'

Mr Razi's eyes moved over Mrs Fars as if he could not recognise her.

'Mr Razi, are you all right? Let's get inside. Come in and have a tea?'

'Oh, no, I don't want to trouble you. But please, answer me again – you didn't tell me what happened to Ms Lili and her family.' He was holding Mrs Fars's thin arm to help her to walk the few steps in her front door.

'Mr Razi, who is Ms Lili? Who are you talking about?'

'The next-door neighbour. I am talking about the next-door neighbour. My next-door neighbour. The girl. There is this young lady, her name is Ms Lili, and in the last few nights she came to visit me.'

Mrs Fars pulled out her arm from Mr Razi's hand. Then she looked at his eyes with astonishment and blame. 'Mr Razi, aren't you ashamed of yourself? You are a respectable man. We knew each other for years. Your wife, your beautiful wife, was such a respectful woman too.'

Mr Razi was annoyed that this old neighbour was questioning his loyalty to his wife, but he didn't have time or patience to discuss that now. He wanted to know what happened to Ms Lili.

'Mrs Fars, I didn't mean that kind of visit. She came to use my internet because she didn't have internet connection and she wanted to talk to her sister in Australia.'

'Mr Razi, I am telling you, there was no neighbour in the house next door to yours for months and months. There is no Ms Lili there, for sure, I am telling you. If there was any neighbour, I would be the first one to know.'

Then she went in.

Mr Razi walked toward the demolished house and stared at the broken tiles and bricks. He stood there until the cold penetrated his woollen coat. He left the debris and went home.

In the kitchen, he boiled the water and made tea. He took two sleeping pills from his coat pocket and had them with his tea. When he had just fallen asleep, the bell rang. He thought his ears were wrong. He ignored it. But the bell rang and rang. He finally got out of his bed, covered himself in the woollen blanket and went out to open the door. He heard the door lock behind him. He fiddled with the door knob, pressed it, pushed it, but the door was locked. Mr Razi stood in the freezing air, but he no longer felt cold.

Where Waters Meet

Jack Latimore

Millie found her sister hunched over the flat grill poking the narrow end of a wooden spoon into a length of hosepipe fitted to the end of the grill's grease tray. The diner was empty except for Peter Hewler. He sat over his steak watching a cowboy movie on the little television mounted to the far wall.

'Chelsea,' Millie called, loud enough for only her sister to hear. Chelsea heard her, but kept working to unblock whatever was lodged in the hose.

'I told you not to bother,' she said.

'I came to walk you home.'

'I know,' said her older sister, straightening. She tossed the wooden spoon across the kitchen into a pair of steel wash-tubs, hefted a bucket of scummy water with both hands. 'Now get out of the way, Big Woman.'

Chelsea waddled towards the screen door, where Millie stood. Millie held the door in, pressed herself flat against the passionfruit vine climbing up beside the doorway. Watched Chelsea edge by and carefully descend the two steps at the end of the concrete landing. The scum splashed over the brim of the bucket onto the toe of Chelsea's white running shoe. Her sister cursed, splayed her feet wider and set off crab-like for the end of the yard.

'I can help,' Millie said, tagging after her.

'Go away,' her sister huffed. 'Go home.'

'You'll scald your foot if it gets inside your shoe,' said Millie. 'I can take this side of the handle.'

*

After they'd emptied the bucket against the same gnarled pepper tree as the previous day, Chelsea returned to the kitchen to sweep the floor. Millie crossed the yard, scattered three crows from the picnic tables.

She watched Peter Hewler climb down the front steps of the diner with a lit cigarette in his hand to stand by the roadside, gazing up and down the old highway. He wore the same grey coveralls he always wore, opened to reveal a silver neck chain and his bare chest. The coveralls made no sense to Millie. He wasn't a mechanic. He'd closed down that side of the business when he paid out Blaze Driscoll. But Chelsea said the customers liked to think it was still a working garage – part of the charm that got them in from the new bypass. So every day Peter Hewler got dressed up in his costume and slid open the big wooden door to the workshop, where everything was covered in as much dust as grease.

George Riley said Peter wasn't right. Right before he barred him from the tavern. And Millie was certain she knew why. Peter Hewler drank too much and he drank too quickly. And when he drank he became so smart he sneered at whoever he was drinking with. He'd also drink until he dribbled on himself. And then he'd just keep drinking.

But after Riley barred him, Peter got a deal with one of the bus lines. Next thing he was hiring people to work in the diner. He opened longer hours. Offered late-night and early-morning shifts. Hired more and more local girls. Then he was hiring their boyfriends and husbands to fix the roof and do his gardening.

*

'Hey, Big Woman!' Chelsea called. She'd changed out of her white work tunic into tight black jeans and a T-shirt that kept slipping off her bare left shoulder. Her straight mousy hair was loose, getting in her eyes as she walked. Millie hopped off the picnic table to meet her.

'You seen Pete about?'

Millie pointed at Peter Hewler standing beside the empty roadside, sucking hard on his cigarette and now staring vacantly at the sunlight flaring off a pale granite bluff high on the eastern ridge.

'Peter!' Chelsea yelled, and when he turned Millie saw he had a glass flask in his other hand.

'I'm heading home,' her sister told him.

Peter raised the bottle in appreciation, staggered back half a pace as he took a steady swallow from it.

*

They crossed a derelict paddock without a word, Chelsea leading the way and treading heavily to ward off any snakes, while Millie plodded behind nurturing her suspicions of Peter Hewler. The sun glowered fiercely in the western sky and both girls were relieved when they reached the shade of camphor trees lining the riverbank. They paused for a few moments to cool off. Dry brush crackled deep inside the lantana thickets. Cicadas thrummed. Mullet slopped in the river.

When they started along the shaded track towards Boundary again, Millie began to mock her older sister's walk. She squared her shoulders, dipped them absurdly. And then exaggerated the seesaw motion of Chelsea's hips. She giggled so loud her big sister caught her.

'Why are you walking like that, Big Woman?'

'It's how you walk,' Millie said and hammed it up some more. 'Just like this.'

The sisters began to laugh at one another.

'I don't walk like that,' Chelsea said.

'Yes, you do.'

'Well, you walk like this.' Chelsea started wriggling her arms and bobbing her head like a rooster.

'No. You walk like this,' said Millie, thrusting her groin frenetically. 'You walk like this for Grinner White.'

'What!' Chelsea protested. 'I definitely do not!'

'Yes, you do!' Millie said. 'Just like this! Just like this!'

Grinner had circled their house for months before Chelsea

started at the diner. Around the block he'd go, doing burnouts in his bombed-out Holden with his shirt off and the stereo turned up real loud. Then he'd park it outside their front door and pound the heavy bass rhythm on his pigeon chest. If he caught Millie staring, he'd grab himself and waggle it at her and tell her to get Chelsea to come outside to go driving with him. Millie knew what he was up to. That heat glistened in his wonky eye. But what really worried her was that Chelsea didn't seem to mind.

*

Suddenly serious, Chelsea warned her to quit teasing.

'I can't stand him,' she said, sternly. 'I can't stand any of them around here. Not one of them. You think I want to hang around here with them? No way. Because that's what always happens. Get caught up and best case, you might make it down the coast like ma. But just look at us, Big Woman. Back in Boundary.'

'Well, sometimes it looks like you like him! Like you want him hanging around,' Millie blurted.

Her sister scoffed. 'He can stand out front of the house all he wants,' she said. 'He can hang around work all he wants. He can bring me all the stupid little things he wants. He can drive me home as many times as he wants. But he's never going to get what he wants. Never. Why the fuck would I like Grinner White?'

There was an opening in the scrub where the old bridge met the northern bank. A patch of cracked asphalt remained, resembled a crocodile skin flecked with dandelion flowers and lanky fleabane weed. The patch of old road was a popular area for snakes and lizards to sun themselves of a morning, but the afternoon's high heat had induced them into the refuge of the undergrowth.

The remnants of the old bridge abutted the bank. A pylon of heavy timber, weathered smooth and coated in pale red silt dust. Crested dragons lazed on the dry woodwork. Sunlight glinted off the river.

Chelsea walked to the edge of the bank, where the busted concrete and bitumen crumbled into a bullnose of gravel and red earth. The tide receded through the reeds below, ebbed swiftly at the base of the pylon's thick posts.

'What do you remember about ma?'

Millie wandered over and stood beside her sister. She looked down at the running water. Watched the tide purl through the long reeds at the bottom of the bank.

There wasn't much. A second-storey fibreboard unit. Faded bed sheets billowing inwards from the windows. Cigarette burns in the carpet. The tide ripping by the rocks along the breakwall.

She remembered her mother's dark, slender hands, the nails so white and her palms almost orange.

'Not much. What Nan's told me, mostly,' she replied.

'Do you remember where we lived?'

'Kind of.'

Chelsea began loosening a slab of the old road with her foot. 'Well, you've lived there and you've lived here,' she said, breaking a piece away. 'That's it. That's all you know. That's all you know of the entire world. Two places, fifty clicks apart.' She stooped and picked the slab up. The water dragons turned their heads, blinked their leathery eyelids. Chelsea weighed the chunk in her hand. 'That's all Ma knew. That's all Nan knows. And that's as much as you and me know. Fifty clicks down that way, and up-the-fuck here.'

The lump of asphalt struck the side of a pole and burst into a shower of bitumen and gravel. Dragons plunged into the water and the cicadas fell silent as the knock echoed upriver.

*

Grumbling green-tinged storm clouds hung low over Boundary when Millie got out of school the following day. The twilight was too early, the heat was heavy and the ground still dry. She walked by the old convent neighbouring the schoolhouse, then cut across St Veronica's churchyard to Mill Street. Riley had paid her two dollars for sweeping the tavern's front verandah that morning and her mind had been set on a couple of cherry-liquorice straps since recess.

The derelict houses along Mill Street were all unpainted, buckled board and rusty tin. Only half of them were still homes. Overgrown wisteria vines and long grass had claimed the rest. She walked to Perret's disused machinery shed and turned up the gravel lane that led to the old stable yard at the rear of Nancy Chisholm's general store. She climbed through the paling fence and crossed the yard. Climbed out into the spare block that ran up the side of the store.

The jars behind the counter were almost all empty. Most of the shelves in the store were empty too. There was milk and newspapers, loaves of sliced bread and cigarettes. The big store up near the new bridge had taken the rest of Nancy's business.

It took an age for the old woman to shuffle in from her living room. She reminded Millie of a river heron. Riley said that before the store, Nancy used to travel with a rodeo. He said she was a famous barrel racer who toured the countryside. But Millie had never seen her outside. Not even out front on Falls Road.

One strap was gone before Millie reached the bottom of the hill. She started on the second immediately. Walked through the empty timber yard spitting goopy red juice on the bare, diesel-soaked ground. White cabbage moths fluttered through the gloom.

*

Riley was hunched over the bar listening to the radio, his big hands buried in the sides of his bushy, pied beard. The bar room was empty, save for Frank Hobbs smoking his foul-smelling tobacco and staring blankly out the back window at the river. Her grandmother was wiping the liquor shelves, wiping under each of the coloured bottles and setting them in their place again. Millie dumped her schoolbag, climbed up on a stool. She knew better than to interrupt the race call.

One race ended and led right into another. She huffed and glanced around at the old photographs of Boundary hanging between the saw blades and bullock yokes and the oil paintings of timbermen in felt hats, puffing tobacco pipes in front of giant tree stumps. There was Perret's machinery shed with smoke streaming out of every chimney. There was the timber yard with piles of hewn poles. Stock drivers carted raw logs down busy Mill Street. Horse buggies and coaches filed along Falls Road.

'What time is Chelsea finishing today?' she asked when the radio finally lulled.

Her grandmother groaned, placed another liquor bottle in place.

'Leave that girl alone,' she said, without turning.

'I thought you'd be down that garage already,' Riley said ponderously.

'I'm going,' said Millie.

'Well,' Riley continued. 'That cross-eyed hoon-billy was in here a quarter-hour back. Said he was headed on over there.'

*

Millie broke from the scrubby bank and darted across the open paddock. The air was dead still. Only the moths stirred in the dismal light below the heavy clouds. She ducked under the hanging tails of the pepper trees. Stumbled onto the lawn gasping for breath. A hard block of light filled the frame of the diner's rear door. Blue steam spilled from the crooked flue, pouring skywards.

'Chelsea,' she called into the kitchen, expecting to see her sister scraping down the grill. But her sister was gone.

Peter Hewler whirled around, a flask of brown spirit sloshing in his left hand. 'Little sister,' he said simply and took a hit of the liquor. The burn made him grimace, smack his lips together. White match-heads of spit formed at the corners of his smirking mouth. 'How's the river run this evening?'

His chest heaved as heavily as hers as he surged across the kitchen floor towards her. His blue eyes glistened like wet shells as he propped beside the doorway and caressed the top of the jamb with his free hand. Sweat stained the underarms of his coveralls. He snapped the door open and Millie teetered back a step.

'Where's Chelsea?'

'Already gone,' he said, grinning. 'Took a ride with that buck-toothed fool.'

'But she doesn't like him,' Millie said.

Peter Hewler snorted, brushed the rump of his thumb down the side of Millie's cheek.

'Little girl, that's got nothing to do with it,' he said, slipping his drinking arm around her neck and drawing her firmly to him. The coveralls smelt of hot grease, booze and cigarettes. Millie twisted her face to the side, tried to squirm loose, but

Peter Hewler squeezed more tightly. The brown liquor danced inside the bottle as he covered her face with the flask.

'Nothing to do with it at all.'

Love, Actually

Brian Castro

'Actually, I don't have to apologize for my not writing, you know after all how I hate letters. All the misfortune of my life . . . derives, one could say, from letters or from the possibility of writing letters. People have hardly ever deceived me, but letters always – and as a matter of fact not only those of other people, but my own.'

Franz Kafka, Letter to Milena Jesenská

Dear Reader,
I forgot to say that Kafka also said that written kisses never reach their destination because they are drunk by ghosts and that in order to achieve natural communication between people we have invented machines of speed and instantaneity like planes and phones. Love is ghostly in the first instance. Not to notice that, not to see how love would end because of the rapidity of communication, is a special form of blindness.

I forgot to say that of course you can look someone in the eyes and not have to write about it. You could have dinner while swooning, tasting flights of wines, talking the talk, serious and light, and then spend midnight to three in the morning reconsidering how stupid you sounded. It would take a week for that to pass. People would say you looked tired and tell each other you must have been having another affair.

I forgot to say how your heart beat faster when you sat down to a letter than when you sat down for a meal or a good bottle of Bordeaux. How everything unsaid and written between the lines seemed so much better than making a reservation for a concert or a table – when actually *being there* took too much concentration over the programme or the menu and how the talk did not matter at all or, worse still, it was either one-sided or too intellectual or you discovered there was no compatibility. In surfaces you thought you saw hearts. That has always been your problem.

I forgot to say that at sixty-two even Casanova called it quits. That when a beautiful woman tried to seduce him he complimented her by saying she was flattering him for his works or his past and that he would have been taking advantage of her by offering a few poor wilted laurels upon which he had bedded down for far too long. He was a man of superb manners. And of course manners and courtesy, which are little practised today, have two advantages: they keep out those who would make you someone other than yourself; they also prevent overfamiliarity and can either be a weapon or a prolongation of intimacy, thus raising the quality of seduction.

I wonder if writing letters in longhand and sending them through the post allows the imprint of the body as well as the mind to write slowly and feel the agony of delay. These days it takes even longer to send a letter through the mail, as post offices are losing money because of emails, couriers, etc. In Los Angeles they have shut down the Central Offices of the US Postal Service.

I wonder when you write 'I love you' in an email whether it means much less than it does, as it is too naked and probably disingenuous and quite certainly self-deceiving because the nature of love is usually weighted more on one side and this declaration, electronically instantaneous, is without much self-reflection or correction. Just like writing xxx for kisses, which no longer works as an oath, when x stood for Christ and people would kiss the oath which stood for their mark or signature. It certainly is not an emotional copula connecting to an erotic future, as you used to think, driving you to return the xxx, which was by then an empty sign.

I wonder if this laptop love which necessitates its sending (since one's outbox is automatically cleared unless you put it into the drafts folder) hides a desire to have it made public (which admittedly is one of the complexions of love – to declare it to the world even if blushingly), but also to destroy ambiguity. So there is nothing between the lines or the ears and the urge to twitter it on an iPhone is even stronger, unconsciously making love social, shared, communal, so that National Security Agencies can find out if you love your country as well.

I wonder if Boris Pasternak was right when he said every novel is a woman. He meant the inspiration for it. You have stopped writing novels. Does that mean you have become a family man?

Where did I read that all love letters are meant to be intercepted, not only as part of a Freudian unconscious, but part of a vanity needing to be published, such as an open postcard where the postman doesn't even ring twice but leaves it in the rain out of disgruntlement, about to lose his job, and love sails down the gutter, perhaps redeemed by a grate or a skateboarder who cannot read but likes the picture.

Where did I read that your ex-wife found your password written in your wallet (since you had changed it so many times you had forgotten the latest one), and got access to everything: not only those quick sweet nothings to someone else, but also your bank account.

Where did I read that a true lover mutters, murmurs, stammers, babbles, blubbers, becomes tongue-tied, unable to narrate with patience his or her desire. That the love letter cannot play the game of writing, caught up in the heat of the moment, unlike a true boxer who knows how to fight cool.

Where did I read that there are at least five different kinds of love which don't exactly fit with our description: *delictio*, *caritas*, *amica*, *amor* and *concupiscentia*, not necessarily in that order. That charity and friendship – such as sending a cheque to UNHCR or having your dog follow at your heels without commanding him to do so – are not loves you can express in a letter.

I remember that in your youth you continually deflected, diverted, detoured from, the object of your desire. That you paid more attention to the target's best friend or anyone in close proximity. You are now sure that this decoy love, which duck hunters employ to lure a flock within range, is not a transference but a fear of directness, a congenital dysfunction perhaps, but probably something honed by manners and the need to write. If reality is sex, as Freud said, then arriving there can be as shabby as a Metro station populated by drunks and crazies. It is better to stay in the carriage.

I remember that it took a long time to take a lover. There were many false starts. You wrote an acrostic poem to your first beloved. The poem began every line with a letter in her name. It was your first year in university and you were about to be conscripted for military service. Impending death put love and war in place. You were very proud of sending it, but no one acknowledged it or made mention of it until one day, just before your psychological interview by the Army, your friends said everyone knew about the poem and that her boyfriend was not pleased.

I remember your awaiting the answer to your love letter. You sat around, moped, read Pushkin, drank a bottle of vodka. You deliberated how long this non-reply should last before you gave up hope and resorted to all kinds of clichés: there are plenty of fish in the sea; throw this one back. Go out and get a life. Love is aleatory and results from bluff, like winning at poker etc. You knocked on her door. There was no answer so you waited for fifteen minutes. Within ten, which is the length of most love-making, you heard voices; both male and female. With your next liaison, you began by discussing Heidegger.

I remember that silence was the best communication. Your mother taught you that. Your father once confided to you that she is capable of love but cannot express it. You didn't think this was true. Just because she didn't speak much English. She expressed through the diving bell of her depression. She wrote shopping lists in asemic writing. When your father died she said, 'What a relief.' She can now speak. Yet she never spoke the word 'love'.

I'm not the sort to put down love letters. Some of the world's greatest writers fell victim to them. I mean, when you read them, they are actually the least interesting in the plethora of their other letters – like those about people whom they hated, or ironic vignettes about extremely odd encounters. It may have been Freud who said the best cure for love is an unanswered love letter. The interesting thing is how few replies to these great writers are ever published.

I'm not the sort to perform love in public. You know that you feel a terrible embarrassment when you see lovers openly displaying their lust or their intimacies. It can be like squatting in a communal toilet outside Shanghai, ten holes in the ground without partitions. Some people use their cheap umbrellas to pretend to privacy and modesty. This is very moving.

I'm not the sort to say 'I' too often. It is best to be brief. Leave oneself out of it. The pen can be a penis. When Peter Abelard fell in love with his student Héloïse nine hundred years ago, her uncle's henchmen crept into the philosopher's room and cut off his private parts. He retired to a monastery and she to a convent. Then she wrote letters to him which were unanswered. She accused him of being inspired by 'the flame of lust rather than love'. Abelard wisely, though perhaps through his disability, devoted his writing to the philosophy of love. This did not stop monkish transcribers from dolling up his early letters, from which an early pornography developed and turned viral, culminating in the Marquis de Sade's prison notebooks.

I'm not the sort to deride pornography. Of course it has a distinguished history. Yet most of it becomes boring after a few pages. Epistolary pornography is a little more interesting. The early communist and foot-fetishist Rétif de la Bretonne (1734–1806) very cleverly wrote epistolary novels in which readers replied to the author and to each other, commenting upon Rétif's books and their own lusts, thus not only inventing a communication between writer and reader, but an illusion of word of mouth in publicising his own works. Fan fiction *avant la lettre.*

I know that Kafka's last lover looked like a raven-haired Ingrid Bergman or a plump Hannah Arendt. It was 1924 and he was dying of TB. The great writer, an insurance clerk so oppressed by his father he wanted to become a cockroach, knew of the cockroach's survivalist qualities. Perhaps the insect wasn't a species of *Blattella germanica,* but a dung beetle, because Kafka is anything but literal. Then again, maybe he was. In any case, *The Metamorphosis* can be read as prophetic of the exterminations to come.

I know that Kafka wrote thirty-nine love letters to Dora Diamant and that thirty-five of these were stolen by the Gestapo in 1933.

I know that Kafka wrote for the last time to Milena Jesenská, the love he had lost, saying he wanted to go to Palestine. He would never get there. This letter mirrors one of Kafka's shortest stories, in which a dying Emperor of China sends a message to an unknown subject. Perhaps it is an amorous message. But the imperial herald is caught in the crowds, trying to make progress through labyrinthine courtyards packed with people (nowadays he would be pushing his way along with what is known as The People's Elbow) and he can never make it out of the Forbidden City, which is the centre of the world. This non-arrival of a message might indicate how words are swallowed up by ghosts. They echo from beyond the grave, but the intended recipient is always absent.

I know that after the war, Dora Diamant ran a restaurant in London's Brick Lane area, catering to the beret and borscht brigade, London's cockney Jews. On her gravestone in East Ham Jewish Cemetery is an inscription: 'Who knows Dora knows what love means.' That, too, is a love letter.

I'm sorry that I promised the world when I wrote to you about Coimbra: *I have been there and have visited the spa at Buçaco. It is beyond beautiful, with a maze of gardens and pink-and-yellow-wash buildings like cream cakes. And in the grand hotel there are wonderful rooms. But I think you need more. You need the beaches in Oporto, the Granja, the Espinho. It is even more beautiful down south. I have a friend with a house in Algarve in a small fishing village called Ferragudo where there is a castle overlooking the cliffs; an old Moorish-style house with a patio, almond and fig trees and a courtyard. She offered it to me when she was busy teaching in Lisbon. And here you can write. The weight of time is sand. And the measure of sand is writing. So when you suggested we meet in Coimbra I was feeling as if something had connected and was disturbed. I can try to catch what was lost, but having only met you twice, good sense suggests I be shy for once.*

I'm sorry that perhaps I was really Fernando Pessoa for a time, the dead poet whose ghost negotiated the steep and rainy streets of Lisbon in deep disquiet. I, in fact, had never been to Coimbra.

I'm sorry that I was a tiger in camouflage, that the psychoanalyst Jacques Lacan was right when he said to beware of the other. Jorge Luis Borges, who was blind for a large part of his life, wrote that though he could not recall the eyes or smile of a woman, he never forgot the colour and splendour of tigers.

I'm sorry that I missed closing time, you said to the head keeper of the Dubbo Plains Zoo who came looking for you; that you had been mesmerised by two tigers, who had suddenly come alive at dusk; by the size of them, by the way they urinated so powerfully while standing in the stream, pissing against the walls of their enclosure while you were composing a love letter in your notebook, knowing that years hence you would be sorry how quaint all your promises were, how you knew well the passions of others and decided you were not the sort to treat them lightly, how you remembered the past incorrectly, conflating it with what you had read, in wonderment and ultimately, in forgetting.

Far From Home

Georgia Blain

High in the hills it was still too hot, although from the back of an air-conditioned car you could almost pretend that it was a European winter, the clouds were so grey and low.

In the front seat, her mother asked the driver the same questions over and over again, mostly innocuous variations of where he was born, or some harmless query about what they were passing. Then, whenever there was a pause, she would lean over to ask whether they had bushfires in these hills.

This last one never made sense to him.

'Yeees,' he said, drawing the word out, like a wide uncertain smile, although it was clear he didn't understand her.

'This ees your lunch hotel,' he said with some relief, as he turned down a narrow drive, bamboo pressing close on either side.

Sione had expected something a little grander, but then the ridiculously expensive was often strangely ordinary, she thought – how lavish could you go before you just trod water and fiddled with the finer details?

The driver gave her a card.

'When you finish lunch, they will call me,' he told her.

In the driveway, an old man swept up dried husks from the palms, long dead leaves from the frangipanis and brown, bruised blossoms. The slow steady brush of straw was a soothing and familiar rhythm underneath the rapid trickle of water from the fountain.

Each morning, in their own hotel by the coast, Sione had woken to this sound; the detritus of the night swept up, the gentle rush of the brooms along the pathways that bordered the gardens around their bungalows. It was always old men sweeping; dressed in dark green trousers and shirts, they would stop in their task and smile at her as she walked down to the seaside promenade before breakfast.

Here, the man was also dressed in the same green, but he did not look up, his eyes remained focused on the ground as they were shown in the direction of the restaurant. She took her mother's hand, the frailness of her wrist and the bruisings on her skin always disarming.

'Slowly,' she said as they approached the stairs, smooth, shiny tiles that were bound to be slippery. 'Take the railing.'

'I'd like to go to the bathroom,' her mother said, insisting that she could manage on her own.

And so Sione let her, partly because it was always a matter of flip-flopping around on the line that divided holding on to some semblance of independence for her mother, and recognising that this was foolish. But the truth was, she was also eager to have any chance to get away from her.

'I wish you were here,' she'd told Louis last night. 'I get so fed up and then I feel so guilty and I know I'm meant to just agree with everything she says, no matter how wrong it is – yes it's breakfast time, even though it's clearly night, sure a backless halterneck would look good on a ninety year old – but I just can't do it.'

'Ah well,' he said. 'If she wants to flash her back let her.'

'When I said I didn't think the dress would work on her, that backless was a little inappropriate, she said no one saw her back anymore. Which I suppose was her thinking that because she didn't see it, no one else did.'

'Maybe it's a spectacular back,' he offered.

She was drunk when she called him. She was often drunk soon after her mother went to sleep. Not that it took much. Two Bintangs by the pool and she veered rapidly from alcohol-induced elation to guilt, sorrow and missing him and home.

Now, as she hovered outside the toilet and peered into the window of the hotel gift shop, she was becoming anxious. After ten minutes, Sione decided she needed to check.

'Are you alright?' she called as she pushed the door open.

'No,' her mother replied.

She was looking up at her from the floor, her face white, another bruise already swelling, and Sione, being hopeless in any kind of crisis, just screamed.

*

The hotel didn't have a doctor, but her mother insisted she was fine. It was just a shock, she hadn't cut herself or broken anything, she just needed to lie down for a little while. Sione should have lunch and then they would return to the coast, where she could go to the hospital if she didn't feel better.

Out on the verandah, Sione sat under a fan, the slow tick-ticking overhead bringing with it the faintest puff of breeze. She could see rice paddies, terraces of fragile green under an oppressive sky, and below that the hotel pool, an aquamarine that spilt over the horizon, glassy in the sharp light of the building storm.

The table behind her was full of Americans. She hadn't really taken them in when she was shown her seat. Two men and a woman, all dressed in white and either pale pink or lemon, speaking loudly of someone in the movies, someone whose career was imploding because of her unfortunate move to Texas. They seemed to be about sixty, although one, a man, was younger, olive-skinned and handsome, his accent not as pronounced.

Next to her was a French family, a mother, grandmother, and two sons fighting over an iPad. The boys ordered burgers and fries. The women, both of whom seemed fresh from botox treatments, had tea only.

And then there was the Chinese honeymoon couple.

Sione glanced across at them as she ordered a *soto ayam* – not quite sure why she wanted soup in this heat, but perhaps it was the comfort factor. The young woman kept taking photos of her meal on a phone that was so overburdened with gold accessories it was a wonder she could hold it up.

Standing at the edge of the balcony, Sione looked down at the pool. Its smooth surface was disturbed by one old man slowly doing breaststroke in a diagonal, the gentle plod of his strokes discernible in the hushed stillness. By the edge, his two tanned daughters (she presumed and then hoped that's what they were) stretched out on sun lounges.

When she sat down again, the Americans were leaving.

Glancing across at the more handsome of the party, she blushed as she caught his eye, and then realised that he seemed to think he knew her.

'Sione?'

She nodded, desperately trying to place his face.

'Michael. Michael Pavlou.'

And as he uttered his name, she really blushed, hating herself for doing so.

She'd been fifteen, staying overnight at her friend Marina's. Marina was a new friend – smart, funny, pretty, one of those sporty, clever, popular girls – a trifecta that invariably led to physiotherapy. Michael was her older brother. He was studying law, she remembered. And he had a girlfriend, a slightly pimply Greek girl, who was also a law student and whose clothes weren't quite in fashion. The four of them had been watching television and then Karla, the girlfriend had gone home.

Lying in the dark, she and Marina had talked as teenage girls did – about schoolwork, friends, movies, and perhaps even a little about Michael and Karla. Sione had thought he was handsome. She didn't quite understand why he was with Karla.

Later, as she hovered on the edge of sleep, Marina's breathing steady and slow in the bed next to her, the whole house still, there was a tap on the door.

'Shh,' Michael told her, beckoning for her to follow him.

His room was at the end of the corridor, his bed unmade, the smell of him, sweet and musty, the sheets still warm from where he'd been lying, the curtains slightly open to the frosty spill of the moon.

Sione had never even kissed a boy.

But she got into bed with him, and she followed each and every one of his instructions to the letter – a rapid sex education, which would have been more enjoyable if he'd been a little less insistent about what he wanted and how.

Perhaps he would have moved beyond the urgency of his own needs if his mother hadn't almost caught them. Sione would never know. Mrs Pavlou had opened the door to his room and he'd pushed her down under the doona with such force that she'd wondered whether she was going to be able to breathe. About five minutes after she left, Marina came in and told her she had to get back to their room – 'now'.

'Mum's wondering where you are.'

And she had pulled her nightie back down and run, as quietly as she could, sliding back into the trundle bed moments before Mrs Pavlou looked in.

She'd been obsessed with Michael, but at least had the sense not to talk about it too much to Marina.

'He has a girlfriend, you know.' It was Marina's only comment to her on the matter.

And then she had embarrassingly got very drunk at a party and cried, telling Marina she loved him and he'd used her, and she hadn't had her period (the last bit was a lie).

Marina was a good girl. She became school captain the following year and was only four marks off being dux. She must have told Michael to ring her, which he did – his words kind but firm as soon as he realised she wasn't pregnant.

'You're too young for me,' he'd said. 'I'm with Karla,' he'd told her. 'I'm sorry I hurt you.'

She hadn't cried. But her voice had squeaked a little when she'd said she was fine, she hadn't even given him a thought, there was no need for him to worry and she hoped he and Karla would be very happy together.

Now as she looked at him, she wondered whether she would have recognised him if he hadn't told her who he was. He wasn't as handsome as she'd first thought – strange how that flickering impression of Mediterranean good looks worked. In his case, it was really no more than a mass of features she thought of as appealing – dark skin, white teeth, dark eyes – but there was something of the ferret to him, she realised. There probably always had been.

'What are you doing here?' he asked.

The waiter placed her chicken soup in front of her as she explained she was just here for lunch with her mother, who'd had a fall and was resting, which was why she was eating alone.

He'd come on a holiday.

'Not the one I'd expected,' he told her, as he pulled out a seat, stretching his tanned legs out in front of him.

She had a slice of bread left and he helped himself, dipping it in the last of the oil. For a moment she wondered whether she'd tell him she'd actually been saving that for her soup but then decided it would be simpler (and more mature) to call the waiter and ask for more.

'Divorce,' Michael told her. 'Or at least staring down the barrel of it. She left me a week before we were due to come here. I came anyway.'

'It's a beautiful place,' she replied, wondering why he'd chosen to sit with her when she hadn't requested his company.

The dark clouds were pressing low and the deep boom of thunder promised a heavy downpour. Overhead, the fan continued to tick, pushing thick sluggish air around with little effect.

She asked him what he did now, where he was living, looking across at him as she spoke.

He was a sports agent in LA. He'd been there for close to twenty years. He leant back in his chair and waved a napkin in front of his face.

If she'd held any illusion that he was going to ask her about herself, she didn't hold it for long. He was simply sitting there, no doubt willing to answer her next question if she had one, but other than that, his contribution to the conversation wasn't going to amount to much.

'So what are the rooms like here?' She regretted the words as soon as she uttered them, dismayed by the thought that he might think she was coming on to him, and she shook her head slightly, grinning as she did so.

'Sorry,' she told him, aware that the heat and her embarrassment were only going to make her blunder further. 'I'm not cracking on to you for old time's sake. I was just curious as to what you'd get for such a large sum of money.' Now she was commenting on his wealth, she thought, but fuck it – she'd seen the small suburban house he'd come from, the room with the Kmart doona cover and faded brown striped curtains.

His laughter was a relief. 'I haven't heard that expression for years.' And then he stood. 'I'll show you,' he told her. 'And I'm not cracking on to you either. Or at least I'm not planning on it right at this minute.'

The bungalow opened onto a garden, each wall seeming to slide back to let in the cool green. The room itself was relatively simple: the floors stone, the furniture teak, a palatial bed in the centre, a throne beneath the wafting white mosquito netting. He took her through to a sitting area that also opened onto a stretch of impossible emerald lawn, and beyond that a pool, which he told her he shared with three other garden suites.

'Top of the range have their own pools,' he said. 'My friends at lunch have one of those. He's a very successful producer.'

'And she's?'

He shrugged. 'His wife.'

She told him it was beautiful.

She should probably get back to her mother, and as she spoke he stepped a little closer, the slight sweetness to his sweat familiar, a glint in his eyes as he smiled.

'What's the hurry?' he asked. 'Someone will come and get you if she wakes or needs you.'

'But no one knows I'm here.'

He shook his head. 'They know, believe me,' he said. 'This is a place where they know – everything you could ever want or need. Before you even know it.'

The heat and the absurdity of the situation made her laugh, the sound more nervous than her usual throaty laughter, more of an uncomfortable squawk as she began to fend him off, putting one arm on his shoulder and stepping back.

'You are trying to crack on to me,' she protested. 'God knows why.' She told him she was in a relationship. She was faithful. She wasn't here for this, she was just on a terrible holiday with her mother who had dementia, and coming here had been a way of trying to pass another day because it was hell sitting by the pool in an endless circle of the same conversation with a woman who'd once been so alive and intelligent and was disappearing before her eyes.

'And maybe a quick fuck with the man that I lost my virginity to would pass a little more time and be part of this entire absurd package, but I'm not up for it,' she said.

He stopped then.

All the swagger in his posture seemed to sag. He sat, legs crossed in front of him and put his head in his hands.

It took her a moment before she realised his shoulders were shaking, and she knelt on the floor next to him, one arm on his and told him it was okay, although she had no idea what 'it' was, other than a single word in an empty attempt at consolation.

He lifted his head and looked at her.

Later, she wondered why she leant forward and kissed him, but it was only a brief moment of wondering because she knew it for what it was, both at the time and afterwards. Neither of them spoke and she felt him hesitantly following her lead, a drowning man holding on to a drowning woman as they both tried to swim back up towards the surface.

When the rain fell it was torrential, so loud that even if either of them had chosen to speak it would have been difficult to hear the other. She was glad of it, all of her intensely focused on his body and her own. She would forget this, as soon as it was over. She would say nothing of it to Louis, to anyone. It was just right here, now, and when they finally shifted away from each other, the heat unbearable, she allowed herself to look at him again.

'Are you married?' he asked her.

She nodded.

'Children?'

She shook her head.

'Did you want them?'

The question disarmed her. She had wanted them. Terribly. But Louis hadn't. And so eventually she had come to convince herself that she hadn't really. And now here she was, just beyond the possibility of it ever happening, even by accident, both feet firmly in a future that did not hold any chance of her stepping over into that other land, the one where she had always assumed she would live.

'And you?'

He told her he had twins, boys, eight years old.

'They'll live with you both?' she asked.

He was sitting up in the bed, looking out at the garden. The rain had stopped, but each of the leaves, the grass, the heavy clusters of frangipani, the tall stems of ginger, the moss that grew in the stone wall, all of it was shining, the weight of that downpour still heavy on every leaf and petal.

The knock on the door was soft, the voice only just loud enough to be heard. 'Excuse me, madam. Madam.'

She stood up, quickly dressing herself as she said she would be right out.

He was waiting for her, the man who had met her and her mother at reception, and behind him another man, both with parasols protecting them from the last of the rain, both looking at her, solicitous, apprehensive.

'Has something happened?' she asked.

She could sense Michael behind her, his arm holding her up, as they told her it was her mother.

'I am very sorry, madam. We do not know what happened …'

She must have held on to him because he stopped her from falling, the rush of green coming up towards her as he scooped her up, holding her steady as they hurried back across that garden, past the smooth surface of that pool, empty now, along the white tiled walkway, the old man still sweeping, and towards the room where they had put her mother to rest, and where she had died, alone.

*

The manager of the hotel took charge.

Sitting opposite him in his office, she tried to take in his words, but all she could hear was the trickle of the fountain outside and the slow brush of the broom; the old man still clearing up the debris from the afternoon storm.

A doctor would arrange for her mother's body to be taken to the morgue in Denpasar. She would need to speak to the insurance company about getting her flown back to Australia.

'Should I go with her?' she asked the manager, wanting someone to tell her what to do.

If she liked, it could be arranged. They would call her driver.

It was Michael who stopped her.

'Stay,' he insisted. 'You don't want to be alone. You can head down there tomorrow.'

Sitting out in the garden, she called Louis, leaving a message for him to get back to her – 'something terrible has happened' – because she felt she couldn't say that her mother had died over the phone, she couldn't leave those words disembodied in a mailbox. And then she called straight back, not wanting to alarm him, but to say that it wasn't to her, the terrible thing hadn't happened to her, even though it had. And so of course she ended up phoning again, her words bald this time. 'It's Dora. She's died.'

'Can I have a drink?' she asked Michael.

He picked up the phone and ordered gin and tonic.

She was relieved to see it was a whole bottle, and a bucket of ice.

He poured them each a glass. 'I haven't drunk since my first year in LA.' He closed his eyes as he swallowed.

She downed hers quickly, pouring another immediately.

They would have been fucking as her mother had died. She could barely bring herself to glance across at him, but after her third glass the gap between being in bed with him and sitting here now began to disappear. She knew him, she thought. She really knew him. And he really knew her.

She was pissed.

'I'm sorry about when I was fifteen. Pretending to be pregnant.' She shook her head as she uttered the words. 'It was a very bad thing to do.'

His swagger had returned. He sat back, legs slightly apart and paid her apology little heed.

'And it was bad to Marina. She must have felt strange knowing I'd run off into your room and had sex with you and that your mother almost caught us. Let alone telling her I thought I was pregnant. No wonder she didn't want to be my friend afterwards.'

The sky had cleared again. The late afternoon heat was unbearable and she stood now, unsteady on her feet and looked at the pool. She didn't say anything to him as she walked towards it, stepping in to her knees at first and then thinking why not? Why not go all the way in? What does it matter? What does anything matter today?

And so she submerged herself, the cool glassy turquoise enveloping her as she cried momentarily, her clothes clinging to her body and floating upwards as she tried to sit on the bottom.

He gave her a towel when she emerged.

She was about to pour herself another drink when she realised she could be sick. 'I think I may need to eat,' she told him.

Again, he picked up the phone and ordered for her.

'It's so sad.' Her voice was softer now. 'For the last year, I have willed her to die. It's been unbearable. Everything was scrambled. Sometimes she would ring me eight, ten times in the morning, wanting to know what day it was, what time, when would I come and see her? Always insisting that of course her memory was still alright. And if I questioned her on how she managed anything – her medication, her money, turning off heaters, any of it, she would get so angry with me. And then there would be days when I would glimpse her again, and I would feel confused. I would think that maybe she was right and I'd just imagined it. And I hated the way I was forgetting all the other versions of her. I'd loved her as a child. She was gentle to me, kind, and she smelt so good. I used to love borrowing her clothes, putting on her sweater and smelling her as I pulled it over my head. It was like sunshine on a tree trunk – warm, solid, real. And she made mistakes, but who doesn't? Oh, Jesus. Look at me here now. I should get home. I should get back to Louis.'

The sun was in her eyes when she looked over to him. She wanted to see him as she had when she was fifteen, when they'd sat in Marina's lounge room watching television and she'd been so aware of him sitting that little bit closer than he should.

She'd known he'd come and get her later. Or at least she'd hoped for it so fervently that it hadn't been a surprise when she'd heard his knock on the door.

She reached out and touched the side of his face.

'Are you going to kiss me again?' he asked.

She shook her head. 'Too drunk.'

'I'm sorry too.'

She realised then that he was on his third glass. His eyes had softened, the darkness of the iris covered by a slight haze of gin and heat.

She looked at the hairs on the back of his wrist and then down to his calves, his feet bare in the lush green grass.

'I was just a boy. We don't think like women.' His grin was rueful. 'Marina had the shits with me. Karla knew too. Or at least she guessed and I denied, convincingly enough to make her forgive me until I did it again with someone else.'

Sione's phone rang and she silenced it. It would be Louis. She didn't want to speak to him, not right then.

She looked across at Michael and smiled as she held her glass up, the condensation glittering in the sunshine.

'Here's to Dora,' she said.

He clinked.

'And to me.'

He raised his glass again, eyes still on her. 'To what we once were and will become.'

She lay down on the grass, the low clouds spinning. 'And to what we are now.' She looked through the glass at him, each feature distorted, before she closed her eyes. 'Fucked, and far from home.'

The Fat Girl in History

Julie Koh

My mother and I are sitting in front of the TV. We're talking about going on the CSIRO Total Wellbeing Diet.

I've filled in a preliminary form on the official Diet website. Based on my responses, it tells me that I'm Overweight, and that if I do the Diet, I could lose up to 8.3 kilograms in twelve weeks.

I feel relieved that I am Overweight and not Obese, because there's less work to do and I'm lazy like that. This sort of thinking is more or less how I became Overweight in the first place.

'If you lose weight, Julie,' my mother says, 'when we walk down the street everyone will turn and say, "What a beautiful girl that lady is walking with!"'

'I'm already beautiful,' I tell my mother. 'All mothers should think their daughters are beautiful, all of the time.'

My mother is becoming upset about her sagging chin and arms, and her sagging everything in general. She's in her mid-sixties but looks like she's in her early fifties.

'You should be grateful,' I say. 'Other women your age don't look as young as you do. Imagine if you actually looked your age. You would absolutely die.'

I remind her that I've never had skin as nice and clear and white as hers used to be when she was young. Everyone ages, I tell her. She should be glad she even got to be pretty in the first place. Some people go through their lives ugly, from start to finish.

She doesn't look convinced. She touches the slackening skin under her jawline, as if to see if it has miraculously tightened.

The problem everyone has with my body is not really that I am heavy-boned for a woman in general, but that I am heavy-boned for an Asian woman.

My university boyfriend, the one I thought I would marry, used to squeeze my arms and legs and call me Chunky Monkey. I was over 8.3 kilograms lighter in those days. He'd probably call me a Fail Whale now.

I once told him I wanted to buy a backless dress. It'd make me look chic, like I was from Paris or something.

'Don't you need a nice back to wear a backless dress?' he'd said.

In that moment, I suddenly became aware that not only did I have thunder thighs and a belly and adult acne and a fat head, but I also had a back that didn't look good from the back.

So I didn't buy a backless dress. I bought a hessian sack that covered my body from my neck to my knees, so that no one could tell if there was a woman underneath or a glutinous green blob with an unsightly green behind.

I'm sitting on a train wearing my hessian sack. I look at all the petite yellow women around me in a tableau determined by seating preferences and station order. Each little woman takes up just half of her blue seat. Overweight can look Obese when you're comparing yourself to delicate yellow peonies who blow gracefully in the wind.

I sit there and think about how they're all so tiny that I could squash them.

I also think about all the white guys I've met lately who have yellow fever. Even they reject me now. I'm not petite and Asian enough. I reject them and they reject me, and we are all filled with horrible feelings of rejection.

At a friend's wedding I'll be attending in the near future, I will avoid the dance floor and instead accost a friend's mother and complain to her about my dating woes – in particular, the phenomenon of yellow fever.

'Maybe,' she will say, 'the overwhelming attraction of some white men to exclusively Asian women is biologically the unconscious subjugation of one race by another.'

I like this theory. I like the idea that I am fighting a civilisational battle using my vagina.

I think that my heavy bones must be an indication that we have had a robust Russian somewhere in the family line, or maybe a Viking.

I order a DNA ancestry test kit online. When it comes in the mail, all I need to do is spit into a tube and post it back.

The lab sends the results by courier. I sign for the box. Inside the box is a pretty snow globe that fits in the palm of my hand. I stare into it.

In the background of the snow globe is the double helix logo of the DNA testing company. In the foreground is a tiny figurine of a big man in traditional Cossack gear. He's standing in the snow shielding a little Chinese woman from the weather by wrapping her in the folds of the coat he's wearing. Her shoes are at least six sizes too small. In fluent Mandarin, he's telling her that she will bear him gigantic, beautiful semi-Slav babies. She smiles and blinks. Snowflakes cling to her eyelashes.

'Of course,' I say out loud. 'My blood's part-Russian, not Viking.'

This should already have been clear to me, given that I've never had any upper body strength. I'm unable to lift a finger, let alone row a boat from Scandinavia to China.

'Can a lab be this specific about my ethnicity?' I ask myself. I revisit the website of the DNA testing company. I realise that the company specialises not only in DNA Testing but also in DNA Wish Fulfilment, and that I've unwittingly ticked the optional Wish Fulfilment box at the end of my test kit request.

I don't care. Because the lab has confirmed my wish that we've had a Russian in the family, I start to drink vodka. I try all the brands.

I am connecting with my roots.

Despite plying myself with alcohol, I have niggling doubts. If the reason for my fatness cannot squarely be laid at the feet of a giant Russian, then I have to conclude that it's probably my own fault.

One evening when I'm not drunk, I go to Fitness Second for an introductory session with a personal trainer.

I distract him from training me by asking him in-depth questions about his personal life. He's happy to talk. He has a girlfriend who was once a client. His father is Greek, and keeps tarantulas.

Despite my conversational manoeuvres, my personal trainer still manages to prepare worksheets for me that set out the different exercises I need to do every day.

When I come back to the gym the next evening, he takes me through the circuit he has designed for me, so that my technique is correct.

We do a lot of work with exercise balls. We also box. I put gloves on and punch the pads he's holding up. After five minutes, I get tired and bored.

'I'm puffed,' I say.

We go to Gloria Jean's instead for iced coffees topped with cream.

This is how I gain fat by going to the gym.

While I'm shedding kilos unsuccessfully, everything turns out well for my mother.

The front door is open when I arrive home after my iced coffee. The porch light is off; the house is dark.

'Is that you, Julie?' my mother calls out.

'What's wrong?'

'Come into the lounge room.'

The lounge room is set up like a photography studio, with a cyclorama where our altar for the Goddess of Mercy used to be. In the near darkness, a woman is standing side on, turning her face to smile enigmatically at a clicking camera.

'Work it, work it, work it,' the photographer is saying.

The woman is slim and beautiful, with fine alabaster skin. She's wearing a black backless gown. A diamond-encrusted pendant on a long silver chain hangs down her back.

'It happened,' she says to me in my mother's voice. 'It's a miracle! I'm young again! And I'm the new face of Chanel.'

My friend Jiao comes back from Hollywood to get rid of the last of his Sydney belongings.

We go to Obelisk Beach on New Year's Day. We aren't really beach people, but lately I've given up hope that one day I'll live in a place that snows at the turn of each year. By going to the beach, I feel that I am embracing my Australianness. I've picked Obelisk Beach because I want to avoid the crowds. Obelisk is apparently one of the most secluded beaches in Sydney. It's also a nudist beach for gay men.

On the way there, I ask Jiao what the rules are at a gay nudist beach. Is it okay to be a woman? Is it rude to wear my swimming costume?

Jiao says it's fine for us both to keep our clothes on.

To access the beach from the road, we have to climb down a huge rock staircase. There are a lot of bushes around. I've read on the internet that men 'cruise' here. As we move down the stairs, I wonder why anyone would want to have sex among rocks and bushes. These are gay men, after all. Don't they want fluffy pillows and thousand-thread-count Egyptian cotton sheets? Who will maintain the world's standards for classy living, if not gay men?

The beach is small and quite crowded. Not all the beachgoers are men, but most are. Three-quarters of the people here are nude.

It's definitely rude to look at all the penises, but I sneak glances anyway. They look so small, and this surprises me because so many of their kind have gone to war and conquered cities and engineered financial collapses and been models for very tall buildings.

Jiao and I lay out our towels, sit down and talk.

'Should we go into the water?' Jiao asks after a while.

'Sure,' I say, nonchalant. I start undressing, down to my swimming costume.

I'm really worried about my big thighs and belly. I try to keep them covered for as long as possible, then I get up and wobble with them across the few metres of sand between our towels and the water. I wade in as quickly as possible.

Two boats are moored just off the beach. One is full of people: men in shorts and a woman in a black dress. They're flying a rainbow flag and playing old-time jazz.

I'm very comfortable here. No one's ogling me, and no one seems bothered that I'm the wrong gender and sexual orientation. No one here is even really swimming. Like Jiao and me, most people are just standing around in the water or floating on their backs. The sand is smooth, except for some occasional rocks. There aren't any violent waves, so I don't feel like I'm going to be pulled under suddenly and delivered to the Kraken. The water just laps in and out.

I'm still curious about the penises of everyone on the beach. The more I consider them, the more it becomes apparent that the penises only tend to look small because a lot of men here have big bellies, which dwarf their other body parts.

I compare the size of each paunch to its corresponding penis. I decide to call it the Paunch to Penis Ratio.

A man with what I am sure is a very high Paunch to Penis Ratio wades over and begins to talk to me. It's not clear to me if he's gay or not. I get more of a paedophilic vibe from him. I remain calm, reminding myself that although I'm emotionally still a child, I am currently the size of an adult.

The man tells me a bit about the history of the area but I don't retain any of it. Something about there being a golf course here in years gone by.

'You look a bit out of place here,' he says.

'Why's that?'

'You look very white.'

'I've been sitting indoors writing,' I say. 'I haven't seen any sun.'

'I guess you and your boyfriend are here having a cultural experience?' he says.

I look back at the beach, at all the other beachgoers. I realise that, in their eyes, Jiao and I must look like we're tourists from China who got waylaid on our way to Bondi and are unsure what to do about it.

'It's a *gay* beach,' says the Paunch. He says the *gay* under his breath as if it's a secret.

'Yeah, I know,' I say. 'I guess I qualify because I brought my gay friend?'

'It's nice you're here,' says the Paunch. 'It's nice to have some eye candy once in a while.'

The water is at chest level for both of us. I realise that, underneath, the Paunch's junk is just floating there, cradled by salt water. I'm not only meeting the Paunch for the first time, I am also meeting his junk.

The Paunch is now standing between Jiao and me, and gradually edging forward. He asks me what country I'm from, and talks about how he spends six months of the year in Thailand.

Jiao keeps looking over, then leaves the water to go lie on the beach.

'What do you write?' the Paunch asks.

I tell him I write fiction but am having a crisis of confidence. A review of my work has just been published in *The Australian Morning Age.*

'The reviewer said my fiction is bland,' I tell him. 'I think it's a typo. I think he meant to type "wild".'

I tell the Paunch that I wonder if my yellow skin and vagina are limiting my chances at being the next big Australian author. I tell him that I stand in the shower sometimes and try to scrub the yellow off but, huh, it turns out it doesn't work like fake tan. I ask him if I can borrow his body and perhaps his mind.

'Ha ha,' he says nervously, paddling backwards.

*

Judy Garland appears on the deck of the boat that is flying the rainbow flag. She gazes down at me. She's in her younger years and is holding a small dog and looking wistful, as if she is feeling very stuck and can't leave.

'I tell you who's funny, Judy,' I say to her from the water, 'your daughter Liza. Is really very funny.'

Judy begins to sing. She sings about a rainbow somewhere. She sings away all the layers of anxiety I didn't even know I had.

I tell her I'm a writer.

'What have you written recently?' she says.

I tell her I've just finished a short story about a young woman who has depression. I finished it on New Year's Eve and went to sleep at nine o'clock, like the woman in the story.

'How much of the story is true?' Judy asks.

'Well, it's about androids in the future, so . . .'

'Uh huh,' says Judy. 'Okay.'

She feeds her little dog a biscuit treat.

'Is your work popular?' she asks.

'I don't think so. I think I'm behind the times. Everyone's writing about celebrities now. Like, inserting famous people into their fiction.'

'Interesting device,' says Judy. 'A bit gimmicky.'

Back on the beach, Jiao is burning. The skin on his back is all red.

We agree that it's time to go, and begin to climb back up the rock staircase.

'That guy in the water,' I say. 'I think he was coming on to me. I also felt like he might be a paedophile.'

'Oh,' says Jiao, 'I thought he was just making conversation. He seemed like a nice guy.'

I am dying, climbing up these stairs. At the top, I try to control my panting so it seems that I'm breathing regularly, like a fit person. I almost keel over.

On the way back to the car, Jiao gives me life advice.

'If I were you, I'd write genre fiction to fund your literary fiction. Vampires or something. And get back on OkCupid. You can't find a partner if you're locked away writing every day. How is anyone going to marry you if they don't know you exist? I don't want to come back and see you when you're forty years old, bitter because all the good guys are married off and you've missed out on finding the right one for you.'

'I hate OkCupid. It's so unromantic.'

'Oh, no,' he says. 'You're not still in love with the Kerouac guy, are you?'

I've had a multi-year crush on a dark-haired guy who's a fan of Jack Kerouac.

He's three years younger than me. I barely know him. Nevertheless, I've tried to woo him with clever variations on the metaphysical love poetry of Andrew Marvell. Unfortunately, the romantic success I pictured when writing those poetic variations far exceeded their real-world reception.

I ask my crush what he likes to read.

'I like *On the Road*,' he says. 'I like that the style was based on jazz.'

I neglect to tell him that I didn't enjoy *On the Road*, and that I like actual jazz – not jazz fiction.

My crush mostly ignores me, most of the time. I wonder if he'll start liking me if I become more like Jack Kerouac. I send him love letters filled with sharp fives and flat nines.

All he says is, 'Thanks.'

Eventually, I realise that he won't start liking me if I become more like Jack. *He* wants to be Jack. He doesn't want *me* to be Jack.

In a surprising and upsetting turn of events, he ends up falling madly in love with my mother, the Chanel model.

He can't stop texting her. He develops RSI in his thumbs from texting her so much. He texts her even while I'm talking to him about the beauty of *On the Road*, and how my fiction could one day be as cool and famous as Jack's.

In practically no time, my mother asks him to move in with her. This means that I have to move out.

'Aren't you troubled by the age difference?' I ask her.

'You're thirty-two,' says my mother. 'You've always had a hard time dealing with reality. Wallowing in dreams is not going to improve your circumstances. It's time for you to wake up and learn to support yourself financially. I am having my second wind. Go and have your first.'

My mother and my crush, a glamorous item, have a big booze-up at their place to celebrate Australia Day. All their smug couple friends are there.

They party all night, but they push everyone out by sunrise. It turns out that, despite my crush's baby-face, he's a four-hundred-year-old vampire. The age difference between him and my mother is no longer an issue.

On my way out the front door, he shakes a long, bony finger at me.

'If you dare write about me in your genre fiction,' he says, 'I will suck you dry and chuck your body in a Woolworths dumpster.'

I tell Jack Kerouac about my woes when he turns up in the front yard of the apartment block where I'm living.

He has reincarnated, and is currently a forty-five-year-old who owns a one-person company that mows lawns in our neighbourhood.

The landlord hates listening to Jack blather on, so I've volunteered to go out into the yard on a fortnightly basis to give Jack the envelope with his thirty-dollar mowing fee.

The beauty of Jack is that he knows all the gossip about all the people on the street. He just offers it without me asking as I'm giving him the cash – as if it's part of the trade. He tells me who's moving in and out, how much all the apartments have sold for, who is having an affair with whom, and who has gone on holiday and killed themselves.

I tell Jack about my struggles as a writer. I remind him of the paper scroll he typed on to produce *On the Road*, and how the scroll sold at auction for more than two million dollars.

'That's about right,' he says. 'But that was literally a lifetime ago. Get with the program.'

Jack isn't interested in Genius or Literature anymore, only Gossip.

I complain to Jack about being a woman and a writer.

I tell him that men are brought up to be bold. That they become the sorts of people who'll put on a pair of boxing gloves, dip the gloves in paint, and then punch art across a canvas. They blaze through and fall down and pick themselves up.

I tell him that women are born bold but then people chip away at them. '"Don't do this, don't do that," everyone says, "or you'll make mistakes. And if you ever get important enough to sit on a stage in front of an audience, for God's sake, close your legs."'

'Stop bitching,' says Jack. 'Start producing.'

I suddenly decide that Jack is handsome, and ask if he'd like to go out on a date.

'I'm in love with Joan slash Laura,' he says.

'Who?'

'You didn't read my book properly, did you? Should've known. Even the way you make me talk isn't natural. If you think *On the Road*'s a mess, this story's even worse. Where's the cohesive narrative? Where's the structure? It's just a bunch of anecdotes about being fat. It's a fucking mélange.'

'Like a mélange à trois?'

'What are you even saying?'

I think Jack is being unfair. I don't know much about him but I know a lot about other writers. Salinger, for instance. I watched a documentary about Salinger once. If Jack were Salinger, this conversation would have been a lot more historically and linguistically accurate.

'Well, this is my advice,' says Jack. 'If you want to succeed, you first have to identify which writers you are having a dialogue with in this country.'

'I'm not sure I'm having a dialogue with anyone.'

'You think you're hollering into the darkness but you're not. You're having a conversation with someone but you just don't know who it is yet.'

'Maybe it's Peter Carey,' I say. 'People say I remind them of Peter Carey.'

'He must be after my time.'

'I haven't read any Peter Carey.'

Jack walks back to his lawnmower and starts it up. 'If you sound like Peter Carey but you haven't read any Peter Carey,' he shouts over the roar of the machine, 'maybe you're reinventing a perfectly good wheel.'

I stand there thinking about what he's said. I decide that the writer I must be having a dialogue with is actually a guy called Tom, basically because I stalk him and we literally exchange words as a result. I also talk to another writer called Eric, who sends me creepy stories about terrariums, and tells me that if I want to be a proper writer, all I need to do is stand on a desk and declare that I am one.

I conclude that making note of actual conversations I've had is probably the best way to keep tabs on who I'm talking to.

Over breakfast, I'm reading an article about current trends in fiction. The author contends that society is now in the throes of autofiction. Everyone is writing it; everyone is reading it. Everyone wants to read about *real* alcoholic fathers, and *real* divorces, and *real* stay-at-home dads. No one wants anyone to make shit up anymore.

The author also claims that the days of postmodernism and pastiche are over.

I don't even know what pastiche is. It sounds like a type of pastie filled with Clag.

I skim the rest of the article and finish my porridge. I decide that I'm going to write an autofictional essay called 'The Fat Girl in History'.

I'm following the hip literary crowd. I'm deliberately in vogue.

I'm selling myself out but at least I'm selling myself to you.

I'm invited to the wedding of one of my best friends.

Everyone is shaking hands in the foyer, waiting to proceed into the ballroom. The women around me are wearing stacks of bangles and beautiful make-up. I can't understand a word they're saying. I used to go to school with them. We used to speak the same language.

'Umf umf umf,' they say, kissing me on both cheeks. The bangles rattle around me.

'Fug fug fug,' one of their husbands says, putting an arm around my shoulder.

'Ik ik?' I ask, trying to blend in. I don't know what I'm trying to say.

They look at me like I'm not making any sense.

I try a different tack.

'Audi?' I say. 'Lexus gucci prada tiffany?'

They smile and nod, and I smile and nod.

I look at them and my brain is a blank field below a blank sky. No thoughts appear; no ideas for conversation occur to me.

They proffer a camera, and I take a photo of them and their husbands and babies. Their arms are very toned, and their teeth are very white.

The bride puts her arm through mine and leads me to the bathroom. We stand at the mirrors as she fixes her hair.

'Am I losing my mind?' I ask. 'Do you understand what I'm saying?'

'Og og *quog* og,' she says, adjusting her sari and refreshing her lipstick.

'Shit,' I say. 'My life is over.'

She smiles at me in the mirror. 'Kidding.'

I smile back. She has the most beautiful face in the world.

'But,' she adds, 'you should stop telling people about Jack and Judy.'

'What?'

'At least Jiao's real, right?'

'You're all real.'

In bed, I watch a documentary on my laptop about women who are extremely fat, and deliberately continue to make themselves bigger. Many have skinny romantic partners who become their 'feeders'. The feeders enjoy feeding their women to fatten them up.

Men make appointments to spend time with these women, just so the women will sit on them.

It's a smart idea. There are a few people out there whom I'd be happy to crush, especially if they paid for it.

When the documentary is over, I lie down and look into the very core of my nature. I discover that I am simultaneously extremely ambitious and extremely lazy. It becomes apparent to me that an ambition appropriate to this core nature is to be the fattest person that ever lived, and to achieve this by being too lazy to exercise.

So I eat. I fatten myself up like a Wagyu cow.

Each roll of fat gets bigger and bigger until it rolls over the previous roll, grows downwards, and puts down roots.

My rolls spread out over the front yard and the whole apartment block.

I work harder at eating and soon the rolls extend across the country. Kangaroos hop across my knees. Black cockatoos make their nests in the crooks of my elbows. Koalas climb up and hug themselves around my pinkie fingers.

I can see how big I'm getting relative to the people who come around to visit. They lift up my arm fat and pop under it and say hello.

They're all so small that I have to squint to see them. Although they start out chatting to me in an upbeat mood, every one of them ends up lamenting my weight. It's like someone's died. Their tears form puddles around my ankles. Platypuses paddle in the salt water.

I continue to expand in ever-multiplying concentric rings of fat, which move outwards across the world. Soon there is no more room for oceans, let alone tears. I am one big beach.

I begin to grow extra limbs and heads and breasts. Nevertheless, my Paunch to Penis Ratio remains nil.

I have so many fingers and arms and legs and necks now that I am able to wear truckloads of statement jewellery. I adorn myself with malachite and onyx, moss agate and lapis lazuli, citrine and smoky quartz. My jewellery becomes beautiful armour.

I become the face of Fat Chanel, and they send a team of photographers to shoot me from every angle. They do so even though they're in the middle of a stressful trade mark dispute over the unauthorised use of the Chanel name.

I wear a backless dress for the key promo shot. The dress is also frontless, shoulderless and arseless.

They build a white temple to contain me. The walls are made of square panels that interlock in an ingenious way, so that new sections of wall can be added easily as I expand.

I grow faster than the little people can build the walls.

Around the temple, under an orange sky, a field of yellow peonies springs up.

Millions of ant-sized people pick the peonies and bring them to me as offerings. They lay them at my feet. They are here to get my blessing – for their newborns and marriages and assorted happy occasions – because I have become a goddess who doesn't care about shit, and people really respond to that.

I gather up all the tiny worshippers and their fragile peonies. I pick up all the people I love and the people I hate – Jack and Judy, and Jiao and the Paunch, and Tom and Eric, and my mother and her vampire, and my friend with the beautiful face, and all the little women with their rattling bangles and words I don't understand.

I wrap my fat arms around all of these little people, and hug them to my breast. I drug them with a lullaby, and nurse them all to sleep.

Snow begins to fall.

In their dreams, the little people call out to me. They call me the Goddess of Mercy.

Because I can nurse them or I can crush them, and the power is all mine.

A Step, a Stumble

Trevor Shearston

The phone rang at breakfast, and again when they were dressing for service. Each time he let it ring out. So early it could only be another reporter.

It was ringing again as they turned in the front gate, they could hear it through the open kitchen window. He sprinted to the porch and was almost to the door with the key aimed at the lock when the ringing stopped.

'Blast!'

Now was different, there'd been time for a second search party to have gone down. He opened the door and, without waiting for her, strode to the kitchen and stood at the phone. People often tried again a minute later. She came in and placed her purse on the table and took off her hat. 'Do you want a cuppa?'

'No, too hot, I'll just have water. Can you wait here while I change.'

He went to the bedroom and stripped to singlet and underpants and put on shorts. She'd left his ice-water on the bench and had unlocked and opened the back door to let in air. He drank standing. Then he picked up the receiver and put it to his ear. There was the customary click, followed by the burr of dial tone. He placed the receiver back on the cradle and folded his arms and stood till she returned in her yellow sunfrock. He asked what she needed from the garden.

As he re-entered the kitchen the phone rang. Both had their hands full, she at the sink shelling boiled eggs. She pointed with her chin to the colander standing on the draining board. He dumped into it the lettuce, carrots, radishes, swiped his right hand down his shorts.

'Mr Newstead – Morey. I tried you earlier.'

'We were at church.'

'I thought you'd want to know, we found him.'

'Yes. Thank you.'

'He arrived down there a lot quicker than we took getting him up. It was quite a slog, especially in this heat. Only blessing, we couldn't find all of him. I'm actually in Katoomba, the hospital – the morgue. I was wondering, seeing you were the last person ... you'd know the clothes he was wearing – I was wondering if you'd be willing to, ah, identify him for us. Officially.'

'Oh – no – I don't think I want to do that.'

'It wouldn't need long, just a quick look, as I say, more at the clothes. They tell me there's no Mrs Childe or a companion, and that he hasn't lived back here in over thirty years. Means I'm chasing next of kin and I've no idea where they are or if he's even got any.'

'I'm sorry, Constable Morey, I think that's somebody else's job. Maybe somebody at the Carrington. Reception, the barmen – any of them would know him.'

He knew what Morey was doing, calling in a favour, confirmed when the policeman let a silence grow.

'Not your job, Mr Newstead, I agree. I was simply asking. I'll follow up your suggestion. You'll be required at a coroner's inquest, though, as you'd probably know.'

'Yes. I was called to one once before.'

'You know the drill, then. So, sad result, but at least now we're sure he didn't plant his stuff and waltz off down the track.'

'What ... that's happened?'

'My word it has.'

She had finished shelling the eggs and was breaking lettuce into the smaller of the wooden salad bowls. She'd guessed they'd found the body and wanted to know what it was he'd refused to do. When told she was outraged. He'd been absolutely right to refuse, what an awful thing to ask! As if he hadn't been through enough! She glittered with anger, clashing plates and slapping cutlery onto the counter until he took her by the arms and said into her face that he'd told the man no and that was an end to it.

He ate fast and went out to the laundry. He got the fork and the cardboard cylinder of derris dust and came out and picked up the brass nozzle from the lawn and walked again to the vegetable beds, the warm hose snaking bonelessly behind him. It wasn't an end to it. But there was a disproportion between what the policeman had done for him and what he'd just been asked in return, grateful though he'd been at the time for the man's help. Well, 'help', it was the man's job!

Back in July, a night cold enough to have him working in overcoat and scarf, a man in his fifties, no coat or hat, had come to the rank, got in and asked to be taken to Blackheath. The few words were enough to fill the cabin with beer fumes. He took the bends out of town slowly, ready to pull over at the first warning the man gave of wanting to puke. Instead the man slumped against the pillar and fell into a muttering doze that lasted to the descent into the village, when he sat up and stared about, then told him to cross the railway and take the second left, Kubya Street. He then asked if he was married. When told yes, he said that was all right, that could be accommodated, then announced that he didn't have the fare but his sister would take care of him, she wasn't all there in the head but she was in the body, but seeing he was married he mightn't like to do the other but that was all right, she was good with her mouth, he used her that way himself. Newstead drove to the police station. Fearing the man might attempt a runner, he parked on the kerb and pumped the horn. The cop who came was Morey, then also a stranger to him. He got out to explain but the policeman was already at the passenger door. 'Save your breath, I know what he's told you.' He opened the door and said, 'Hello, George,' and hauled the man out and spun him and pushed him hard against the trunk of the tree growing on the footpath and held him while he went through his trouser pockets, extracting change and signing to Newstead that he come closer and cup his hand. 'What's he owe you?'

'Three quid.'

'That'd be half anyway. That do you? He don't carry a wallet.'

'Not worth court for the rest. Thank you.'

Still holding the man pinned, the policeman extended his other hand. 'I run the shop – Jim Morey.'

'Henry Newstead. Harry.'

'Katoomba, are you?'

'Yes.'

'Nice bastard isn't he. You'll know his face next time he ventures down your way.' He gave the man a light cuff to the back of the head. 'Won't he, George.'

At the lookout yesterday Morey had done almost the identical thing, taken the worn leather pocketbook from the inside vest pocket of the professor's coat and asked what he was owed, for the ride and the wait. When he demurred, Morey kept the pocketbook open. 'You're not going to get your money otherwise. Once I take this to the station you're buggered.'

Newstead had named the amount. Morey drew out the notes and gave him.

'Whack it in your pocket before we get company.' He'd then removed and counted the rest of the notes. 'Fifteen pound ten?' Newstead nodded. The policeman tapped the notes straight and slid them back into their compartment, then drew from another a folded single page, which he opened and read, before holding it out to Newstead.

'Witness if you would, Mr Newstead. Letter of credit on the Commonwealth Trading Bank for three hundred pound in the name Vere Gordon Childe.' He lowered and refolded the letter. 'That the name you knew him by, the man you brought here?'

'The surname. At the rank we just called him Professor. My partner in the taxi, Fred Benham, he knew him better. Today was the first time he rode with me, he mostly rode with Fred. They're closer in age. But Fred's told me a fair bit about him. He liked the black Wolseley. He told Fred it reminded him of the taxis in London.'

'What was he professor of? He tell Mr Benham?'

'Yes, archaeology. But he told Fred he'd got interested in geology. Why he was coming to places like Govetts.'

'And why the compass.'

'I suppose so.'

'He normally a good pay? Apart from today?'

'He paid above the rate, yes.'

'He certainly has today, Mr Newstead. If the signs are correct.'

He swung the nozzle to the rows of newly emerged beans and as he watched the soil blacken and drink wondered whether Morey had even then been thinking ahead to the request he'd be putting. His own mind didn't work that way. But he wasn't a copper.

'Well, don't forget he needs you, too,' he said at the beans. To not say anything that complicates matters. And you managed that with Toohey. So he's had his return there.

What was eating him, though, wasn't the veiled demand, it was his own failure. If going over the edge had been intentional, why had he not sensed anything of the man's intent? Because he hadn't, not a hint. They'd shared the cab of the Wolseley for long enough, twenty minutes. The year before last he'd become a minor celebrity when he'd saved a woman, a Mrs Barry. She got in at the rank, told him she'd come that morning from Sydney in the train, and asked to be taken to Echo Point. They were words he heard, on good days, nine or ten times in a shift. She'd seemed outwardly calm when she settled herself and spoke, but when she looked up and found herself in the mirror's eyeline she'd slid across to the opposite window. Then as they'd descended Katoomba Street what he could describe later to the cops and to Toohey's predecessor and to Joyce only as a sort of electric charge like the static before a storm had started in the taxi and grown until the air between the front and back seats seemed to him alive and humming. He'd dropped her at the Point rank, then gone straight to the kiosk and rung the police, telling them what he believed she intended and waiting till they got there so as to describe her. They'd found her on the clifftop near Spooner's Lookout and stopped her. Her husband had written him, care of the police station, an emotional letter of gratitude and included a cheque for a hundred pounds. Joyce had bought them a new bedroom suite.

He'd picked up no such static from the professor. After stating where he wanted to go, the man had busied himself with filling his pipe and getting it to draw, then with riffling through the sheaf of papers he'd brought. He'd kept his Australian accent, but half-swallowed words as if having to speak was a nuisance. Newstead prided himself on not being like Fred, who couldn't sit in a silent cab. He let his passengers choose whether and how much they wished to converse. In this he believed himself more professional than his older partner. You were not driving a person as a friend and equal, you were providing a service. The professor spoke only twice again in the twenty-minute run to Govetts Leap. When passing along Bathurst Road he'd asked whether Newstead thought the taller of the houses would have a view of Mount Banks. He'd answered that he'd never been in one, but that it was more than likely, if they weren't blocked by the trees on the other side of the railway line. At Medlow the man had taken the pipe from his mouth to comment that he'd never had any interest in staying at the Hydro Majestic, it had the famous view but was in the middle of nowhere. Newstead replied that he'd had other people say the same, that they much preferred the Carrington, where the Professor was, in town where you had the cafes and the pictures and a bit of life on the streets.

'Harry?'

He jumped, spraying the path. The hot concrete drank the water as greedily as the soil. She asked if he wanted a cuppa or something cold. Something cold, he said. When she went back in he drank from the nozzle, then ran water into his hand and slooshed his face.

She brought out two glasses of iced Milo on a tray, and a plate of ginger nuts. He fetched the hose spike from the corner of the bed and drove it into the middle where the spray would fall on the lettuces. His mother had rung, he was in the late editions of both papers. She was sending them over with the neighbour's kid.

He dusted the cabbages and cauliflowers for aphid, then began on digging compost into the bed he'd left fallow. But after half an hour the knowledge that the papers would probably now be lying on the kitchen table pulled him to the tap at the back door.

Joyce was baking, the table floured and waiting for the pastry mix she was turning in a bowl. The papers lay side by side on the benchtop, each unfolded to the front page. She said, 'You're not much, just a couple of lines.' He leaned on his damp fingertips and skimmed both accounts. They seemed identical. He chose the *Herald*, read it standing. ***Body Of Professor Found 1,000ft Below Top Of Cliff*** *Katoomba, Sunday – The body of Professor Vere Gordon Childe, 65, famous Sydney-born archaeologist, was found today below*

Govetts Leap at Blackheath. Police believe that he fell over the leap about 8.30 am yesterday while taking a compass reading near the Bridal Veil falls. A 15-year-old boy, Malcolm Longton, of Blackheath, found his body in dense scrub on a ledge 200 feet above the bottom of the falls. He jumped ahead to his own name and was astounded to find himself reported in words he didn't recognise, that the professor had told the taxi driver, Mr Harry Newstead, *he was going along the cliff top to study the ranges and would not be long.* The man had said nothing of the kind, only stood for a very long moment looking out over the Grose, then turned back to the open door and said, reaching in for the papers he'd been shuffling and reshuffling for the whole trip, 'I will take these.' In the next paragraph he, Mr Newstead, was reported to have become *concerned* when the professor had not returned by noon. It was a stupid word and he never used it. 'Worried', he'd said. And the *visitor from Sydney, Mr Brian Darragh,* was now the one who'd alerted Blackheath police. The whole bloody thing was twisted! He had walked back there with the Darraghs, seen the professor's things, then driven to the police station. Reminded, he moved his eyes over the article for any mention of Morey. There was none, apart from *police said.* He supposed that was standard, only members of the public mentioned by name. Morey, though, after making a statement to Arthur Toohey and answering questions, had stayed at his elbow when Toohey turned to him wanting to know what the deceased's – assuming he was – what his mental state had been on the ride there. Morey had stepped in before he could open his mouth.

'Arthur, Mr Newstead's not a psychiatrist. He's told you the facts you need from him, I've given you the facts at the lookout and what the police believe happened. Now I hope you'll appreciate that Mr Newstead has lost most of a day but still has a living to earn, and I've got a search party to organise to try and get down and up before dark. If you've still got state-of-mind questions I suggest you wait for the coroner's.'

Toohey had looked at him, then back at the policeman. Newstead remembered the man's eyes, amused, as if newsgathering was a game of wits, no more.

'I won't trouble him for more than a sentence or two, Senior Constable.'

'Good day, Mr Toohey.'

The man conceded with a tilt of the head and closed his notepad.

'You don't mind if I come back after I file this and walk round to the lookout?'

'It's a public track, Arthur, you're a member of the public. But be so good as to not pester my officer there to be allowed up to the edge. For our sake as well as yours – we don't want you landing on us.'

Toohey broke into a merry laugh.

He'd turned towards the Wolseley to hide his anger, but caught at the edge of his vision the policeman make a damping gesture with his hand to the man.

'It's all right, Mr Newstead,' Morey said, 'we haven't forgotten why we're here.'

He read to the end of the article. The final paragraphs described the climb, the men carrying the stretcher with the body forced to relieve one another every hundred yards. They were protecting their readers, he supposed, calling it a 'body'. Immediately below was a story as boldly headlined, ***Tulloch's Owner Not Decided About Cup***. What was that about? He'd planned to put a few quid on the wonder colt. He began to read, then stopped, disgusted with himself. He was as bad as the two yesterday. He folded the papers together facedown on the benchtop and turned. She'd rolled out the pastry and was stamping out circles with a floured tin to make turnovers. The rhubarb and apple filling was in a saucepan on the table, a spoon sunk in it. 'Don't you dare,' she said without looking up. For a second he didn't understand, both teasing and food far from his mind. She lifted a white finger towards the papers. 'Why on earth would they take a boy of fifteen?'

'I suppose he just took who he could get.' At fifteen he'd have put up his hand too. He walked to the sink and filled a glass. 'I'm just going to sit outside.'

'Harry.'

He halted and looked at her.

'No – come here.'

She kissed him on the mouth, keeping her floured hands above the table.

'Don't brood. There's nothing you could have done.'

The concrete wasn't hot, only the air. He dragged one of the heavy patio chairs into the shade of the laundry wall and sat and stood the glass between his bare feet. Don't brood. She might as well have said don't think. Don't breathe. He wondered how Fred was coping. He wouldn't be brooding but he'd be upset, especially being behind the wheel. He'd rung him yesterday afternoon from the police station, not wanting one of the other blokes ringing to say he'd been missing from the rank for most of the day. He'd told him only what the evidence said, that the Professor had been off along the cliffs at Govetts taking bearings with a compass like he'd done all the times he'd gone out with him, Fred, and probably stepped too close to the edge not wearing his glasses and had gone over. 'What – yous found his specs?' Fred had shouted down the line. 'Why would he take his specs off? You seen him – the thickness of them – he couldn't cross a footpath without them, let alone a bloody cliff! Did you tell the coppers blokes had goes at him because he looked a poof? Some bastard could have pitched him off and made it look an accident!' He'd told him, keeping his voice as calm as he could, that neither he nor the police thought that was what had happened. The lookout wasn't on the main track, it was down a loop. The police had examined for shoeprints and other signs of anyone else having been there and found none. The specs were sitting on the rock with the lugs open like you'd do to pick up and put on again, and his pocketbook with fifteen pound was still in his coat. The line went silent, he thought for a second it had gone dead. Then he heard Fred blowing his nose. When he spoke he was still choked up. 'I'll miss driving him, Harry, my oath I will. The knowledge that man carried in his head. He could take you to the Stone Age and you'd reckon you were walking round there.'

'You've said, yes.'

'Jesus Christ. Eh? You reach my age and the world can still kick you in the nuts. I'd reckon knock off, son, bring the car here and have a whisky and go home.'

A whisky would be good now. He looked at the glass between his feet. They kept nothing in the house, and he wasn't going near the pub with his name on the front pages. He'd thought the first time he saw the man come down the Carrington steps he had something wrong with his hips, but Fred was right, it was his eyes. They gave him a strange prissy way of stepping, a bit like a chook, as if he wasn't quite sure the ground would be under his foot each time he placed it down. Yesterday he'd stopped on the steps and tilted his hat back to peer at the sky and nearly toppled over. And that was with his specs *on.* Morey had never laid eyes on the living man. Maybe he should have said, I've watched him come down from the Carrington, constable. Just this morning he nearly tripped over his own feet. 'You didn't because of him being a cop,' he muttered at the concrete. But why couldn't something like that have been what happened? He hadn't said it to Morey but he would say it to the coroner. The clack of a beak made him look up. A magpie had landed in the newly-turned soil of the fallow bed and was stabbing for worms. He clapped and it started, but stayed where it was. He half-rose and threw his arm, get out of it! and the bird reared into flight and fled over the back fence. It struck him that even something with a bird wasn't far-fetched, him without specs and a maggie or a rosella diving past his face. 'You bloody don't want it to be the other, do you,' he muttered. Because then he was back to asking himself why he'd sensed nothing. The signs he was putting together now – the shuffling of papers, the furious puffing on the pipe, the hesitation at Govetts when he got out and saw the immense blue trench that was the Grose – all of it was hindsight. The man had been perfectly calm and natural, appeared to be anyway, when he stopped at the bottom of the Carrington steps. Despite the promise in the sky of another hot day he was wearing bow tie, vest and coat. Fred said that on most days he walked to Echo Point, sometimes as far as Narrow Neck, so Newstead was expecting him to turn right and head off down Katoomba Street. Instead the man had looked both ways, then crossed the footpath and bent to speak through the open passenger window. Newstead had never seen him up close. The specs *were* like bottle glass and his nose, as Fred had also said, *was* a pale blue, webbed with fine veins. 'Ah – not Mr Benham.' 'No,' he'd replied, 'I'm Harry Newstead, Mr Benham's partner.' 'Ah. Well, are you free to take me to Govetts Leap, Mr Newstead?' There was a standard response but he'd felt unable to give it to a man probably above common humour.

As he'd told Morey, he always looked at his watch when he arrived at a fare's destination and he'd parked the Wolseley at the Leap at three minutes past eight. There was one other car, a two-tone blue Ford Anglia, but the lookout was empty. The professor seemed surprised to see they'd arrived, he didn't move for a few seconds after the motor was turned off. Then he'd got out and walked a few paces towards the fence, extended his wrist from his coat sleeve and stood staring at his watch. Newstead had presumed he was calculating how long the wait might be, to tell him. But the man dropped his arm and lifted his head and stared then towards the Grose. After what seemed fully a minute he'd turned abruptly back to the open door and said as if thinking aloud, 'I will take these.' He'd gathered up from the seat the papers he'd got in carrying and what Newstead saw for the first time was a brass compass, which he slipped into his coat pocket. He set off towards the cliff track without goodbye or instructions and without closing the door. Newstead wondered if he'd forgotten he was with a new driver and thought he was with Fred, who wouldn't need instructions. Fred had told him though, the man expected you to wait. He stretched his arm to its window winder and pulled the door closed, then chose a tree at the other side of the carpark and drove the Wolseley into its shade, knowing how hot the car got in a longish wait, being black.

He took the slice of fruitcake Joyce had put in his box and walked over to the lookout, pausing for a moment to remind himself of the date on the stone obelisk, before continuing towards the fence and stopping a yard short of the railing. He'd been coming to Govetts since he was a child. He didn't remember the first time, which was probably as a baby. The time that was imprinted on his memory as the first, his father had gripped his hand and dragged him screaming and struggling to the fence, pinning him against his legs and demanding that he look down while repeating into his ear that he was safe, daddy wasn't going to let go of him. That day returned whenever he stepped through the stone arch, but now he could choose where he halted. The air was clear and blue, he could see all the way to where the cliffs blurred together and he knew Richmond to be. Wouldn't that be a walk, five or six days of vertical rock each side and a strip of sky above. He craned forward to look at the trees along the river. They were far smaller than matchsticks, they looked like the pile sticking up on a carpet. He felt his breathing shorten. He turned and saw he no longer had the lookout to himself and made himself walk calmly to the nearest of the plank benches. When he'd eaten the slice of cake he walked back to the Wolseley. At nine the first of Barker's omnibuses arrived with the pickups from the guesthouses, followed a few minutes later by the omnibus from the station. He folded the newspaper and put it back in the glovebox. He'd always been able to pass time watching people. By ten, though, he was restless. To work it off, stretch his legs, he walked to the top of Horseshoe Falls and back. By twelve he'd lost all interest in the Sydney toffs and the women in their sleeveless cotton dresses. When Fred said you waited he surely couldn't have meant this long. He fetched his hat from the boot and locked the car.

At the steps on the other side of Bridal Veil he was forced to wait for a couple coming down. They were red-faced and sweating, wearing identical white caps and with hankies knotted round their necks. When they reached the bottom the man gave him a quick grin. 'You lost your fare?' Newstead was surprised, then reasoned the man must have seen him earlier standing by the Wolseley.

'Yes. An elderly chap in a green coat and bow tie, very thick glasses.'

They shook their heads. The woman said, 'We've been to Evans Lookout and back, we saw no one like that. We had a drink and a bite there, but we were sitting in view of where the track comes out.'

'We did see a coat lying over a log.' The man turned to her. 'It was sort of a green wasn't it?'

'A bluey green.'

'Would your chap have had a compass? There was one on the ledge at the lookout just back there. We left it, of course – we thought the owner might have just ducked into the bushes.'

Newstead felt his balls contract.

'Would you be able to show me?'

The man glanced at his watch, then at the woman. 'Ah … certainly.'

They introduced themselves. He apologised for making them climb again. Don't be silly, the woman told him.

They mounted the stairs, then climbed through a din of cicadas so loud there was no point trying to speak. Where the track levelled they came to a fallen tree with the professor's coat neatly folded lengthways and laid over the trunk. He patted the breast and felt the hardness of a pocketbook. Brian Darragh pointed down a path leading off the track to the cliff edge.

The lookout was a promontory of bare sandstone with a front fence and wing fences of waterpipe and rusty chainwire, beyond the fence on two sides nothing but air. Joyce had forced him out onto similar places. They were awful. He halted. So did the Darraghs. The man was his charge. He breathed in deeply through his nose, blew it out, then descended the cut steps, trying to limit the circle of his gaze to the feet of the fence posts. The professor's brown felt hat and his glasses, the lugs open, and beyond them the compass, were on an unfenced portion of the promontory to the left, a couple of yards outside the wire. The compass sat on a small square of cardboard, one corner of the cardboard resting on a folded piece of paper to level it. He crept to the end of the wing fence and, not caring how it looked to the man and woman, squatted and waddled past the hat and glasses to the compass, trying to keep his eyes fixed on it alone but keenly aware that eighteen inches beyond was the lip of the cliff. His father had taught him to read a prismatic. He didn't need to, he knew that, but it might become evidence. He took a stabbing glance along the line of the needle, refusing to see the blue immensity to either side. It was sighted on Pulpit Rock, two degrees east of north. In pencil block letters on a sheet of Carrington notepaper with a lichened stone weighting it were the names *Mount Banks, Mount Hay, Table Peak, Pulpit Rock.* He drew in a breath and raised his gaze to the edge, searching for a disturbance, a scuffmark, or, and he prayed not, anything that suggested fingers scrabbling for a hold. The stone's grey patina was unmarked, the fine sand pooled in depressions along the rim bore only the ripples left by wind. There was no sign that anyone had been closer to the edge than he was now. He lowered his gaze and shuffled backwards on his haunches until he could grab the wire of the wing fence, then hauled himself to his feet and stepped into the enclosure. Brian Darragh arched his eyebrows. He shook his head.

'I don't know. There's no marks. It's hard to say.'

'So ... what do you want to do? We'll have to leave you, I'm afraid, we're expected at friends'.'

'Yes – sorry – thank you both for your help. You'd better give me an address, though. Where you're staying.'

'Of course.' The man reached to the straps of his knapsack.

He walked with them back up into the cicada din to the track junction, thanked them again and shook their hands. He waited till they were out of sight, then cupped his hands around his mouth and shouted, 'Professor!' A pair of rosellas burst squawking from a banksia and skimmed away towards the valley. In seconds the cicadas flooded back in. He wondered how far into the bush his shout had even penetrated.

He set off towards Evans Lookout, halting every fifty yards to cup his hands and shout into the trees, at the same time feeling a fool. He hoped no one came along the track. Where the flat walking ended he stopped and shouted down the steps, then turned without waiting for a reply, knowing none would come, and broke into a half jog.

He stopped at the coat and laid his hand again on the breast to feel the hardness. Some dozens of people must have passed by and, like the Darraghs, looked but not touched. If, as it was seeming, the coat too was evidence, it would have to be left, pocketbook and all. He backed away for two or three steps, willing the thing to remain, then spun and broke again into his jog.

He was back at Govetts in thirty minutes with Morey and a constable his own age named McShane. Morey questioned him as they descended to Bridal Veil about events from the time 'this professor fellow' had come to the rank, and about what he knew of the man. At times neither could hear the other above the cicadas and had to repeat questions or answers. He wanted to say, *couldn't we save the questions and get a move on*, but Morey seemed in no hurry. When Newstead glanced his frustration at the younger man, McShane shrugged to say, *that's how he is mate.*

He was very relieved to see the coat still lying over the fallen tree, and seemingly untouched. Told of it, Morey patted for the pocketbook, but left the coat in place and told McShane to stay with it. 'Down here?' Newstead nodded. The policeman started down the loop path, not even glancing to see whether Newstead was following, his eyes fixed on the ground. But he'd heard, because he flicked a hand to indicate that Newstead steer to the edge of the path to avoid what Newstead saw then was the print in sand of a heeled shoe, headed downhill. He wondered at himself that he hadn't thought to look for the same thing. All the distinctive heeled prints headed down, none up.

At the lookout the policeman strolled out onto the unfenced rock as if it were a patio. Warnings crowding his tongue, he forced himself to watch. The policeman threaded a path through glasses, hat, papers and compass to the edge and peered over, then stepped back again behind the compass and knelt and read the bearing. He picked up the hat and turned it over. Even from the steps Newstead saw the initials cut deeply into the leather sweatband, *VGC*. Morey placed the hat down as it had been, ran a finger along the frame of the glasses, then stared out over the valley. He spoke looking towards Mount Banks.

'What sort of mood was he in, would you say, your man?'

Newstead waited to see if he would look round. When he didn't he spoke to the back of his head. 'Well ... bit hard to judge, not knowing him. All he said on the trip up I've told you. Only thing strange I thought was he gave his pipe a pretty fierce workout, but he maybe did that all the time. I don't know.'

Morey pushed on his bent knee to stand and came back inside the wire enclosure. He leaned his forearms on the pipe railing and spoke down at the items on the rock. 'Bit like a display, eh Mr Newstead.'

'I'm sorry?'

'He'd be a clever man I take it, an archaeology professor. I'd reckon you'd have to be good at telling a story from bits of evidence. Bit like a copper.'

'Again, I couldn't say. But I gather he's clever, yes. He told Fred he was top dog of some institute in London. And he's published books. Fred's read one. Before the war. Not archaeology, about politics.' He didn't repeat that Fred had told him the Professor was a well-known Red. That on their several trips to Kings Tableland and the longer drive to Bell they'd talked about Joe Stalin and about events last year in Hungary. The professor had been upset by the photographs of Russian tanks in the streets of Budapest. He and Fred were Labor, no further, but hadn't much liked the photographs either. He had no idea what the policeman's politics were.

'Well, Mr Newstead, I'd say your man hasn't stumbled or tripped. For whatever reason, or reasons, he's stepped off.' He turned his head and pinned Newstead with a stare. 'But you keep that news strictly to yourself. Not even to your better half.'

Newstead's mouth filled with an indignant 'no'. Not to the demand but to the verdict so blandly delivered. He managed to stammer, 'Of course.'

'But you don't believe it, do you, everything says the opposite. That's how I know. But it's not what I'll be telling the coroner, and neither will you. Unless there's a note turns up in his room, which I think's unlikely. So what I just said's between you and me. Now go up top and stay with his coat and send McShane down here, we need to make some notes and measurements.'

The anger that had swelled in him yesterday swelled again, he pushed himself up from the heavy chair and strode out onto the grass, needing to be moving. He'd felt dismissed, not sufficiently adult to be there if he'd been so completely taken in by the 'display'. He stalked to the lemon tree and tore off a yellowing leaf. Damn thing needed iron again. He flicked the leaf away. He hadn't told Joyce directly the policeman's verdict but he'd hinted at it. He wasn't having any uniformed bastard telling him what he could and couldn't tell his own wife. She'd backed him up, that without a note or a witness not even a policeman could say what had really happened. They could look at the evidence but they couldn't look inside a person's mind. He was as sensitive to people and their quirks as anyone wasn't he, driving a taxi. He believed he was. He'd picked up on the woman going to the Point. Morey had never laid eyes on the living man. He had. Seen him half a dozen times at least stroll down from the Carrington, smile at people, tip his hat. He'd shared the cab with him for twenty minutes. He'd got no sense from the man, absolutely none, that he was knowingly taking a one-way ride. That he wouldn't be sitting in the same corner of the seat on the return, puffing furiously on his pipe and reading through whatever notes he'd made. No one could be that good an actor if it wasn't their actual job. Yet a sentence of Morey's had stuck. *I reckon you'd have to be pretty good at telling a story from bits of evidence.* The policeman had meant telling in the sense of inventing, not reading a story already there. He turned from the lemon tree and walked in a straight line to the back door. He needed to talk to someone else who'd observed the man.

He recognised the voice as soon as she said good afternoon. 'Carrington Hotel, how may I help you?'

'It's Harry Newstead, Mrs Clooney.' Habit proved too strong and he added, 'How are you?'

There came a wet click, then a pause.

'I've been better, Mr Newstead. How about yourself?'

'Likewise. Finding it a bit hard to stop pacing around. So I was wondering if you maybe could tell me who was on either Friday night or yesterday morning who might have, you know, seen or talked to him. And if I could come up and have a chat. If they're on again today.'

There was another, this time longer, pause.

'That would be me, Mr Newstead, I did from two till ten Friday. And I understand very well what you're saying. I finish at four, if that suits.'

He looked quickly at the new electric wall clock. It was twenty past three.

'I'll just get changed. Thank you.'

'I'll be in the lounge.'

He went into the sunroom. Joyce was sitting in the armchair facing the wireless. A baritone was singing in what sounded like Italian. She paused the needles. He told her where he was going and why. She lowered her hands to her lap and studied him, then nodded and asked whether he'd be back for when Fred dropped off the car. He said if not to tell him he'd go round later and do the take.

He walked up the lesser-used side of Katoomba Street as far as the church before he crossed. When he came near the Carrington he slowed and studied the rank. The Wolseley wasn't there but Bert Mayle and Tom Harradence were standing smoking at the fender of Tom's Chrysler, Tom with his foot up on the bumper. He stepped to the window of the jewellers' and watched from the side of his eye till both men turned to look at a passing Jaguar, when he skipped to the closer of the stone pillars at the hotel's vehicle entrance and slid round it and started up the driveway, keeping to the stone kerb rather than have the crunch of his shoes in the gravel.

He looked at his watch again before he pushed open the door to the lobby. Five past. She'd have handed over. He knew the woman behind the desk to nod to. She returned his nod and didn't enquire when he continued walking. Only two or three times had he been further into the hotel than the lobby, and never into the lounge. A sign with a gold-gloved hand pointed the way.

The barman smiled at him and stepped to the taps. 'Be with you in a tick,' he said. The man executed a small bow and stepped away. At the far end of the lounge the lower sashes of all the windows were fully raised, the blue of the Jamison and the ranges to the south framed, then rooftops entering the frames as he advanced. Three tourist couples were sitting together on curved divans in the centre of the room. She lifted a hand to him from a leather armchair in the right corner. As he changed course he took in the marble fireplace. It was huge, four times the size of the one at home, ironbark logs laid in readiness for one of the sudden changes in weather the Mountains were famed for. She nodded when he entered the embayment of chairs but didn't smile. An empty glass stood on a coaster on a low marble table. She sat upright to take his hand. He'd always been slightly awed by her, not anything in her manner but by the fact that she was nearly as old as his mother yet looked half that age, having flawless olive skin, jet-black hair and a large sensuous mouth accentuated by the scarlet lip paint she habitually wore. Her hand was long-fingered and cool. His, he realised, was probably sweaty. He slid it free and pointed to the glass. 'The same again?'

'Thank you, a gin and tonic.'

He felt as he walked back to the bar in some vague way flattered that she hadn't thought he required an apology for starting without him. He'd have preferred a schooner but ordered a whisky and ice.

He chose the chair to her left, out of the window's glare. He'd practised openings on the way up Katoomba Street. But with the moment upon him he realised that everything he'd practised relied on her already knowing what he knew. She was leaning forward in her chair trying to see his eyes, he'd fallen into his schoolboy habit of staring at the teacher's feet. He sat straight. 'Sorry. Just a bit hard to know how to start.'

'Let me help, then. I had a Senior Constable Morey from Blackheath here a little after lunchtime. You've also had dealings with him, I gather.'

'You could call it that.'

'Quite. Not that I know what he said to you, and it's none of my business. But he pursued with me a line of questioning that had behind it a "theory" I considered to be tripe and I told him so. His words to me *then* were that I'd grabbed the wrong end of the broom, he was simply trying to establish the professor's movements while he was here. I told him as I'm now telling you – that Professor Childe was here on and off over a period of weeks before yesterday morning. He went out twice to Bathurst to stay with another retired professor and his wife, a Professor Stewart of Sydney University, and he told me he was looking forward to visiting there again. I explained that he told me he'd become very interested in geology as well as his own field of history and archaeology, especially the geology of the Mountains, and he was planning a book on the ages of the various strata, why he was going about to look at the cliffs. He seemed actually very excited by the idea. He lived up here for a while as a child, at the end of Falls Road he told me.'

He felt some contribution from him was due and said, 'Yes, my partner, Fred Benham, said.'

'I know Mr Benham.'

'Course you would. Sorry.'

'And I should apologise too, I sound as if I'm setting myself up as some sort of ... confidante.' She lifted her hand to forestall him. 'Understand that I'm speaking now just to you, Mr Newstead, not our policeman. I think he was far too private a man to allow confidences. But I believe we became passing friends at least. Quite often in the evening he sought me out for a chat if I wasn't too busy, or even if I was, or became so, he'd stand until we could continue. I very much enjoyed those chats, and I believe he did too.' Her voice broke and she stopped. 'Excuse me.' She took up her glass and swallowed a large mouthful and set it back on the coaster, dabbing her mouth with the back of her other hand, then, realising what she'd done, glancing at the skin to see if she'd removed any paint. He'd never driven her but knew where she lived, in a large well-kept weatherboard in Lovell Street she'd shared with her late husband. He'd been dead some four or five years and the word was, among the blokes at the rank anyway, that she was on the prowl again, why she'd started at the Carrington. He didn't think the professor would have qualified as prey. *And you can shut up with stuff like that,* he told himself angrily, *you're not here for jokes.* He glanced and saw she wasn't looking, she was studying her hands held clenched before her chest. It so resembled prayer he wondered was she a churchgoer, and if so, where. 'So – Friday.' She raised her face to him. 'About half-past eight he came out of the private bar looking a bit red and flustered. He didn't say anything but Douglas the barman told me later that some men in there – I won't call them gentlemen – were making loud remarks about his appearance. He came to reception and we talked for about half an hour, or rather he talked while I did things. If you've been with him you know.'

'I been with him only the once, yesterday, but Fred says the same – like you were in a library with the books talking to you.'

A sad smile lit her face and vanished. 'That's it exactly. Anyway, he excused himself and went upstairs. A few minutes later he was down again with his portable typewriter in its case and said he wanted me to have it. I'm sure it was a genuine impulse, but I thought it one he might later regret. I told him I couldn't possibly accept, he needed it for his book, but he repeated what he'd said to me a number of times, that he hated typing, he preferred to write longhand, and he wanted to give it to someone he knew would use it properly instead of him with two fingers. It's a very good Olivetti. When I told him again I couldn't he began to grow distressed, so I accepted and thanked him. My intention was just to put it in the safe and give it back. I only managed to do one of those things.' She choked on the last words and closed her eyes.

'Would you like some water?'

She rubbed the backs of fingers across her lids and opened them and reached down to her purse jammed between her hip and the arm of the chair. 'Why don't I give you the money and you buy us another round, and yes a glass of water please.' She saw his mouth open and hushed him. 'I earn my living too, Mr Newstead.'

She'd drained the glass when he returned with the small tray. She lifted the empty aside for him to place the fresh gin and tonic on the coaster, then took the water from him and sipped. She waited for him to sit and arrange his legs.

'I didn't tell our Constable Morey what I just told you, Mr Newstead. About the typewriter. For the simple reason he'd have twisted it to mean the opposite of how it was intended. I did tell him, however, that no matter how long Professor Childe chose to stay with us he settled his account weekly. He was scrupulous about it. I believe if he was planning something ... something untoward, he'd have settled with me on the Friday evening. He would not have left the foyer yesterday knowing he owed the hotel money.'

Keenly aware that his shyness had forced her to do much of the talking, he told her the professor hadn't paid at Govetts either. He began to describe events from when the man had got out and stood looking into the Grose, but she stopped him, shaking her head. 'Please, I'd rather not know.'

They sat in an awkward silence. He really didn't want to walk her down to the rank, have the blokes see them together, but he'd have to offer. Finally he said he should be getting home, they generally ate early on a Sunday. He'd walk her down to the rank if she wished. He tried not to let his relief show when she thanked him and said a friend was coming for her.

'I hope I've eased your mind a little, Mr Newstead.'

'Well, you obviously saw much more of him, Mrs Clooney. So it's been good to hear things from your angle.'

He placed his glass on the tray and reached for hers and she told him to leave them, it was the barboy's job. She offered her hand. When he took it she enfolded his with her left and squeezed.

'We were granted the great privilege of meeting him. I think that's something we should both of us treasure.'

Joyce was flouring salmon rissoles. Having whisky on his breath he kissed her on the cheek and she kissed him back keeping her hands in the bowl. When he turned he noticed the newspapers were gone from the counter. They were somewhere, she wouldn't have chucked them. He got a glass of water and sat at the table.

He told her what Marj Clooney had said, trying to recount as much as he could in her words rather than his own. She floured the last rissoles. He was not distracted by her moving about as he talked, it was the pattern of his arrival home on days he'd worked. She rinsed the sticky flour from her hands and dried them on her apron, glancing up at the clock so that he did the same. If he hadn't copped a last fare Fred would be on his way. She picked up the kettle and carried it to the sink and poured out the old water and refilled it. As she turned off the tap she said at the window, 'I'll save my questions because he'll be here any second. But tell me this –' she looked at him over her shoulder – 'because it doesn't sound to me like this talk with her's settled anything – are you going to be thinking of nothing else for the next week but this Professor Childe?' She turned with the kettle in both hands.

'I don't know, Joyce.'

'That's not exactly an answer.'

'Because it's too fresh to say! If I close my eyes I can watch the whole of yesterday.'

'Well I wouldn't call that a good sign for going to bed. Would you?'

She drew breath to say more but they both heard the distinctive sighing growl of the Wolseley shifting down into second, then the squeal of the back springs as it bumped over the gutter and up into the driveway. She walked to the stove and picked up the flintgun, lit the gas.

The flyscreen door slammed and Fred stumped into the kitchen. He was fifty-one, short, and now cow-gutted after years of sitting. He'd never married. He and Newstead's father had been best friends. In their early twenties they'd bought a second-hand Chevrolet and gone into partnership. There was a photo on the lounge room wall in his mother's house of both men grinning into the camera, Fred behind the wheel of the Chev and his father, for the joke, braced with both hands on the handbrake lever. They'd volunteered for service on the same day and Fred was rejected, as both must have known he would be, his left leg shorter than his right. Despite the heat he was wearing his fawn cardigan. He dumped the takebag on the table and pulled out a chair and sat heavily. 'I'll give tea a miss, Joycey, got an appointment up the club with a schooner.' He turned to Newstead and tapped the belted leather bag, which had a healthy fatness to it. 'Bit of heat brought them out. So, how are you?'

'Still a bit rattled. You probably saw they found him – not yesterday, this morning.'

'Yes. The compass and stuff hasn't stopped the idiots though saying he jumped. Tom for one. I said to him, where'd you bloody hear that nonsense –' he glanced towards Joyce – 'pardon the French. A fare from Medlow. And where'd this fare hear it? He didn't say. And he's telling this to me who carried the man five times in the last fortnight! I told him to his face he was an idiot. He didn't like it much. I said to him, you'd be jumping off a cliff, would you, if you were the top in the world at your game? You could afford umpteen weeks at the Carrington! He was a bit stuck for an answer you won't be surprised to hear.'

Joyce flashed him a look, *get rid of him Harry if you know what's good for you*, and disappeared into the hallway.

Newstead rose and fetched the ledger from the dresser, which diverted the man. They counted up and Newstead entered the amount and the petrol dockets while Fred did the split. He spoke as he opened his wallet on the table and began ferrying the notes and coins into it.

'If I thought it'd be anywhere close, I'd go to the funeral. Like I said on the phone, I'll miss him – and I'm not talking about the splash he made in the kick. But it'll be in Sydney I'd say, where his professor mates can get to it.'

'No reason for it to be up here.' He stood. Fred called goodbye towards the hallway and followed him outside, his limp more pronounced at the end of a day.

She fried the rissoles in the oil she saved from sardine tins, served them with white sauce containing diced carrots and parsley. He found himself ravenous and ate six. Afterwards he made tea while she spooned pears and ice cream into bowls and they took their bowls and cups outside to the chairs on the concrete. The sun was setting. White cockatoos were making earsplitting screeches from the pines along Ada Street. Next door the three Craig kids were still out in the yard chasing one another with the hose, their screams nearly as shrill as the cockies'. The cold of the ice cream on his teeth and the imagined cold of the hose jet suddenly brought into his mind the hospital morgue. He was seeing, he knew, a crime photograph from the *Post.* The floor and walls were tiled white. The professor's body was on a steel table, covered with a sheet. Through it he could see they'd arranged the recovered pieces into a semblance of him. But where the face should have been the sheet was nearly flat, just small bumps and hollows. His heart began to race. He needed to set down his bowl and walk but she'd straightaway be asking what was wrong. He turned his head as if he was studying the peeling paint on the laundry eaves and breathed through his mouth. She was speaking to him. 'Sorry, what?'

'I *said*, Fred would do tomorrow if you ask him.'

He'd had the thought several times already and each time dismissed it. Not for the reason he was about to give. 'I can't. He's got pennants Saturday, he'll be wanting to put in time on the green.'

'Darling, it's only Sunday – he's got two other whole days.'

'Yes, but right now he's probably arranging with the other blokes. I'm not sick.'

'I'm not saying you are. But you could give yourself another day. Couldn't you.'

'I still have to front up to the rank some time. It might as well be tomorrow.'

There – he'd more or less stated the reason. She stared at him, then looked away at the darkening pines. 'Where do you think this other story's come from?'

He waited for her to turn. When she didn't he spoke to the back of her head, the flash coming to him of being forced to speak the same way to Morey at the lookout. 'Hard to say. Maybe the Carrington staff making guesses from the coppers searching his room and the questions they asked, and then the story's moved down to the rank.'

She turned now.

'When you first got there, Harry – what did you believe had happened? What did you honestly think?'

'I couldn't think! I had a dozen things in my head at once. I suppose I was hoping he'd left his stuff and gone off to do business with a gum leaf.'

'Don't, please. I'm serious. You sensed something had happened. That's you, I know you.'

He leaned back, exhaled at the eaves.

'When I saw the specs I thought he'd gone over. Either missed where the edge was, or stood up too fast and got dizzy.'

'And that's what any sensible person would have thought. I don't care what this Morey believes! You don't know that he isn't full of himself, Harry – that he wasn't just puffing himself up at your expense.' She rocked her head knowingly. 'Of course *you* all see the obvious –' she'd deepened her voice to a man's – 'you have to be me to see what *really* happened here.'

That shook him, sat him up. It hadn't occurred to him.

'You've been a worrier as long as I've known you, right back to school. You'll be telling yourself soon the other story is right and you should have guessed what the man intended and stopped him. Well that's nonsense. It's nonsense, darling. And even allowing for a moment it *might* be right, the man must have been a better actor than anyone up here has met before, and that includes you.'

He washed up while she had a shower. Then he had his. When he came out again into the kitchen in his pyjamas and dressing gown she'd turned on the small wireless. They had cocoa and listened to *The Pied Piper*, even he hooting with laughter at the scandalous answers Keith Smith extracted from the kids about members of their families. Beneath the laughter, though, he was dreading bed.

The cool smell of mist was drifting through the window when they got in, a change come. She kissed him and gripped his hand and was quickly asleep. He remained lying on his back. The Craigs' dog was yapping but he'd fallen asleep to its noise before. He'd needed something stronger than sugar in his cocoa. The blokes at the rank would be straight onto him, wanting his take on what had really happened. No, he had to get off that! He made himself begin mentally going over the Wolseley. They'd have to think seriously soon about getting the rear springs done. And the clutch. Even in second she was beginning to slip going up Katoomba Street. A new plate and assembly would set them back. Fred could try his mate in Penrith for a recon. They had enough in kitty for that.

He woke believing he'd been awake. He was crying. He clapped a hand over his mouth and lay his sleeved arm across his eyes. It lasted some minutes, easing off then he'd be blubbering again. When he'd properly stopped he lowered his arm to his chest and looked at Joyce. She had the covers pulled up to her ear, all he could see was her hair. She'd spoken from love but she was wrong. The man had known how far above them all he was, that he was dealing with children. Morey was the only adult among them, not the blowhard she'd painted him. The short film returned of the man when he'd stepped out at Govetts and walked his few paces towards the fence and stared out over the Grose. His eyes welled again. The only comparison in his own life to what must have been going through the man's mind was the first time he climbed the tower at Catalina pool and shuffled to the edge and looked down. He'd known he was going to hit water and swim to the side but he'd still felt like spewing. What had the man felt, looking at where *he* was going? The only clue he'd given was how long he stood. That was when he should have spoken, asked if everything was all right. But the man had been perfectly businesslike when he turned and came back for his papers and the compass. The only concession he'd made to fear was when he was alone, standing on the ledge. He'd taken off his specs.

The alarm clock was on the floor. He groped with his hand and found his watch on the bedside table. It was twenty to twelve. He drew his legs from under the covers and swung them so he was sitting on the edge of the bed and looked over his shoulder. She didn't stir. He stood and moved in bare feet to the door and took his dressing gown from the hook and walked out into the hallway.

He closed the kitchen door and turned on the light, then took a glass from the dresser shelf and walked to the sink. He drank looking at himself floating in the dark pane. Then he came round the table to the bench and lifted the phone and slid the book from under it. Katoomba police station was on the wall but not Blackheath. The phone rang five times before a man's voice answered, croaky from sleep. 'Blackheath Police, Constable Hollis.'

'Hello constable, sorry to wake you up, my name's Harry Newstead, from Katoomba.'

'Yes, Mr Newstead, I know who you are. How can I help you?'

'I'm wondering if Constable Morey's there.'

'Senior Constable Morey will be in at eight tomorrow morning. Is it something I can help you with?'

'Not really, no. He asked if I'd do him a favour. You can tell him if you would please that I've reconsidered. That's if he still needs me. I'll ring him a bit after eight.'

He lifted the phone and placed it back on the book. Then he pulled out a chair and sat. Morey had asked that he look just at the clothes but a proper identification required looking at a face. If, for whatever his reasons, the man had had the courage to step off, then he, Harry Newstead, should have the courage to confront what was left and put a name to it. They'd have cleaned him up he supposed. His hair would have survived, and probably part or all of the ginger moustache. That would be enough. He'd just have to try not to take in too much else. He'd need a whisky before he went in. He'd have to find his father's hip flask. He could get it filled at the Carrington. They sold mints over the bar, too, he thought.

Good News for Modern Man

Fiona McFarlane

When I began my study of the colossal squid, I still believed in God. The squid seemed to me then, in those God days, to be the secretly swimming proof of a vast maker who had bestowed intelligence – surprisingly, here and there – on both man and mollusc. I've discussed this with Charles Darwin, who visits me daily at sundown, always punctual and a little out of breath. His cheeks are red, his hair white. He looks nothing like a ghost. He puts his feet up on the rocks and look out over this small corner of the Pacific, calm at sundown and partially obscured by a mosquito haze. We sit above the tree line and consider the movements of the colossal squid in her bay below. She moves this way and that; she floats and billows in the tide. She reminds me of my mother's underwear soaking in a holiday basin. Her official name, her name in polite company, is *Mesonychoteuthis hamiltoni*. We've named her Mabel and together we plan to free her.

It's no easy thing, this freeing of a colossal squid. It was difficult enough to imprison her in the first place. There is the issue of her size.

'A colossal squid,' I tell Darwin, 'makes a giant squid look like a bath toy.'

He agrees with me, although as far as I know he has never seen either a bath toy or a giant squid. He remains surprisingly unexcited by my account of Mabel's capture: the months-long hunt with smaller squid for bait, the boredom and fussy seasickness,

Mabel emerging from the sea with her hood pink in the sudden sun. She flailed at the surface, she swam and sounded, smelling as much like the sea as anything I have ever smelled. But we hooked her, and we panicked her, and she raced ahead of us, right into this bay, through a narrow channel that we were able to block. And now she spends her days here, rotating among her many arms, and I spend my days watching her. They're going to build her a facility, so there's money to raise and laws to change. For now it's just the two of us – and Darwin.

Darwin first appeared on my 402nd day on the island. We often disagree, but in a neutral, brotherly sort of way, and I appreciate his company. The sun sinks into the sea, but we also see it rise from the sea. This makes the world seem very small, even though we're two hours from any town. There's a Catholic school higher up the mountain and we see the girls walk down to the water and back up again. I hear their singing in the early morning and it surprises me; at sundown it makes me sad. Late in the afternoons they swim in the white sea – far out into the lagoon, where I often see bullet-shaped sharks. Darwin and I take turns peering through my binoculars. It's an innocent and companionable lechery. Although he's a ghost, he leaves sweat around the eyepieces.

I've been thinking for some time of taking one of the monthly supply boats back to New Zealand, then a plane home. At home the rain will be cold, pigeons will grow fat, there will be supermarkets. I've refused replacements and talked up the malarial solitude, and now they won't come, not even over-eager graduate students with an itching for the Pacific. But this is my 498th day on the island, and lately I'm troubled by headaches and abrupt changes in temperature. There's something feverish about this air. It's not only the headaches, although they're bad enough; my major symptom is a kind of vertigo, a frequent and sudden awareness that the universe is expanding out from me. This feeling begins with my feet, as if the ground – the planet – the galaxy – has suddenly dropped away from them and I'm floating untethered in space, only space doesn't exist, and neither does my body. I can only describe the sensation as the suspension of nothing in nothing. But I look down and there are my feet, dirt-brown, and there are Darwin's, sensibly shod. Below our feet swims Mabel. It's only while watching Mabel that I feel tied to the earth once more, and a sense of order is restored. Still, that moment of vertigo is briefly and terrifyingly glorious. It reminds me of the way, when I was younger, I used to feel my body respond to the singing of hymns: an interior fire, a constriction of the heart that I took for a visitation of the Holy Spirit. I never mentioned this sensation to anyone. Maybe other people feel it. Perhaps the schoolgirls on the mountain feel it, singing in their concrete church: the large feeling of singing toward something that sings back. I often wondered if sex felt that way, undernourished adolescent that I was. And now – the quiet sky, the patient waiting, the tick of time in the bones, until the world rushes out and the vanishing of the cosmos presents itself again, magnificent.

I've told Darwin of my troubles. He suspects malaria, which is possible; I stopped taking my meds on day 300, partly because of the dreams they gave me, bright crystal dreams of exhausting flight. Sitting here, atop our hot rock, we might be the last two survivors of the flood, chosen by Noah: a pair of scientists, two by two. But the Ark broke up somewhere along the Line and left us stranded with a squid for company. Darwin regards me sadly when I say this, stroking his diluvian chin.

'Geology,' he says, 'disproves you.'

'I know,' I tell him. 'It's a joke.'

*

I live in a small astronomical observation station owned and, until recently, forgotten by the New Zealand government. It's partway up the mountain, and I can walk down to the sea in thirteen minutes. Paths have been cut into the rock, as if this were a holiday beach frequented by sure-footed children, but it's still a relief to step out onto the sand from the mountain path, to see the sea spread wide and to my left the smaller inlet that is Mabel's temporary home. The clear water is deeper than it looks from above. When I say the water in Mabel's bay is clear, I don't mean it's transparent, but that it's see-throughable, and Mabel is see-able there at the bottom. I feed her fish thawed from a deep freeze, or freshly caught if I'm in the mood, and these she grasps at the end of her tentacles and rolls up toward her beaked mouth. The coral sand is sharp and clean and my feet never feel dirty. When Darwin accompanies me (which he usually does on those days I'm feeling my worst) he only removes his shoes to wade into the shallows, and then his feet are the delicate brown and blue and yellow of Galápagos finches.

The view of Mabel from the shore is more intimate than the bird's eye view from my station fifteen metres above. It's impossible to take in her vastness or the pattern of her tentacles and arms, so it's her eyes that fascinate me. They interest Darwin as well. They're hard to avoid. Mabel has the largest eye in creation, and it looks like ours, although its structure is entirely different. This humanoid appearance far out on the lone branch of invertebrate evolution gave scientists pause, at one time; they paused over Darwin and his theory of natural selection. The eye of the squid once gave Darwin a great deal of trouble. Now Darwin and I stand on the shore and consider the vertebrate appearance of Mabel's canny eye. It looks so very God-given. Impossible to assume that such an eye doesn't think, or ponder, or dream.

I think about squid too much. Darwin cautions me.

'A squid is not a human,' he says.

'A human is just another animal,' I say.

'Oh no,' says Darwin. 'The highest of the animals.'

'Careful,' I tell him.

We argue about this – the concept of progress, the tricky politics of supposing one thing higher than another. He's impatient with the twentieth century on this point. He doesn't seem to have noticed the twenty-first has begun, and I don't tell him. I do tell him that whenever I spend an extended length of time with Mabel, peering into her large eye from the rocks on the shore, I find myself shaking off the feeling that there's a person inside her, watching me. Darwin mocks this as sentimental. He says this sensation is so typical as to be 'fatally unfresh.' I suppose my desire to free Mabel is similarly unfresh. But there are no fresh desires.

Today I feel very well. I feel an immense good health. Today I feel with great certainty my precise location upon the earth, the latitude and longitude, the position of the sun. This is good, because today we free Mabel. The date is September 23rd, but that's elsewhere. Here on this island we've dropped out of time, although once, I believe, the island was within time: when it was first created, it was a definite volcanic event. Then the rock subsided, the sea settled, the coral multiplied, and the powerful boats of the islanders came. Whalers and traders, adventurers, missionaries, and gentleman naturalists endlessly agog at the taxonomic world. Mabel's arrival might qualify as an occasion, a specific point on a timeline, except that the strangest of sea creatures must come butting up against this place in secret, yesterday and today and tomorrow, and usually there's no one here to care or notice. No, the real things of the world take place elsewhere. And yet today will be an eventful day, and yesterday was too. So these are the end times.

Yesterday I visited the Catholic school. I have an arrangement with the school: I go there once a month and am driven into town by the school's driver. We travel in a primordial jeep. In town, I pick up the supplies shipped in by my research group and send my month's data home; then we drive back to the school. It's a suitable arrangement for everyone, worked out in the distant days in which I was apparently capable of dreaming up such things: the school, which seems to exist in a state of immaculate fundlessness, gets some of my grant money, and I don't have to go to the trouble of maintaining a vehicle. I order in treats for the schoolgirls: lollies and biscuits, novelty erasers, books. These I pass on to the head of the school, Father Anthony, who always wants me to come to his office for a chat; I always refuse him. Every month I anticipate these trips with an obscure dread.

For the last few months, Father Anthony has been inviting me to address his students on the subject of marine life. I declined at first. It felt false to arrive at the school and pose as an expert when a) I no longer believe in God; and b) to this date my most significant contribution to the science of the squid is the observation that male colossal squid probably do have a penis. I discussed my qualms with Darwin and he rejected them immediately. First of all, I am a scientist, and these priests and nuns and children are not. They don't know how many papers I haven't had in *Nature*. Second, I'm invited to speak on marine, not heavenly life, so my lack of faith shouldn't interfere. And third, I have a problem that I need help with: namely, freeing Mabel. It was

Darwin's suggestion that the school may be able to provide this help. He has a tactical mind.

I delivered my talk yesterday, after my usual visit to town in the jeep. The driver of the jeep, Eric, is a sinewy man of tremendous energy. I understand that he does various kinds of physical work for the school: gardening and maintenance as well as driving. When he talks, which is rarely, it's mostly of the branch of his family who moved to America long ago and is thriving there as if having discovered a taproot from which they were once dramatically severed. Eric speaks of America with an ancient nostalgia, but refuses to go because he was born on this island and his unlucky father lives here. His energy is badly placed behind the wheel of a car. He sits in tense near-sightedness, coiled, attentive, as if he's offended by the stillness required in order to travel so far so quickly. The roads are covered at all times in blotchy fruits that, when crushed, spill out slippery seeds. Apparently, the animal that would once have eaten them – a large bird with a frighteningly hooked claw – is so near extinction it now trembles with evolutionary neurosis in the quietest corners of the forest, eating less perilous fruits. This is the road we travel – viscous, birdless – into town. Town: one store and five drinking establishments. When the supply ship docks, the entire place seems doubled in size. I like arriving with Eric. He knows everyone, and with him I'm greeted like a brother. Without him I appear to go unnoticed, which I know is not the case.

Yesterday, everything was quite normal – my crates were stacked on the dock, already clear of 'Customs' – except for the presence of five white women, all young and dressed in T-shirts and baseball caps. They sat together on benches by the dock, fanning themselves with the necks of their shirts and glowing with satisfaction at their evident discomfort. The girls rested their heads on each other's shoulders and took self-portraits with their mobile phones, and no one paid them any attention. They looked to have been sitting there for some time.

'Who are they?' I asked Eric.

'Students,' he said.

'Students? Where from?'

'Who knows?'

'Someone must know!' I said. 'What are they doing here?'

'They're waiting for someone to drive them.'

'To drive them where?'

'Around.'

After our errands we went to a bar, where we found the young men who clearly accompanied the girls outside. They were discussing this question of a driver with the patrons. Their American voices and emphatic gestures lacked economy in the midmorning heat. Eric expressed no interest in interacting with the visitors, so I lost interest in them too. All kinds of people come through this place, just as I've done. They're none of my business. We drank, we drove the slippery roads, and Eric delivered me back to the school in time for my presentation.

This is how I prefer to remember all my contacts with civilisation: as briefly as possible.

Fans revolved idly in the school's lobby. A row of African violets butted up against each window, brown in the heat, and a small table was stacked with copies of a pamphlet called 'Good News for Modern Man'. I read it while I waited for Father Anthony, and it reminded me of the church I grew up in: the primary colours and cheerful messages, the merry heaven and blotty, yellow hell. 'For God so loved the world,' it told me in a bright, responsible voice. I felt a small nostalgia. I had one of my headaches and all the angles of the world seemed wrong.

'Dr Birch!' cried Father Anthony, arriving. Father Anthony seems always to be arriving: there is a perpetual commotion about him. I've also never met a pinker man in all my life. His face is rose and his ears are salmon. His neck folds into itself like certain kinds of coral. His hands sprout from the ends of his arms, anemone-like and gloved in pink.

'Dr Birch!' he cried again.

'Call me Bill.'

'Bill, Bill,' he said with delight, shaking my brown hand with his pink one. His was smooth and cool; mine was damp. Father Anthony has a gift for the comfortable use of names. He dispenses them like small gifts, as if they've been prepared lovingly in advance. I've seen this delight people, and I can imagine it – this small recognition – feeling large enough to turn a soul back to God. I believe that Father Anthony's God is an old friend to him, gracious and prudent, with a priest's sympathy, a compassionate memory, and a steady heart for his flock's misgivings and undoings and hurts.

'This way, Bill, this way,' said Father Anthony, ushering me along with his hands. I wonder if, like certain corals, they glow all the pinker in the dark. 'We're proud to welcome you. The sisters are very excited, as are our students. This is quite a treat. What a treat. We have so few visitors. The bishop once – what an occasion. This is in my lifetime. Well, my tenure here – a lifetime in itself. Ha, ha! This way, this way.'

He ushered me into a small, overcrowded hall in which nuns quieted students and drew blinds over windows. They went about their tasks with a sensible bustle I found intimidating.

Father Anthony introduced me to the students as Dr William Birch, eminent marine biologist. I introduced myself as Bill Birch, malacologist.

'A malacologist,' I explained, 'is a scientist who studies molluscs.'

It occurred to me for the first time that this title of mine is extremely ominous, belonging as it does to the list of distasteful words beginning with 'mal': malcontent, maladjusted, malformed, malicious. I wanted to explain that, until my passion for the colossal squid blotted out my love for all other marine organisms I was a conchologist, which sounds much safer. More avuncular; sort of bumbling. Instead I loomed above them, malacologist, and ordered the lights out.

The students watched my slideshow presentation rapturously in the semi-dark. Their crowded bodies gave out a smell of warmed fruit about to spoil. It seemed to me as if their dark hair was filling up the room and muffling my voice, and when I felt prickles of fever up my legs and sweat behind my knees, I couldn't be sure of the cause – sickness, or girls?

A tiger shark swam across the screen in the dark room. The girls all breathed together, softly, 'Shark.' An anemone appeared, and they sang together, 'Anemone.' 'Starfish,' they sighed, and 'Seahorse', 'Eel'. I showed them a beach camouflaged by thousands of newly hatched turtles, and they inhaled collectively (we slow-breeding humans are always astonished by the extravagance with which sea creatures, seasonally awash in salt and sperm, reproduce themselves). I showed a photograph of myself in the observation station, taken by my departing colleagues. I paused on this photograph for too long because I was struck by the plump health of my former self, with his tan and his professionalism (he stands in the station doorway in prudent boots and his posture is in no way diminished by the tropical mountain rising above him). Then I showed pictures of Mabel in her bay and the students giggled. They know Mabel, although we have taken care not to publicise her. They know I'm the man who watches Mabel in the long afternoons and then watches them with his long binoculars. They laughed at her, friendly, and they laughed at me.

'Thanks to the wonders of technology,' said Father Antony, 'you have shown us the goodness of creation.'

The students can walk for minutes through the goodness of creation to see first-hand, in the blood-temperature sea, the same wonders I had just displayed. Since leaving them I've found myself repeating their breathless catalogue: shark, anemone, starfish, seahorse, eel. A children's book of the sea. And I think of the waste involved, the sea full of death and the dying: all of creation's necessary hunters fanning out among the reefs and rocks and sunken ships, all of them hungry and if not hungry, dead. What if I'd discussed this in my talk? A Lecture On the Origin of Species? But Father Anthony seems a sensible man. Perhaps the students are taught evolution. I suspect we think similarly, all of us trapped yesterday in that hot room: we're worried, daily, by the vast number of unredeemed things in the world.

Father Anthony took me to his study after my presentation. A white room with a view of jungle trees and, above the window, an ivory Christ on an ebony cross. Sun-faded copies of 'Good News for Modern Man' filled a low bookshelf. The sun ages everything so quickly that they may have arrived on last month's supply ship. Even Darwin looks a little more worn around the edges than when he first arrived a few months ago, glumly agnostic. Only the thirsty trees seem to resist the sun, growing greener by the day, sweating out a greenness that hurts my eyes and forces me to keep them trained on the sea. The mosquitos, also, seem unaffected, but I suppose they hide from the sun in the daytime.

'May I ask you a question?' said Father Anthony.

'Of course,' I said.

'Are you a man of faith, Bill?'

'That seems like the kind of thing you'd ask *before* letting me get up there in front of your girls.'

'Our students are not necessarily young women of faith, Bill. And we would never keep you away from them on the basis of your beliefs.'

This implied – I was sure of it – that Father Anthony had considered keeping me away from them on some other basis.

'Well, I'm not a man of faith,' I said. 'No, I'm not.'

And because this seemed so definitive – because this was the first time I had said anything like it aloud to a living man – I wanted to qualify it, immediately. I said: 'I used to believe, you know. God, the maker of heaven and earth, Jesus Christ, conceived by the Holy Spirit. The third day he rose again from the dead. You know, all that. The Church of England.'

'But not any more?'

'Not any more,' I said. 'So I suppose that means I'm going to hell.'

And I regretted this immediately; it was such an amateur thing to say. But my head was bad and I was worried I might have an attack – a vertigo attack – right there in his office.

'God knows your heart better than I do,' said Father Anthony. 'I thought you might be a believer, because in your lecture you said the way a squid eats is like a camel passing through the eye of a needle. Ha, ha! I found that very funny. It's rare these days to come across a good Biblical joke. Can I order you some tea?'

Father Anthony is a kind and good-natured man, one of those beaming, healthful men who truly believe drinking a hot liquid in insufferable heat will cool you down, and my heart went out to him – broke for him, really – and I loved my fellow men, and wanted to sail home to them immediately. I wanted to have sailed already. And why hadn't I? Mabel, I suppose, whom only I could save. I was also embarrassed for having said so much. I was talkative in my guilt and sorrow, and would admit to anything.

'No tea, no thanks,' I said. 'Sorry.'

'If you don't mind, I'll have some. 'A "spot of tea", yes? I'll ring the bell. Something cool for you, perhaps, Bill?'

His hand was poised in mid-air, holding a small silver bell. Did I mention we were both sitting, he behind his desk, and me in front of it? It was like being at school again.

'Yes, something cool,' I said.

I pressed my hand against my forehead, and when the something cool came, I pressed the glass against my forehead too. Father Anthony looked concerned. He looked on the point of ringing his little bell again.

'When you agreed to give this presentation today,' said Father Anthony, 'you asked for something in return. You said there was a scientific matter we could help you with. Is it to do with your squid?'

'With Mabel, yes,' I said. 'Strictly speaking, of course, she's not *my* squid. She's not anybody's – not even God's. Do you see? I want to free her. That's what I want your help with.'

'You agree, then, with those young activists in town?' said Father Anthony. I realised he was referring to the young people I'd seen at the port in their T-shirts and caps; I understood that Mabel was no longer a secret and they were here to protest her captivity. This explained why Eric had been so unforthcoming with me.

'I don't know who they are or what they believe,' I said.

'They want the very same thing you do – to release your squid. You could ask for *their* help.'

I thought of the boys in the bar and the girls on the beach, of their sincerity, their photogenic martyrdom, and the primary colours of their T-shirts, and I said, 'Tomorrow, Father Anthony, it has to be tomorrow. Before they find her and turn her into something she isn't.'

'Turn her into what?' he asked.

'Do you know very much about colossal squid, Father Anthony?'

'Only the information you presented in your lecture today,' he said. 'Their brains are round with holes in them, like donuts. They have eight arms and two long tentacles.'

'The most important thing I said about colossal squid today, Father Anthony, was that we don't know anything about them. And even though I've been watching Mabel for over a year now, I still know nothing. It's even possible that Mabel is still immature, that she could get bigger. How can we be sure of the true size of the colossal squid? Who knows what we'll fish up some day – the gargantuan squid? We might have gone a step too far, calling this one colossal. Soon we'll run out of superlatives. Wouldn't it be better just to leave things be? They've recorded a mysterious bloop, you know, coming from somewhere underwater, which could only have been made by an animal of unthinkable size. I hope we never find it.'

Father Anthony waved his hand in the direction of his tree-crowded window as if mysterious bloops were none of his business.

'The squid an infant – interesting,' he said. 'But wouldn't it look different if it were a baby? Forgive me, but you must know that, at least? You scientists?'

'No!' I cried. 'It's impossible to tell. Darwin talks about it in the *Origin*: "there is no metamorphosis; the cephalopodic character is established long before the parts of the embryo are completed". A squid is always a squid, right from birth – so we talk of mature or immature squid, but never of infants. The squid has no infancy, which means no nostalgia. It has no Romantic period. Squid think Wordsworth is full of horseshit. They have no childhood! None at all! They're born adult, and the only change they undertake is death. There is no metamorphosis!'

At the end of this speech I felt as pink as Father Anthony looked. There was a ticking in the room; I thought it came from the ivory Jesus crucified on the wall.

Father Anthony drew a long breath. 'Do you like it here on our island?' he asked.

'Actually I'm thinking of leaving.'

'Do you crave human company? That's only natural.'

'I want to be surrounded by people again, but I don't have much desire to talk to them.'

'But you have so many ideas to share,' said Father Anthony. 'If you'll excuse my asking, do you feel quite well? Not everyone can withstand this climate. I myself, many years ago, spent an entire year prostrate on my bed. The heat, you see, and it led to a sort of spiritual crisis, a lack of faith, you might say, in the sustaining hand of God. I thought I may have dreamed winter. It was only prayer that gave me strength, Bill – the strength of God against the burden of His creation.'

'Prayer!' I said. 'Can I ask you a question? Doesn't faith feel to you like a deep-down knowing, something you've discovered rather than made? And what do you do when you've lost that *knowing*? Hope that praying to something you no longer *know* will get it back for you?'

'Would you like me to pray for you, Bill?'

'I'm not well,' I said. 'I have headaches.'

'I understand,' said Father Anthony, reaching out a hand, and I was able, then, to imagine him laid out on a bed, dreaming winter. 'Why not leave?'

'Mabel.'

'Mabel is the squid, yes?'

'She belongs in the sea.'

'And what do you propose?'

I explained that the net with which we'd plugged Mabel's bay was impossible to move with only two men. I corrected myself – one man. Of course he didn't know about Darwin. Can a priest see the ghost of Darwin? Unlikely. But if all the students came down to the bay and we worked together, we could unfasten the net and, very swiftly, move it from one side of the bay to the other, so that Mabel, on escaping, wouldn't tangle herself in it. (Confession: when I imagine this, I have in mind a delirious scene from the Marlon Brando version of *Mutiny on the Bounty*, in which the girls of Tahiti, bare-breasted, hold an enormous net in the water, into which the native men drive schools of fish.) Father Anthony seemed concerned about this plan. He asked if there would be any danger. I told him no, there would be no danger – unlike octopi, squid are not dangerous to human beings. All those old etchings of whaleboats embraced by monstrous tentacled creatures are completely false. I said this, but we don't really know. No one has ever swum with a colossal squid. But just to be on the safe side, it's my plan to feed Mabel all the fish I have while the girls move the net. I'll enter the water to distract her if I have to. I'll get so close I'll fill her clever eyes.

'Select your strongest swimmers,' I said to Father Anthony. 'Those girls will take the end of the net farthest from the beach. They'll be the ones to swim across the entrance to the bay.'

'I see you've thought this through. Would you excuse me for a minute? I must consult a colleague.'

I let him go with regret. It had begun to grow cool in the room, if it's possible here to have any sense of what cool truly is, and I fancied that this relief emanated in some way from Father Anthony. His pink skin suggested not clammy heat but the smooth, cool skin of a baby. I was content, sitting there in that office. My presentation had gone well. I was acting on my belief that Mabel should be free. It was good to talk to another man again. And, as if offended by this betrayal – who was he, if not another man? – Darwin appeared at the window with the air of someone casually strolling by. He peered in.

'It's safe,' I said in a loud whisper. Then I gave him the victory sign, at which he looked puzzled.

'Where is he?' asked Darwin.

'Gone for help.'

'Help for whom?'

Darwin ambled away from the window and out into the trees, but I could see the bright camel colour of his naturalist's coat among the greenery; he hadn't gone far. Sitting comfortably in that cooling office, I considered the ways in which Darwin had never been particularly helpful to me, despite the initial promise of his appearance. After all, to a man – a scientist, no less – who has recently lost his faith, the ghost of Darwin could be a rich resource. We might have sat and talked a little about God's sovereignty, and then about its dissolution: a little of God vanishing into the dodo, a little into the long-lost ichthyosaurus. But he seems impatient when I raise these topics, and I've come to avoid them. I used to think of Charles Darwin in the same way some people think of Jesus Christ: he was a real man who existed in a specific historical time and he taught some valuable lessons, many of which I could adopt with no sense of contradiction. In short, I was a sensible man. I was no Creationist. I was reconciled with Darwin. I weighed it all up, and with the same clever hands I held something else entirely: that joyful faith of mine, impregnable.

I was once quite certain that God so loved the world. How sudden it was, on day 282: God's absence upon my shoulders, like a heavy flightless bird that can still hop to a height. How sobering to pass from Dr William Birch, beloved of God, to Bill Birch, organism. Just to be there on my sticky cliff and feel this way for no specific reason – it was a kind of grief. And I saw Mabel differently after that. How could I help it? She has nothing to do with me. I can't eat or fuck her. She's without complication. I was sure of one thing, until I was no longer sure; now my conviction is that Mabel must be free. And not for her own sake, no; although I love her, I would have put her in a tank and watched her in it for the rest of her life, or mine. But now I think she should remain a mystery. There must be some things in the world that no one sees and no one knows. Some monsters.

I began to worry about Father Anthony. Why was he taking so long? I rang the silver bell and a girl appeared. She was about sixteen, neat and shy behind heavy hair, and I felt like a *Bounty* sailor encountering beauty for the first time. I thought of the one mutineer who had the date he first saw Tahiti tattooed on his quivering arm.

'Hello,' I said.

'Hello,' she answered. She was solemn, and so was I. The heat had returned.

'Who are you?'

'I'm Faith,' she said, and she was so allegorical, standing there, she may as well have been draped in white robes, placed on a plinth above a plaque that read 'Faith'. I laughed, which startled her.

'Is that really your name?' I asked. 'Or did Father Anthony ask you to come in here and tell me that?'

She was confused but pleased. I knew I wouldn't touch her – I'm not so mad as to touch her – but I wanted to. I want to. Oh, Tahiti! Was Darwin ever there? No, I don't think so. He preferred dustier places, godforsaken places like the Galápagos, prehistoric with tortoises. This girl and girls like her would come to the beach with me and draw aside the net.

'Do you like to swim, Faith?' I asked.

'Yes,' she answered.

Father Anthony entered the office, and behind him was Eric, the driver.

'Faith!' Father Anthony cried, as if overjoyed to see her, and he ushered her merrily out. She looked back at me very quickly, the way she might look over one shoulder while swimming. Where had she appeared from, and where would she go now?

Father Anthony went behind his desk but didn't sit down. Eric leaned against the bookshelf.

'Now, Bill,' said Father Anthony. 'You mentioned headaches. The brain is a very delicate thing, which you as a scientist would know very well. The brain and the mind – two different things, yes? Both very delicate. If we're going to help you, I'd like you to do me a favour first.'

'I already gave the lecture,' I said. 'You owe *me* a favour.'

Father Anthony laughed.

'Very true, very true,' he said. 'You're right. But perhaps you'd consider doing this favour anyway. For my sake. Let me just tell you what I have in mind. I'd like you to see a doctor about these headaches of yours. Symptoms that seem harmless enough in other places become much more serious on an island like ours. When I first arrived, I was reluctant to see doctors. I thought I could cope with all the discomforts. But things escalated until I was in the grip of a brain fever.'

'You called it a spiritual crisis,' I pointed out.

'It was, Bill, it was,' he said, smiling, pinker than ever. 'I want you to travel back to town with Eric. There's a doctor on the supply ship, and he's willing to see you. It's either today, or you'll have to wait another month. Why suffer needlessly?'

'And the squid?'

'You see the doctor,' said Father Anthony, 'and then free the squid.'

'It has to be tomorrow,' I said.

'Tomorrow,' nodded Father Anthony.

Of course he was transparent; a man like Father Anthony always is. He was perched on the edge of his desk, becalmed in his own solicitude, hoping I would submit without fuss to his will. So I did. I allowed myself to be ushered out, I allowed him to assure me that my supplies had been refrigerated, I allowed myself to be seated comfortably in the jeep. Father Anthony followed the jeep as Eric backed it onto the road, he waved us off as if with a valedictory handkerchief, and I turned my head at the first corner to see him walking toward the school with his arms behind his back, his head lowered, as if in prayer.

Around that first corner I offered to pay Eric to stop the jeep.

'No, no,' he said, intent on the road.

'Please, Eric. This is important. How can I make you understand?'

'Forget it,' he said. 'I'll lose my job. You know how hard it is to earn money here if you want to stay legal? I have a Bachelor of Commerce from the University of Auckland, and this is the only work there is. I'll drive you into town. After that you do what you want, I don't care, and if anyone finds out it's not because I've told them.'

We drove on. Soon afterwards I noticed movement in the trees alongside the road. There was Darwin, running. I've never seen a man move so fast. He couldn't quite keep up with the jeep, although he managed it for stretches of a minute or two and at times seemed to extend his right arm out to reach the car door. Perhaps he was trying to warn me of what I already knew. Faithful Darwin sped beside us, the wings of his coat flying out behind him, his feet a blur and his face a study of determined strength. We lost him shortly before town when it was necessary to cross a river and he made the mistake of plunging into the stream rather than waiting to follow behind us on the narrow bridge. I turned to look and saw him thrashing at the water with the incredulous fury of an Olympian who's just lost the final.

Eric and I parted in town. He made no reference to the doctor, but also no promise of a lift back to the school. I walked through the sandy streets to the end of the beach farthest from the dock, observing the population as I myself was no doubt observed, and I hoped that once I left the island I would never see a place like it again in my life. I longed for escape. The supply ship sat smugly in the harbour, equipped with its doctor, and I was tempted to board it waving a white flag. But who then would free Mabel? If she doesn't belong to God, she belongs nowhere. I must remember to write that into my grant report.

I thought I might find Darwin on the beach, but I found the protesters instead. They talked in groups in the extended shadows of the palm trees. I walked toward them with my hands in the pockets of my trousers, and when they saw me coming they stirred with hope and indignation. I stopped a few feet from them, and despite the failing light they peered up at me with their hands cupped over their eyes, as if the absurd sun of the island's midday had forced them into a permanent habit.

'Good evening,' I said.

'Hi,' they chorused.

A blond boy stood, handsome, a kind of voluntary Achilles. He advanced toward me. 'Maybe you can help us,' he said. He seemed to be wondering aloud. A ripple of assent went through the group: yes, yes, they seemed to sigh, maybe he can help us.

'I hear you're looking for transportation,' I said.

'Do you have a car? Even better, a truck?' said the boy.

'A bus?' called one wag, and they laughed.

'Where is it that you'd like to go?'

'We need to get to the other side of the island,' said the boy. 'Do you know of a scientist, a Doctor William Birch?'

'Bill Birch, yes. Sure I do.'

'And you're not him?'

'Me? I'm no scientist,' I answered, and for some reason they all laughed again, perhaps in relief. The boy began to explain to me that he – that they – objected to the work Dr Birch was doing with a certain captive squid. He was guarded, but furious. They'd all been together on some kind of ecology project in the Cook Islands when news of Dr Birch's work broke, and had talked their way onto the supply ship.

'That was only three days ago,' the boy said, with pride. 'We're here before the media.'

'So you want to get to Dr Birch,' I said.

'No one seems to know where he is,' said the boy. 'It's like he's a hermit or something.'

It thrills me to know the locals protected me from that lovable, good-looking, deluded band.

'I know where he is,' I said, 'and I'll do what I can to get you to him.'

They rose up as one then, and surrounded me with their relief and zeal and exhaustion, shouting names at me and asking mine.

'Eric Anthony,' I said. 'Now tell me, what would you have said if I'd been Dr Birch?'

'We'd have said we were marine biology students,' said Todd, the Achilles. 'Who wouldn't want to see a colossal squid if they got the chance?'

And they asked me to take a photo of them, all together on the beach; it was a beautiful picture, sand-lit, and they pressed together inside its frame with such health and trust that I wanted to – I did – like them, very much. And I knew they would help me if I asked them to; they would swim out across the bay, they would remove the net, they would farewell Mabel with me, sending her seaward, and every second of her escape would be captured on their phones. Mabel would swim forever in a digital sea. She'd be free, but all the world would know her.

In town, I had more luck than they had finding transportation. I paid for the use of a utility truck owned by a friend of Eric's, and the crusaders climbed into the tray with their knapsacks. I even bought them supplies and checked the batteries in all their torches. The townspeople watched us. It pleased me to think that the only person they would betray me to was myself. Todd rode in the front with me. He asked me what I did on the island, and I told him I taught in a Catholic school near Dr Birch's camp. I told him we would pass the school, and that they should walk up to visit me there whenever they needed to get into town. He asked if I lived at the school, and I said yes. He asked if I was Catholic, and I said yes. This all came very easily. Todd is an earnest and admirable young man. I'd be proud to have a son like him. But he plays no part in my vision of freeing Mabel, and my principal concern was to cause him as much inconvenience as possible. To accomplish this, I dropped him and his cheerful gang at the head of a trail leading to a beach a few bays east of my observation station and told them that Mabel, far from being trapped in a small inlet, was enclosed by the coral reef and had the whole lagoon to move around in.

'Don't go swimming,' I said. 'She's probably pretty angry by now.'

'Are colossal squid dangerous?' asked Todd.

'Deadly.'

I told them Bill Birch moved his camp from place to place in the jungle, so they might have trouble finding him at first. I said that he was essentially harmless, that the machete he carried was only for cutting paths; I warned them, too, that he was hard of hearing and jumpy when startled. I said I knew they were responsible kids and would act with appropriate caution. We unloaded their gear onto the road. I moved the car so the headlights shone down along the trail. They remarked on the audible ocean and seemed much less nervous than they should have; they said goodbye, they expressed their gratitude, and then they plunged off into the humid trees. When they were far beyond the beam of my headlights, Darwin bound into the road like a stricken kangaroo.

'There you are,' I said.

He climbed into the car and sat rigidly, ecstatic with terror, like a boy waiting for a rollercoaster to descend its first hill.

'You've never been in a car before, have you?' I said.

He shook his head. I gave him quite a ride. There are some hairpin bends on this old volcano that could knot your intestines like a skilful sailor. By the time we'd climbed down to the observation station we were both giddy as schoolboys. We walked out onto the cliff and looked down at Mabel. It was dark, of course, and colossal squid are not, to my or anyone's knowledge, phosphorescent, but I would be willing to swear that I saw her outline glowing very faintly from the bottom of her bay.

That was last night. I slept late this morning, day 498, and spent the afternoon writing this account. Now Darwin is with me, and it's pleasant to see him in the fullest light of the day; he seems more definite, and in this way more ordinary. The weather is clear, so we amuse ourselves by pretending we can see New Zealand. I don't know what's become of Eric; I don't know what report he's given Father Anthony. No one has come looking for me. I imagine the supply ship has left by now. I imagine I'll spend the next month in town living on this newly discovered goodwill of the locals, just another oddball wanderer. The protestors will find me, eventually, and we'll make friends; we'll laugh together when they hear what it is I've done, and one of the girls, less pretty, perhaps, but kind, will take pity on me. I'll resign my position, of course. I'll take the next ship; I'll go home. Darwin says he won't come with me. He's scornful of Australia and talks of England with the adoration of exile. This is all as it should be. Unless, unless, I get too close to Mabel, and she takes me with her.

In these last few minutes I've felt the swimmy brimming that precedes an attack of vertigo. I feel it as a pressure in my feet. Soon, I know, the earth will fall away from them, and this too is as it should be. My head seems to press outward. To myself I say,

Shark, anemone, starfish, seahorse, eel. My main concern was that if Eric raised the alarm, Father Anthony wouldn't permit the girls to take their daily swim. But here they come now, down the mountain. They're singing, of course, and Faith is among them. She's singing softly. She likes to swim. She'll wade out into the water and the other girls will follow her. What is it about being immersed in water that's so exciting, so vital to us? We all experience it – this thrill of feeling the medium we move in as something dangerous and contingent. It reminds us of the artifice of oxygen and gravity, the sheer unlikelihood of their provision. We feel the water close around our arms and legs and we make our way through it with difficulty and determination, singing and proclaiming and making promises, kneeling and rising and sitting and standing. It feels like the unbearable presence of God, His hands on our submarine chests. A blowfish might waft past, inflated, with a look of dumb surprise on its face. I have basketfuls of fish ready to feed to Mabel. The girls will take hold of the net; I'll watch as they rise through the sea with it into the air. The light will billow and flare around them in the bright wind, and their hands will reach out to heaven as if strung on trapeze wires. I'll wade through the shallows, wet to my stupid waist; then I'll kick downward and swim. Darwin will observe from the shore in his nineteenth-century socks. And Mabel will fly seaward, holy and beautiful, a bony-beaked messenger bringing no news.

Alpine Road

Jennifer Down

Mornings were when they were most forgiving of each other. When they fucked now, it was first thing, when they were still kind.

Before Clive got sick, he was always up early. He worked at the power plant in Hazelwood. Even when he'd been on night shift, he'd get up and make the coffee.

These days he might not get out of bed at all. Mostly Franca woke when Billy wormed his way between their bodies, smelling of sleepy toddler. She'd lie there feeling his hot belly pressed against her back, his fingers in her hair. She'd go to the kitchen and do the kids' lunches, make the coffee. Clive'd be where she left him. Sometimes the blanket was too much for him to lift. He'd stopped saying *sorry* a long time ago.

He was having a good week. Franca heard him moving around the kitchen. The front door slapped shut. She sat up and looked through the blinds. There was frost on the lawn. Clive was barefoot, shirtless, carrying two plates of toast across the yard to the caravan, propped up on its bricks, where the older two slept. He banged on the metal with his fist. He shouted *Gendarmes!* It was a joke the kids wouldn't understand. The door swung open. Emily stood with a half-smile, wiping sleep from her face. Her mouth moved. Franca couldn't hear what she said, but it might have been *I knew it wasn't Mum.* Franca never brought them toast with jam in the mornings.

*

'There was a spider the size of a five-cent coin in the caravan,' Clive reported. He sat on the end of the bed. 'Kurt was carrying on the worst.'

'Thanks for getting them breakfast.'

Her shoulders were wet from the shower. The house was so cold she could see her breath.

'Listen, I'm getting Cate to pick up the kids from school today,' she said. 'There's a meeting about the bargaining agreement after work.'

'I can get them.'

She bunched her stockings at the ankles. 'It's okay. It's probably best to ask Cate. So we know for sure. You know. If you start to fade by then.'

He was gracious. He said nothing.

'I'll pick them up after five,' Franca said, 'then come and get you and Billy.'

'We still going to your parents' for tea?'

'Only if you're up to it. Otherwise I can just go with the kids.'

'I'll be right.' Clive scratched his ear. 'What'd you say it was at work?'

'The meeting for the bargaining agreement. I haven't been able to get to the others.'

'What's the go?'

'It's all still a bit over my head. I know they're talking about changing our pay from fortnightly to monthly.'

'Well, that wouldn't be the end of the world,' Clive said. 'We always work something out.'

Franca felt that sudden rage rolling in. 'Who does?'

'What?'

'*Who works it out*, I said.'

Clive looked at her steadily. Franca dropped her head.

She went to Billy's room. He was awake, one fist clenched at the corner of his sheepskin rug. He was two and a half and he'd had a name all along, but they still called him *the baby*. He sat up, beamed at her.

She made the lunches. She wiped the crumbs from the bench. The house needed restumping so badly that when she'd dropped the frozen peas last night, they'd rolled and collected in the corner of the kitchen by the door. The kids had crouched, pinching them between their fingers. Kurt said, *See, Mum, woulda been worse if the house wasn't falling down. At least they're all in the one spot.* He and Emily slept in the caravan because it was warmer than their bedroom with its rotted weatherboards, the hole under the window spewing damp Insulwool. They were good at making adventures of things.

Franca took the scraps out to the chooks. She stood by the caravan and tried to decode the conversation inside.

'Look! The sun fell!'

'Can you stop putting it in my face?'

She tapped on the door. 'Are you two showered? We're leaving in ten. Get a wriggle on.'

When she went back to the bedroom, the baby was in bed with Clive, in the curl of his arm. They had the same face.

'It's a real sickness,' Clive said. 'I'm really crook.'

Franca was helpless. She stood holding her coat. 'I never said you weren't.'

In the drawer beside his bed were a bible, a broken watch, his prescriptions and some foreign coins he kept to prove to himself he'd left the country. There were photos, too – mostly of the kids, but there was one picture of Franca from before they were married. She was naked, standing in front of a curtain. Shy pubic bone, one arm tucked behind her back politely. Franca didn't like the photo, or didn't recognise herself in it. She looked too much of a child.

After the second baby she'd gone away, left him with the kids. When she came back Emily was eleven months old and didn't recognise her. Clive knew nothing about where she'd been or what she'd done that year. She didn't know if he'd ever trust her again.

*

Franca worked four days a week at the Latrobe Valley Magistrates', all pale blue glass and clean angles. It had been built ten years ago, but she still thought of it as new. She was a stenographer. She liked the solemnity of the courts. She liked the drive to and from work. There was comfort in the skinny poplars, the long driveways, the husks of burned-out cars in front yards, the gutted petrol station, the paddocks, the roadside signs to tiny cemeteries. This time of year, canola – fields of sunshine. The mountains. On Fridays she worked at Bairnsdale, closer to home. It was a smaller courthouse, set down by the brown river. The road was unmade, two streets back from the grand brick building and the motels.

Clive hadn't worked in two years, but before, they could coordinate their lunch breaks some days. It was about ten minutes from the court to the power station. She'd meet him in the car park and they'd eat their sandwiches in the station wagon beneath the brutal concrete building, like something from the pages on the Eastern Bloc in her high school atlases. It had eight towers, set in pairs, and red capital letters spelling out HAZELWOOD. When she'd been on maternity leave, she'd sometimes taken the kids to the lake next door. Its water was used to cool the station.

It seemed like all the men in the valley worked there, or at the Yallourn plant, or else in the coalmine. Franca used to be reassured by its hulking brown shape on the horizon. You could see it from the highway for miles. In the right weather, you could see the plumes of shit it belched out into the atmosphere. Now when she saw it, it meant other people's husbands.

*

The end of the day was the wrong time for the meeting. Franca could barely follow. She'd been concentrating on voices and words all day. The union rep was a young man, impossibly articulate. He said things like, *There has not been a pay rise commensurate with the cost of living in five years. Waiting an additional year for that increase is problematic.*

Franca wanted to ask the right questions but she was giddy. Plenty of employers are going with monthly pays, the IR lawyer was saying. It's to do with compliance costs. Workers can adapt. It's the same amount of money.

It's not the same, Franca thought. The union guy was already saying it for her. It seems punitive to move from two weeks to four when you know you're working with people already in a low-wage bracket, who possibly already have to budget very carefully—

Everyone was talking at once. The room was too full, too warm.

'Right,' someone said, 'we'll get the minutes out early next week. Anything else?'

'I just wanted to ask about carer's leave,' Franca said. The room of faces turned to her. 'I saw in the last transcript something about medical certificates.' Her hand hovered by her ear as if she were a schoolgirl with a question.

*

She drove past Stephen's on an impulse. His car was in the driveway. She tapped on the door and watched his figure approach through the bubble glass. He asked if she wanted coffee. She said, *I have to get the kids.* They fucked in a hurry. He held her wrists and pinned her down. His face hovered over her. His features blurred when he came. She thought, dimly, that there was something pathetic about the two of them, her thighs clenched around his hips.

Afterwards she fell asleep. It was only a few minutes but she woke panicked, scrambled to sit up. His heavy arm fell away from her.

'Whassatime?'

'Ten past six.'

Franca lay down again, jackhammer heart.

'Have you been here the whole time?' she asked.

He stared at her. She felt foolish, dazed.

When she left the sky was paper-coloured. All the cows had started their journey home, their tender ears flattened. She parked out the front of Cate and Sonja's. No one answered when she knocked. She heard the high cuts of the kids' voices out in the yard. She pushed through the side gate.

'That baby, I mean, she had lead rings under her eyes,' Sonja was saying. 'They had to get out of the city.'

The two women were sitting on the deck, rugged up against the thin sun. They looked like royals surveying a kingdom: their sloping lot, the ashy grass, the kids kicking a footy at the bottom of the yard. Franca did a small wave.

'Hullo!' said Cate. She spread her arms. She had a quilt around her shoulders. She was holding a glass. 'Do you want some? It's Tasmanian whisky.'

'I'd better not,' said Franca. 'I don't like drinking when I've got to drive with the kids.'

She sat down. Sonja slid her a smile. She worked at the Koori ressy care facility in Bairnsdale. Once she'd told Franca, *Sometimes when I finish I need to be alone for a bit.* She had wild pale eyes. *I just know if I go home and the kids and Cate are hanging off me, I'll do something awful.*

Franca liked to think they understood each other.

'How's Clive?' Cate asked.

'Oh – not good today.'

'Have you heard of anyone else from Hazelwood with it?'

'No. He's lost touch with a lot of the blokes from work.'

'I imagine,' said Sonja, 'that'd be the sort of illness that men don't understand.'

'I was thinking. Remember all that talk about asbestos a couple of years back?' said Cate.

'You don't get chronic fatigue from asbestos,' said Franca.

'I know that. You just can't help wondering if somehow – if there's something—' said Cate.

'*Anyway*,' said Sonja. She began to rake her hair into a braid.

Franca watched her brown hands working away. 'It's not that we're really struggling,' she said, 'it's just that we've got no safety net. If the car needed a new windscreen tomorrow, we'd be buggered.'

*

The wind had picked up by the time they were heading home. On the radio there was talk of storms and flash flooding.

'Know what Cate told us today?' Emily asked.

'Hmm?'

'"You can't bullshit a bullshitter."'

'No,' said Franca. She craned her neck to check if it was safe to pass the car in front. 'That's true.'

'Mum, Emily said *shit*.'

'It was in direct speech,' Franca said, batting at the indicator. She could feel Kurt's foot through the back of her seat.

'She said it twice. She said, "You can't—"'

Gold headlights streaming towards them, the dull blare of a

truck horn. One of the kids shrieked. Franca jerked the wheel, overcorrected. The car behind honked its horn, too. Someone was crying.

'Will you two *shut up*?' she said. 'We're fine. Nothing happened except this *fuckhead* in front is travelling thirty kilometres under the limit and I'm trying to get home.'

Her arms were weak with shock. She could hardly hold the steering wheel. She wondered if this was how Clive felt all the time.

*

The house was unlit. The kids dropped their schoolbags at the front door. Franca heard the thud of their bodies against the beanbags, the fight for the television remote.

Clive and Billy were as she'd left them. There was a box of Duplo upended at the foot of the bed.

'Have you two been there all day?'

'We had some lunch,' Clive said. 'We played Lego. We watched some footy on YouTube,' he said, 'didn't we, mate?'

Billy smiled at Franca, then burrowed his blond head into the pillow. He looked dopey, stunted.

'He needs sunlight, Clive.'

'I'm sorry. I had a bad day.'

'So he could have gone to childcare.'

'We don't have money for that more than once a week,' Clive said. 'You're the one keeps saying it.'

Franca knelt to gather the coloured blocks. They made a hollow clatter.

Clive's face appeared above her. 'Sorry, babe,' he said.

'I'm going to mum and dad's for tea,' she said, 'remember?'

'Oh, yeah.'

'I said you didn't have to come if you're not up to it.'

He touched her hair. 'What if I stay here with Kurt and Em. I'll make us dinner. You just go with Billy.'

*

Her parents managed a motel in Omeo. This time of year it was filled with people on their way to and from Hotham, rich people who stopped overnight before they fitted their snow chains and drove up the mountain to ski.

Used to be that Clive always drove up from Bairnsdale. Franca hated driving the Great Alpine Road at night. She still hated it – the seventy kilometres of high-beam light, the sudden twists, the narrow places – but she had no say in it anymore. Clive hadn't been up that way in months. She wished he could see it now. It looked healthier since the drought had ended.

Her mother cooked a roast. Franca was embarrassed, turning up with only Billy in her arms. There was far too much food.

She tried to talk to her parents about the meeting. She thought if she could explain it, she might understand it better. She thought of the lawyer. *That's why the CPI forecasts are low; everyone knows that.*

She felt sick.

'This happens time and again,' her father said. 'Remember how worried Clive was about the carbon tax? Thought he'd lose his job? It all blew over.'

'He lost his job anyway,' Franca said.

'Well, not because of the tax. All I'm saying is, the agreement might still get voted down.'

'We could move closer,' her mother said, 'and look after Billy.'

'Don't be silly.'

The rain fell in sheets.

'I should move the car. I parked under the big tree,' Franca said.

'Do that. Then sleep here tonight,' her father said. 'No good going home now. It's bloody cyclonic out there.'

She stayed in one of the motel rooms. It smelled of eucalyptus cleaning product and old carpet. She undressed Billy and tucked him in. She turned on the television. The football was just finishing. At home, the kids would be watching the same match. Maybe Clive would have made it to the couch, too. The muscles in her thighs had begun to ache.

*

She waited all night with the baby in her arms but the sunrise didn't happen; the light just got grey. She stripped the bed so the cleaner wouldn't have to. She washed Billy's face. She rubbed a flat cake of soap between his tiny hands. She sat at her parents' table. Her mother scrambled eggs in the microwave. On television they were reporting the storm damage.

'Lucky you stayed here,' her father said. 'They've had trees down all along the highway. Flooding from Traralgon to Paynesville.'

'They just had a bloke in Bairnsdale,' her mother said, 'reckons almost the whole town's without power. You spoken to Clive?'

Franca shook her head. 'His phone might be dead. If there's no power, he won't be able to charge it.'

There was a tree across the road at Doctors Flat. She stood in her parka, hopping from foot to foot, while the SES crew finished clearing it.

She stopped for petrol in Bruthen. She tried calling Clive again.

'Was your power out?' she asked the guy at the servo.

'Nah, we were fine, but they were rooted in Sale,' he said. 'You been listening to the radio?'

The roads were slick with water that hadn't drained; flooded in parts. Franca pictured the footy oval in town. It'd be marshy. Maybe Kurt's match would be called off. She hoped their spouting at home had withstood all the bark and leaf shit, but she was sure she'd be up there all afternoon with a pair of gloves and a garbage bag, clearing out the muck.

She saw it as soon as she pulled into the driveway. The great dead red gum had come down. It lay across the yard, priestly trunk like a spear. The front room of the house was caved in; roof beams exposed, weatherboards splintered to matchwood.

The caravan, the kids' room, was cleaved in two. It looked absurd, the metal folded into itself.

Franca yanked the handbrake to and heaved open the car door. She saw a striped doona cover beneath a sheet of corrugated detritus. She saw her daughter's gumboot. She started to run. Suddenly she was on her knees in the mud, calling for Clive. He was in front of her. His mouth was moving. He helped her up.

'They're okay,' he said. He was shivering. Franca clutched at his arms. 'The kids are inside,' he said. 'They're okay.'

Coca-Cola Birds Sing Sweetest in the Morning

Elizabeth Tan

But Audrey is partial to the Panasonic birds, a cheaper but no less handsome variety; they acknowledge the dawn without extravagance, *pip pip pip pip pip,* little notes of fixed widths, such deft, even spacing. They are not meant to be here in the city; Audrey suspects they have migrated from Russet Hill, a network over a hundred kilometres away, renowned for wildflowers. The birds have a talent for evasion, as Audrey has never seen them at the reassignment plant; just as well, perhaps, for to crack open such a tender body, to see the inert parts that produce the sound of her dawn – it would surely be an act of violence. Audrey slips into the morning – or perhaps the morning slips into her, like a suggestion, *pip pip pip pip pip* – opens her eyes to a crisp blue sky, so bleeding-edged in its clarity. It is the kind of sky that reminds her that she was once loved.

The traffic is not so loud that she can't discern the Citrus Man cycling down the street, the clicks of his wheels, the brittle music-box tune that pings from his gramophone. That old song – *oranges and lemons say the bells of St Clement's.* She has never purchased fruit from the Citrus Man, but, as with so many things in this city, she cannot help but have affection for his presence, a belief in his importance: that not one part of this city is dispensable, not him, not the birds, not her, as she slides her legs into her overalls, fills the kettle with water, scoops black tea leaves from a battered tin.

Gently caffeinated, Audrey turns the locks of her apartment, exits briskly to the streets with their striped and creaking awnings, passes the buoyant results of the stock exchange. A man punches a code into an automated teller machine, removes the bright bills; a publican overturns bar stools. Audrey can still hear the Citrus Man's music box, camouflaged now by the eight-fifteen tram, the Coca-Cola birds, the queues shuffling through the bureaus and banks and offices, the shop bells ringing with their first customers of the day.

At the reassignment plant she punches her card and crosses the first floor, where workers disassemble birds and insects and amphibians so that the parts can be reassigned; they clean the cogs, bolts, circuits, screws; they sort them according to grade and size. No part is ever judged unfit to be repurposed. Someday the parts will be reincorporated into new wholes, inserted into new networks, sponsored by a different corporation; maybe the Panasonic birds to whom Audrey listens so keenly in the morning contain parts that once belonged to Coca-Cola birds.

Audrey ascends to the second floor, where mechanics like her collect their day's allotment in closed wooden boxes. Before the animals are sent to the first floor for disassembly they are delivered here, their last chance to be repaired and reintegrated into their network. Mechanics receive a commission for each animal restored, though Audrey believes that there is some inherent reward in clipping the parts together, resetting the animal; some satisfaction to know that it thrives in some distant network once again conveying pollen, regurgitating nectar, lubricating soil.

Today Audrey opens her wooden box and finds it empty. She checks that it is indeed her box – it says AUDREY KWAI on the label – and opens the lid again. A cold memory revives itself. But then Cornelius the second-floor supervisor leans out of his office, his spectacles already lit with dust: *Ah yes, Audrey – the return machine on Cambridge is out of order. Mind taking a look?*

*

She did not always work at the reassignment plant: in another life she repaired ticket machines, all kinds, but mostly the ones at train stations, their buttons polished smooth by generations of hurried fingertips. She used to wonder if commuters appreciated the sound of a coin rolling through the slot, the rich clunks as it navigated the machine. A crisp new ticket, an unrepeatable date and time. In this other life, Audrey was a collector of tickets, everything from the theatre pass to *Le Sacre du printemps*, hole-punched by an indifferent usher, to the forked slip she pulled at the delicatessen counter, number 25. She liked transport tickets the best: their sharp corners, inkjet smell. Their typeface optimised for legibility, to be understood by tourists, locals, ticket inspectors alike.

It is because of this past life that Audrey now arrives at Cambridge Street with her toolbox. She has a letter of authorisation from Cornelius, but Audrey thinks she is unlikely to be questioned: a school, a church and silent apartments are all that comprise this corner of the city. Audrey has borrowed a broken Cadbury frog from the reassignment plant to test the machine. When she places the frog in the slot, the machine does not accept it. No numbers click the scales, no coins tumble from the chute.

Audrey pockets the frog. She loosens screws, opens the face of the machine, observes the maintenance sticker that says that the machine was inspected and emptied one month ago. A clutter of animals and animal parts has accumulated like irregular confectionery, not enough to cause a malfunction; nonetheless, Audrey unfolds a basket and empties the shaft.

Return machines are not at all like ticket machines – they are reverse vendors, the recipients of goods in the user–machine transaction, complicating the axis of trust. When Audrey repaired ticket machines, it was not uncommon for her to discover one or two counterfeit coins amongst the legitimate tender – *slugs*, were what her colleagues called them. Though ticket machines are adept at recognising slugs, swallowing the counterfeit and refusing to dispense a ticket, over her career Audrey amassed a sizeable collection of slugs in her toolbox, some nothing more than crude washers, others with an astonishing resemblance to their authentic counterpart, down to the grooves on the circumference.

Sometimes, when Audrey is tasked with repairing an actual slug at the reassignment plant, she remembers that other kind, the slippery connotations of both.

There is a sound coming from Audrey's basket, the slightest articulated tremors, *rrrp, rrrp.* Audrey carefully shifts dislocated heads and abdomens to find the source: a bee, legs flailing as if riding an upside-down bicycle, too small for Audrey to determine the sponsor. She supposes it belonged to a park in the city, for bees cannot fly far. She wonders how long it has been inside the machine, kicking and kicking. She extracts a pin from her toolbox, flips her magnifier over her eye. Inserts the pin inside the bee to deactivate it.

Her mechanic's eye is always drawn to the wholest animals, hypothesising causes of malfunction, possible solutions. The sky is still blue, the street is still silent; somewhere in the city the Citrus Man still cycles, and Audrey's most significant days are those that begin like this one, without portent, glowing with the kind of ordinariness on which she leans entirely. But today her eyes fall upon a bird in the basket; as she lifts it from the pile, something in the universe pivots quietly, creaks imperceptibly, like the wheels turning in a cassette tape.

She has not seen this bird before. Her first suspicion is that it is, at long last, a Panasonic bird, but as she turns the body in her hands, she knows this is incorrect. She twists her magnifier and searches for the sponsor name – birds, the largest and most recognisable animals, *always* have a major sponsor – but there is no identification.

She turns the bird. No facet of its design suggests a manufacturer. Without opening the body she cannot ascertain what the bird's network purpose was – to disperse seed, pollen; to monitor; to sing. Ten minutes pass before she realises that the bird has no activation pinhole.

Across the road, the school siren rings. Audrey looks up at the gaping machine, for a moment lost in its very insideness – the belts, pinions, coils. Bolted to the machine's exterior is a sign that reminds citizens that it is a criminal offence to vandalise or steal from a return machine, and in the style of the train tickets she once collected so attentively, the sign is typeset plainly in capital letters, to be understood by tourists, locals, machine inspectors.

Still, it has to happen, on this empty street, on this unremarkable day – Audrey turns the bird a final time, wraps it in a handkerchief, and pushes it deep within her pocket.

*

Nobody knows what compels the animals to migrate, but also, nobody knows, *truly* knows, what it was that caused the original crisis. A disaster of first nature. The day that bees were falling out of the sky, suddenly turned flightless. Is it a real memory of Audrey's – an infant at the time – this image of bees twitching on the ground in their thousands, their brittle, feeble buzzing, or did Audrey absorb the image much later from a schoolbook? Or is it, perhaps, that this is the memory passed down, made true through its insistent reproduction, a cultural heirloom?

Or could it be that, since the day that Audrey threw out her ticket collection – save one, a faded ticket for the river ferry, softened at the edges – something had happened to Audrey's memory itself, a quiet transformation, heaving weakly to accommodate a vast and unimaginable trauma?

At home, after work, Audrey snaps on her desk lamp and unwraps the bird. It is not an ugly bird, but it resists comparison to the birds she fixes at the reassignment plant. As if someone studied a bird and replicated it from memory, with none of the inferiority one associates with replication; as if 'bird' was just a reference point, a figure from a dream.

Audrey angles the lamp, probes the exterior until she detects an interruption. The right tool and the body yields, halves asymmetrically, intimate as a dollhouse; there is something endearing about it, this private arrangement of parts. They all fit together, in an inexact way. Some of the connections are tenuous, and in fact Audrey sees that the bird is inoperable not because of a single fault but a number of parts that have worn away as a result of their imperfect tessellation. She cannot, still, discern the bird's purpose.

There are hobbyists, she knows, who assemble animals, though the Department of Second Nature prohibits their activation in public. While this bird might well be a hobbyist's work, Audrey finds the premise unconvincing: something in the humbleness of the arrangement, the absence of an activation pinhole. Audrey unearths a yellowed pad of graph paper and a pencil, transposes the bird onto these squares, numbering the parts; tenderly, she dismantles the bird and soaks the pieces in white vinegar. Across the night, through her quiet window, it is time for stray frogs to open their throats. Samsung, Toshiba, Cadbury: their creaking dialogue, all the tongues of industry.

*

Again, the Panasonic birds; again, the Citrus Man; again, the reassignment plant. This time, Audrey's wooden box contains a series of silkworms. All morning she has replaced spools, tested salivary glands; at ten o'clock, Cornelius approaches her workbench, asks if she might know why the weight of the animal parts did not match the reading on the return machine from yesterday. *A discrepancy of about sixty grams*, he says; she responds that the scales had malfunctioned, and as Cornelius nods, scribes on his clipboard, she admires the ease of the lie, gliding like a gear with perfect teeth. She returns to her silkworms, sends the inoperables down the chute.

The diagram of the bird is folded in her bib pocket. During breaktime she studies it in a restroom cubicle, commits the dimensions of the required parts to memory, returns to the plant floor and slips candidates into her pocket. Yesterday's chill of opening her empty wooden box still hovers – somewhere, a ticket machine explodes quietly, not so deep in the past that its reverberations can't disturb the present.

After the silkworms, a wasp. After the wasp, a moth. Through the window, the sky is an imitation of yesterday's, an unsatisfactory facsimile, like a perfume sample in a magazine.

How distant, that blue sky – how faintly persistent – under which Audrey once stood, holding a boy's hand on the river ferry. The world was bright and forgiving then; time was worth marking with tickets. She remembers how the dragonflies floated like helicopters, kissed the reeds at right-angles. That day, she didn't know that those particular reeds are pollinated by the wind, not by insects, so the dragonflies must have migrated from another network; but, whatever their origin, they were witnesses to her short-lived good fortune; she was, to someone's eye, indispensable.

*

She can still detect it, that facsimiled sky – turning mauve now – as she walks home from the reassignment plant, rotating a stolen cog in her pocket. The diagram of the bird creases against her chest every time she breathes. Cornelius had smiled at her as she clocked out and it pains her, his simple trust, the paper-cut sting of it.

She is relieved when the sky exhausts its colour, and the ferry is small on her memory's horizon.

She notices, then, the broken window of her apartment. A single, decisive puncture. At first she thinks it is a trick of the light, ghostly as an autostereogram, but it refuses to be blinked away. Audrey grips the cog in her pocket, slides it between her fingers. She climbs the stairs two at a time. The arrival takes forever.

Turning the locks, bursting over the threshold, to her desk – the toppled beaker of vinegar, rocking in the intruding breeze. Shipwrecked on the liquid surface: two bolts, a screw, a pair of tweezers. Parts have been dragged through the spilled vinegar, spiking the puddle's edges; she can even perceive a trail of pronged footprints, determined as arrows. And the bird, which she had left open on the bench, is gone.

Audrey's hand moves over her heart, to her bib pocket, expecting the diagram, too, to have vanished; she flounders to extract it, confirms: the bird was *here* – then scrunches this tangible memory along the wrong folds, clutches it to her chest like a mourner's handkerchief, while the cold afternoon hurtles through the window's wound.

*

Before he left, he had the nerve to ask her to exchange some notes for coins, so he could purchase a train ticket to the city where the other woman lived. A thorn which sunk deep, piercing some vindictive vein Audrey did not realise she possessed. She performed this favour anyway, and on that last morning handed him a ziplock bag of coins, buffed to a deceptive shine: slugs, all of them.

It was not meant to have consequences, this feeble revenge; she supposed it would take not more than two attempts before he realised. When the slug rolled through the slot nothing was meant to happen, absolutely nothing, but it was as if the machine was animated by her indignity, summoned to act beyond its regular function; the explosion sent unprinted tickets pummelling through the air, coins flashing – that's what the witnesses remembered the most, coins strewn like dying bees, although Audrey also heard about the young man thrown off his feet, the blast propelling, with malevolent accuracy, a slug into his temple, a shard of which remains lodged in his skull to this day.

The investigation labelled the event a freak accident, but she resigned all the same, fearing the day when she'd be cut loose. Ticket machines are not supposed to explode. But Audrey wonders if machines are themselves part of second nature, if they are categorically the same as the birds and insects that toil away in their networks – all of them lively, wilful, migrating out of turn; enacting, in their quiet malfunctions, an unauthorised evolution.

*

Sometimes, Audrey gets the notion that there is nothing outside the city, no farms, no fields, no vast harmonious networks. In this vision, the animals that the mechanics repair and ship out of the city are all redirected to one factory, where an assembly line opens the animals, roughens the parts, ships them back; some parts are scattered in parks and thoroughfares for unwitting citizens to pick up, redeem for coins at return machines; the only real things are the sponsors, the benefactors of this operation, while the stock exchange results are algorithmic fabrications of the Department of Second Nature. But then Audrey thinks: where does the honey come from, the fresh flowers, the vegetables and fruit? – and the vision disappears, but not wholly.

Audrey, woken on this new morning not by the Coca-Cola birds, nor the Panasonic birds, but by the whistling of the broken window, a disruption to her routine waking. She listens for the

Panasonic birds, receives their *pip pip pip pip pip* with the scantest relief; listens ever more keenly now, desiring the city's wholeness – there, the Citrus Man, *oranges and lemons say the bells of St Clement's.* The air is still soured by vinegar; she has not swept the glass, and for all her expertise Audrey cannot discern whether the hole was made by something exiting or entering. She had fallen asleep with the lamp on, and her fingers still grasp two things: one, her river ferry ticket, her last mark of time; two, the pencil diagram, the vanished bird.

Pip pip pip pip pip – Audrey, overwhelmed by the liveliness of objects, holds the ticket to the light, against yet another crisp sky, relentlessly blue. Sometimes it seems that everything in this city conspires to remind Audrey of her impermanence and obsolescence, from the blue sky to this smallest ticket, inkjet-fragrant, words still legible despite the intervening years. It's some kind of amazing, the things that outlast us.

A Review of *Over There* by Stanislaus Nguyen

Michael McGirr

Over There is the third volume of Stan Nguyen's comic memoirs. For a man who, in the course of this book, celebrates his fortieth birthday, that's not bad going. Socrates said famously that the unexamined life was not worth living. If he were alive today, he might have said that the unlived examination is not worth much either.

This new book focuses on a period of less than a month in which Nguyen, now teaching in a prestigious independent school that he calls Grace Grammar, accompanies a group of about a dozen senior students on a 'justice tour' to South Africa and Kenya. Nguyen was a reluctant participant. He notes that Africa had enough problems already without adding him to the list: *Mandela had only recently died. I hoped they weren't looking to me to fill the gap.*

He treats his students in the same dry manner:

> There was an application process. They were all pretty good at this because they all had part-time jobs, usually in the fast food industry. One of the boys most anxious to join the trip, Andy, had a proven record of working hard to feed the hungry. In three years, I had never seen him without food in either his hand or his mouth or, most of the time, both.

After a few skirmishes of this kind, Nguyen settles down to deal with some real concerns. He writes about a girl he had taught who landed an internship with a large accounting firm because she had been on a trip to Africa, a fact that gave her an edge, a kind of X factor, in a competitive market: *I reckon this is the colonial experience all over again. Go to Africa, get what you can for yourself, come home and make a profit out of it.*

He also tells a story of being at a school assembly soon after his arrival at Grace Grammar. Some of the students had recently returned from a trip to Cambodia, where they had visited an orphanage and spent three days painting the main building. One after the other, they had said how good they felt because they had made a real difference in the lives of people who needed their help. Nguyen was bemused that young people could step into a desperate situation and come away in high spirits because they had played a few games and painted some walls.

> Surely to Zeus, if you are going to run these trips, you at least want privileged students to feel muddled up about the way the world works or doesn't work or only works for a few. If the situation is bad, we need them to feel bad.

When Nguyen writes about such things, there is pepper in his ink. The second volume of his memoirs, *Over Here*, describes the poignant journey of his parents from Vietnam. His father, Aloysius, trained for a time to be a Catholic priest but, in an illicit romance, had already fallen in love with Teresa, a girl from his village. The couple married in secret and had two sons, Noel (born on Christmas Day) and, ten years later, Stanislaus.

In June 1976 they left Vietnam and crossed the South China Sea on what was little better than a raft, coping with hunger, thirst, sunstroke and the threat of pirates. After seven tense days, and two years in makeshift detainment facilities, they arrived in the refugee camp on Palawan in the Philippines. For the whole voyage, Teresa and Aloysius took turns holding their two-year-old son, Stan, whom they protected from the sun with a broken umbrella. They had left Noel behind with an uncle and never saw him again. *Over Here* is a beautiful book because it shows a brash young writer struggling to express the grief of his parents. It marked a leap beyond the crusty gags of his first book, *Over It*, a shallow account of working in real estate. That book was so bad it sold like crazy; Auction Arnie became a minor cult figure. *Over Here*, on the other hand, had the gentleness of honesty. Re-reading it allows you to see why Nguyen is suspicious about those who have the luxury of choosing where they go.

Yet Nguyen also writes with compassion about the quest of the young people with whom he is travelling. He knows that quest himself. In *Over Here* he speaks with both humour and affection about the Catholicism of his parents, about their rosary before sex and the way they always boiled the holy water they brought home from church just to give God a hand in keeping any germs at bay. *They believed that if holy water wasn't going to perform miracles, then at least it shouldn't cause any harm either.*

But, underneath the jokes, there is at least a pale green envy in Nguyen's portrait of his parents. They held the same pair of rosary beads all the way across the South China Sea. *It's a wonder I wasn't strangled to death by them.*

Over the years, until they died, each of them prayed daily for their son Noel, kneeling before a plastic crucifix. Nguyen writes that if he could have one prayer answered, it would be to share something like that view of the world. His second prayer would be for next week's winning Lotto numbers. Deep down, he says, he knows that his students want to go to Africa because they, too, want to believe in something other than themselves.

*

Over There is a long book. It carries a lot of baggage and the narrative is heavily populated. If this were a novel, Nguyen would need to have chosen a smaller cast of characters and given them more space to develop. Fourteen people in a minibus is, by crude reckoning, 182 separate relationships, and that's before anybody starts to notice the thousands of people on the other side of the window, leaning in, trying to sell stuff, trying to catch a glimpse of another world. One of the myths Nguyen denies is that travelling as a teacher overseas with teenagers is some kind of junket. It's hard work.

Nguyen often adopts an attitude of superior bewilderment. The best of the book takes place when his uncertainty defeats his powers of irony and disengagement and he gets tangled up in the lives of people he'd rather watch from a safe distance. He is never sure why he goes to Africa. A colleague pulled out of the trip and the principal put the hard word on Nguyen to take her place; Nguyen wanted his contract position to be made permanent and thought a few brownie points would help. Even then, Nguyen may have stayed home except for the fact that the trip organiser, Imelda Yorac, swept him up in what he calls a 'tsunami of enthusiasm'. Yorac, a bundle of energy even in her late sixties, is an enigmatic figure throughout the story, a cross between Mother Teresa and Hillary Clinton. Nguyen has a deep admiration for her and she becomes a kind of mother figure for the expedition. He also notes that some people have such a powerful vision that it can be blinding. It's not clear what he means by this.

Nguyen lets us know early in the story that he has split up with Lauren, the partner he met at the end of *Over Here* who challenged him to write about his parents. He never says much about the split-up but he thinks a trip might distract him from himself. Lauren is mentioned a few times but she is mostly powerful in her absence. You get the impression that after a while she found Nguyen remote and hard to reach.

'Sometimes people need to leave home to find home,' says Imelda Yorac when Nguyen finally signs on. Yorac often speaks in the pithy language of greeting cards. But she means every word she says, even the clichés. Nguyen enjoys that. He never seems able to find words he can wholeheartedly believe. For him, the words *yes* and *no* have always meant *maybe.*

*

In some respects, the hero of *Over There* is Andy, the boy who has sat for a year at the back of Nguyen's English class with a plastic bag hidden somewhere, trying to sneak food into his mouth like contraband. 'Have you ever thought of trying to let the poem feed your hungers,' Nguyen once suggested, but Andy just picked his teeth.

Andy is the younger brother of a girl who was the champion athlete at Grace Grammar, breaking many of the school records and going on to knock on the door of the Olympic team. Andy decided he could never match those achievements so, rather than fail, he has never really tried at anything. Nguyen had seen some of the artwork he did in the margins of his English texts and thought that he might have a career as a cartoonist if he could put his mind to something other than drawing Lady Macbeth in lingerie. When Andy was lining up for the third time at the counter of a burger chain in the international airport, Nguyen was surprised. Not that Andy was in the hunt for junk food. More that he was on the tour in the first place.

On the plane, Nguyen sat beside Andy, who vomited and blamed it on the African water, even though they hadn't yet set foot on the continent. Andy reduces Nguyen to some of his worst one-liners: *Andy being sick was far worse than Lauren being sick of me.*

During the next few days, Andy's head keeps poking out of the narrative. The group found themselves in Soweto. Nguyen knew the story of these streets back to front and inside out because of his parents. They fled Vietnam in 1976 in the very month in which the thirteen-year-old Hector Pieterson was killed in protests about education, marking the start of a new wave of uprising against the apartheid regime. The famous picture of Pieterson's body being carried by a friend hung over the Nguyen family altar, beside a baby snap of the missing Noel:

> Throughout my childhood, I could have been forgiven for thinking that Mandela was Vietnamese. Mum and dad adopted the apartheid struggle because South Africa was always on the news whereas there was never any real news for them from home. So they barracked for Soweto against Pretoria.

Nguyen was expecting or hoping to find a connection with the streets in central Soweto. Vilakazi Street in Orlando was home to both Nelson Mandela and Archbishop Tutu, a man so good that Nguyen's parents excused him for being an Anglican. The street was violent enough to have created two winners of the Nobel Prize for Peace. He felt a shiver of something like reverence as he saw familiar names starting to appear through the windows of the minibus as they approached the area; he became quiet as Imelda Yorac shared facts and figures with the group about its brutal history.

The reality troubled Nguyen more than he would have imagined. Across the street from Mandela's modest former home was a row of prosperous bars and cafes, full of tourists, paying their respects now that everything was safe. There were buskers and endless souvenir sellers. Three or four doors from Mandela House, he noticed a car wash specialising in luxury cars, mostly imported from Europe.

The group sat down for a meal in a place that felt just like any pizza joint back home. They had a perfect view of the Mercedes and BMWs blocking the road outside Mandela's former bungalow as they waited to be shampooed, perfumed, waxed and buffed.

Once again, Nguyen found himself next to Andy, who was busy with the calculator on his phone. 'You know something,' he said. 'A pizza costs exactly the same here as it does back home.'

Yorac explained that there were still plenty of 'informal settlements', and they had arranged to visit some of the families who lived in them.

'Informal settlements are slums,' she continued.

'That's called a euphemism,' added Nguyen, the teacher.

'Indeed, "good neighbourliness" was a phrase sometimes used for apartheid,' she continued.

'Another euphemism,' stressed Nguyen.

Andy wasn't listening. He was googling. Googling, says Nguyen, is the deafness required to hear what the whole world has to say without tuning into anyone in particular. He wonders if any of his students ever left home; they always need to know exactly what's happening at every party on every weekend back in their suburbs.

'You know there's a huge shopping mall near here,' said Andy. 'It's called Maponya Mall.'

'It's built on the site of what used to be informal dwellings,' said Yorac.

'They have a food court with free wi-fi,' replied Andy.

*

If this entire expedition could be summarised in a single day, that day might well be Nguyen's fortieth birthday, a Saturday near the end of the trip when the group has reached the small city of Eldoret north of the equator in Kenya. Everyone is tired. The students, to be fair, have been forced to think about the great lottery of life. In Nairobi they encountered kids who got a meal at school on Friday and then didn't eat again until school on Monday. One of the successes of the book is the way Nguyen documents microscopic changes in Andy's attitude, small changes being more believable than impassionate slogans about the unfairness of it all. Even better are the changes in Nguyen. As Andy becomes less focused on himself, Nguyen finds a freedom to move in the other direction, to mention things that matter to him.

In Eldoret they spent time in a community supporting people living with AIDS. Here they divided into small groups to visit people in their homes. Andy, Imelda, Nguyen and a few others were taken around by a tall volunteer called Oliver, a lanky gentleman with a winning smile and a colourful wardrobe. Oliver explained he was fifty-one years of age, the proud father of six children, and had been living with HIV for ten years. He caught the virus from his wife, Angel, who, in turn, contracted HIV when she was out collecting firewood and was raped by three strangers. The offenders were arrested but used bribes to ensure their release. Both Oliver and his wife had TB to start with and it wasn't long before Angel passed away.

'Oh,' said Andy. He seemed to be listening now.

Oliver was left with six young kids and the stigma of an illness that is bad enough even before it gets loaded with the moral judgement of others. Oliver found that potential employers all demanded a health check and would not take on anyone who was HIV positive. He was out of work. So he began as a volunteer at the community, paying home visits to the sick and helping people with their medication. He was particularly concerned about a number of evangelical churches in the area that do damage by convincing people they are able to perform miracles and cure them of HIV. This was good for church business but dreadful for the people who get conned and stop taking their medication. East Africa was a religious supermarket. Nguyen wondered aloud how Oliver can still believe in God when so much fraud was committed in his or her name.

'I guess he has to do something,' says Andy.

Oliver takes the group to meet Melody, who is dying at home but still welcomes visitors. With the support of the community, she was able to afford the antiretroviral medication, but kept giving what food she had to her four children. This meant the drugs were not nearly as effective as they could have been. She lived in a shack that measured three metres by three, a place that reminded Andy of his family's shed, the place they put stuff that was in the way but too good to get rid of. With children, grandchildren and others, there were eight people in the space, for which Melody paid about $35 a month. She was two months behind with the rent and the family was about to be evicted. One daughter had to sit at the door of the classroom because Melody was behind with the school fees as well. Melody was now thirty-nine years of age and too weak to stand on her own. Oliver didn't think she would live to see her fortieth birthday.

'See, sir,' said Andy. 'You need to stop complaining about growing old.'

'What do you mean?'

'Well, getting old is better than not getting old.'

Nguyen says that he wasn't aware that he had been complaining. Nor that he was getting old.

That afternoon the group had the opportunity to drive for about an hour to a place called Iten where they could meet some of the most famous runners in the world and watch them train. The world 800-metres champion, David Rudisha, was going to be there and they had been promised the chance to meet him and ask him questions. The students were really excited.

'Can we take selfies of him?' someone asked.

'I thought a selfie was just of yourself,' said Imelda.

'Oh, don't be silly. You can take a selfie of anyone as long as you're in it.'

'They'll be perfect for the school website,' said someone else.

'Is it compulsory to go?' interrupted Andy.

'Why?' asked Nguyen, suspiciously. His fatigue was making him sarcastic. 'Are you hungry? Would you prefer to stay here and eat something? I'm sure they have food at Iten.'

'I've seen plenty of runners,' replied Andy. 'I grew up with bloody runners. I never understood why one second should make the difference between misery and happiness. I'd prefer to visit Melody again.'

'Really?'

'Yes, really. I want to give her something to help with the rent.'

Imelda thought this was a great idea. She had wished Nguyen a happy birthday, telling him that forty was too old to run and too young to slow down. Once again, Nguyen wondered if he should be writing down the things she said. *The Collected Wisdom of Imelda Yorac.*

So Andy and Nguyen spent a long afternoon sitting in Melody's shack and took turns holding her grandchildren and trying to remember jokes to share, no matter how corny, because the attempt to be funny would make Melody smile more than any punchline. Nguyen noticed that there was a plastic crucifix on the wall beside a calendar with a picture of the Eiffel Tower. The crucifix was almost the same as the one his parents used to have. There must be millions of these things, he thought.

Andy was quiet. He didn't eat anything. The eldest daughter helped Melody get to the toilet in the pit outside. One by one, Andy did a drawing of each of the children and grandchildren and handed it to Melody, who kissed the page, then laughed, then cried. Andy pinned them around the crucifix.

As the evening closed in, the house was blanketed by shadow. There was no electric light to compete with the darkness, just a single candle in an old tin. Before long they could no longer see the walls. The room felt suddenly bigger because there was no knowing where the shack ended and the night began. The space became as big as the whole world; they could even see stars in the gaps in the unlined tin roof. When he thought no one was looking, Andy took Melody by the hand and held it softly. She smiled again.

Out of nowhere, Nguyen began in his mind to compose a love poem for Lauren.

*

Over There is more a personal essay than a memoir. Nguyen sets out to write about what is called 'volutourism': *The ultimate consumerism is to shop for meaning or purpose in the suffering of another.*

At the start of the book he cites research that suggests orphanages in countries such as Cambodia are expanding because Westerners need to 'add value' to their travels. An increasing number of parents are leaving children in them and one of the reasons is the money and attention that come from overseas, especially from well-meaning schools. Furthermore, students visit the so-called 'orphans', form bonds that are then broken at the end of the week or fortnight. So the orphans live in an unending churn of attachment and abandonment. Yet after a month, Nguyen is having more than second thoughts:

> There are some people who simply need to meet each other. And sometimes those people happen to be a long way apart. But unless they meet, nothing in the world is going to change and, even worse, no one is going to change.

Young writers used to start with short stories, graduate to novels and, at the end of a distinguished career, feel entitled to produce a memoir. Now it's the other way around. People start with memoirs and, if they become very successful, they may eventually reach such an eminence that they can publish short stories. The assumption of too many writers is that the whole world needs to be interested in them.

Stanislaus Nguyen has been a bit like that. There are people he needs to thank for his rescue. The list would include his parents and Lauren and Andy and Imelda Yorac, who we last see giving every item of clothing in her bag away, and then the bag itself, as she travels to the airport for the flight home. Somewhere along the way, Nguyen became bored with himself and interested in the world. This book is a hymn against narcissism. It took him three books, but *Over There* shows how one man finally got over himself.

Where Her Sisters Live

Kate Ryan

Emma's sisters say things. Emma listens in, standing outside rooms or sitting very still in her spot reading on the verandah. She hears them.

They say:

'Mum, you should get her some decent clothes. She's not ten anymore.'

'Mum, you should put a hat on her. Do you want her to end up with skin like Dad's?'

They say:

'Mum, you treat her like a baby. Why don't you get her to do some jobs around the house?'

They say:

'Mum, what the hell goes on in her head?'

*

On Sunday nights, the first thing Emma sees when her mother exits the freeway in the Holden to take her sisters back to their share houses is the writing on the wall. It is very white, in capitals, on a brown cracked wall: 'RAPE IS POWER'.

The back seat of the Holden is scratchy with seams and the seatbelts are grey with white stitching and the buckles are either freezing or boiling. In summer Emma always wears a T-shirt and shorts, bare feet. She likes to come on the drive even though her dad is at home and she could stay with him; the journey is equally scary and exciting. The writing on the wall speaks of another world. It is not the world of Emma's leafy suburb, where at night the trees breathe and cool the streets, and the lawns receive the tick-tock of sprinklers again and again.

Where her sisters live, the streetlights pick out the peeling terraces and the crabbed dry gardens, a few geraniums in a pot or a half-dead rose marooned on concrete. Emma looks out as if from a ship, a capsule – the figures at the fish-and-chip shop counters, the souvlaki joints, the pubs spilling out laughing boys – here and there caught in the light. She hears music and sirens, sees cars leaking black exhaust, endless traffic lights, petrol stations fluorescent-lit and ghostly. Where her sisters live, the Tip Top factory casts its yeasty smell and at night only the bitumen breathes.

Emma's sisters wear overalls with tight, colourful T-shirts underneath or flowery, floppy dresses and Dunlop runners. Their arms are long and brown and they fling them around and laugh. The rooms in their shared houses have pinboards covered in Liberty material with postcards stuck all over them – of women, naked and very white or dressed in old-fashioned dresses with high collars and brooches at the throat, tight waists, long hair in buns on top of their heads. There are blue and white flowery plates and candlesticks with blackened melted wax. Bicycles have scraped the walls and the halls smell of damp, of old curries and coffee brewing.

Every Sunday, just before lunch, Emma's sisters come with their baskets of washing, their haircuts, long and short, their smell of adult girl and hot cotton, their eye-rolling opinions and irritations, their stubble of underarm hair and Spray Fresh deodorant. They sit at the big oak table and scoff the hot roast, the nubbly potatoes, the corned beef, pink and moist. Emma jiggles her feet along the bar that runs underneath the table and looks down at her thigh. She imagines the insides like corned beef; if she sliced it open perhaps it would be just like that.

Her father argues with her sisters endlessly, pointlessly, about Student Fees and Immigration and Women and America. His mouth gets tight and his face bright and their mother says, 'Darling, why do you always come down so hard?' after one of them has stormed off – usually Lizzie – and Emma presses her cold potato into the plate's cherry pattern with her fork and looks up at her mum. Her mum says, 'Okay, darling,' and Emma slides off the chair as quick and smooth as melted butter just as her dad is launching into another rant and Imogen has pulled her chair back from the table abruptly saying, '*Fuck it, Dad*, why don't you ever *listen*?'

By the time Emma hears the screen door clack behind her and grabs her bike she can hear Lizzie somewhere upstairs crying and her father shouting.

*

When she gets back from her ride, though, she knows the house will smell of her sisters' hot clean sheets swirling in the dryer, they will be drinking tea, pushing their stomachs against the bench, her mother placing each dish carefully on the drying rack, their father shut in the study with a copy of *Surgery Today*.

Emma is twelve. She can do things. Roam the streets with her friend Caroline. She can lie smoothly to her mother, though her sisters usually guess. She can throw a ball so it hits the back wall hard and bounces back at her. When she catches it, it claps hard into her left hand; she knows it will.

Emma's arms and legs are wiry and they seem to connect with the other parts of her body strongly, like Meccano. There is no hair anywhere weird yet, no bumps. Not yet.

Her sisters. She watches them. She hears them. She knows from them that life cannot be explained by the snap of a catch in her hand, the scrape of her ankles against the pedals. What will come she does not know.

*

It has been in the paper every day and Emma is scared. A teenage girl was dragged into one of the houses at the back of the school. It is one Emma likes to look at as she walks home. The garden is lush and almost tropical, its looping foliage creates a mini-rainforest that almost obscures the house from the street. The house itself is picture-postcard perfect, a cream Victorian with a tiled verandah on three sides. This is where she ended up, the girl, bleeding, lost, raped at four o'clock in the afternoon. She is only fourteen.

Then it happens again in the next suburb, another private schoolgirl, fifteen this time, an attempted abduction. Emma sees it on the news – the policeman nodding, his face sombre, the mother tearful, warning people. Emma's mother tells her to walk home along the main road, a couple of days in a row even picking her up after school in the Holden.

All the girls at school talk about it and go into horrible graphic detail. One girl, Stacy, whose mother is president of the tennis club and who seems to know everything, tells Emma that a man has been circling the school in his car. He beckoned to Stacy and when she went over, the man had only a black stocking over his dick. Emma feels sick when she hears this but Stacy just laughs. 'That's what my mum says to do,' she says. 'Just laugh and run away. They hate it when you laugh.'

*

Emma's sisters come again the next Sunday and Emma listens to them talk to her mother when they stand in the kitchen after lunch.

They say:

'Mum, you need to talk to her about this sort of thing. She's so naive.'

'Mum, you know there are creeps everywhere.'

'Mum, you need to teach her to be more self-protective.'

'Mum, this is the real world.'

*

They have caught the man. Emma breathes out slowly when she sees him on the news. Her father snaps off the TV – 'Bloody pervert,' he says – as Emma slips off her chair and out of the room.

*

As they drive to the inner city, her sisters talk at her mother about their dad.

They say:

'He needs a hobby. He's probably depressed. He's impossible.'

They say: 'Mum, you need to get a life.'

*

Emma thinks of the man. He looked small and ordinary, a pathetic gingery moustache, like the man who fills the Holden with petrol every week. For a second, seeing him on the news, Emma had been afraid it *was* him. But it wasn't.

But who are they, she wonders, these different men?

*

The Holden glides off the freeway and Emma half closes her eyes as she sees the letters so they are faint, less like letters than currents, lines moving inside her brain:

'RAPE IS POWER'.

*

She wonders about the words, each one, and about her sisters, how they know about such things and yet they go forward into the world again and again. She winds down her window to feel the hot bitumen breeze.

Martian Triptych

James Bradley

I

It comes with a sound like a river, the noise so loud in the silence of the observatory he turns for a moment to see if Clyde has heard it too, only to realise Clyde is not there, that he left hours ago. Through the door he can see the trees outside, dark against the fading sky, hear the wind in the trees. And then the sound is gone, as quickly as it began.

It is more than twenty years since he first came here, led up the narrow path to the butte by the agent. He knew the agent – what was his name? Tompkinson? Thomas? Thompson? – thought he was a fool but he didn't care: even then he knew what he was doing, knew this empty hill high in the cold air of the mountains was the place he needed, the place that would bring him closer to the stars.

That night, back in his room in the hotel, he took out Schiaparelli's maps, traced out the pattern of lines that bisected them. And as he did he understood something he had not before, understood what it was that had made him want this so badly. It was not simply the same restlessness that had taken him halfway round the world to Japan and Korea, it was something deeper and more profound than that. It was that same feeling he had when he stood under the desert sky and saw the massing light of the Milky Way move overhead, that sense that this is not all there is, that to look beyond the Earth is to glimpse the possibility of other lives, as yet unknown.

As the building grew he took to working on the site at night, his telescope mounted on the floor, the half-built dome of the observatory rising about him. Overhead the stars so clear in the desert air he sometimes thought he might lose his purchase on the Earth, fall upwards into the emptiness of space. It was cold, of course, but he forgot the cold as the Martian surface flickered into life in the lens, the lines on its surface resolving one by one.

Schiaparelli had called them *canali*, meaning channels, but the more he studied them the more certain he became they were not a natural phenomenon but the canals the Italian word suggested, things carved into the landscape of the planet to bear water like the aqueducts of the Romans or the irrigation ditches of the Egyptians. Why else, after all, would they be so straight, why else would they darken and fade with the turning of the seasons?

Yet who were these people, what did they look like? Why build such things? Why were there no other signs of civilisation, no cities, no roads, no lights on the darkened surface? The canals spoke of a people who tilled the soil, who had transformed the low Martian lands into fields and paddies surely such a people would not live underground. So where had they gone? What calamity had befallen them?

Then there was the night he understood. It began with the fact the canals did not stop when they reached the seas, their lines extending on, into the basins. It made no sense to him. Why do that unless the seas themselves were retreating? But then he saw it, saw it all almost at once. The seas were receding, drying up, and the canals were not the work of a civilisation in full flower, but the creation of a people fighting a losing battle against their dying planet, a people desperate to water the spreading deserts. A people noble, and wise, yet doomed.

There were those who complained his results could not be replicated, that his ideas were little more than fantasy, the lines he saw merely illusions created by flaws in his telescope or the ghostly networks of capillaries branching out across his retina. Yet, as the years passed and he watched and wrote, he only grew more certain he had stumbled upon something that mattered, something that spoke of the impermanence of life, of its fragility. Faced with the evidence of this ancient race's labours, their long fight against the inevitable, how could humanity fail to be reminded of the grace and wisdom of peace and the brotherhood of civilisation?

More than a few mocked him for it, but he did not care. Once some wit called him the Martian Ambassador, the name designed to sting, yet instead it pleased him so much he took it for his own, referring to himself as the Envoy of Mars or the Martian Envoy. They could not see it, that was all.

He could though. Sometimes alone in the quiet of his study he felt almost as if it might be possible to close his eyes and be there, his body translated across time and space as quick as thought, as if the familiar things of his study, the books and papers and furniture, had no more solidity than the resisting tension of water. He imagined cities carved of stone, old as time and more beautiful, pyramids, patchworks of dusty fields stretching out towards the horizon. And the steady whisper of the breeze, the sound of a windmill turning in the quiet.

He is falling now, or perhaps has already fallen, is lying on the ground. Time no longer seems true to him, a thing that spools and flows like water spilling out along the channels of a delta, flowing fast and slow and then away. He is not afraid, which surprises him, he has so much still to do. Perhaps there is something else he has not understood. Perhaps they needed him to see, to understand. Perhaps they were simply waiting for all of us.

And then he realises they are already there. Silhouetted against the night they are so strange, so shy, their tall bodies and thin limbs both graceful and awkward, like those of a child or a giraffe, designed for life on a world older and lighter than this one, their skin green, like chlorophyll. Their noseless faces too, he sees now, like those of an African mask, impossibly long and yet elegant, their black eyes featureless beneath heavy brows. As they draw near they seem to hesitate, then with a new confidence step closer, the tallest extending one three-fingered hand as if asking him to come with them, to join them, their voices like no sound he has heard, like the whispering of the wind, like the knocking of sticks. Like the sound of approaching water.

II

Sunset is still a quarter of an hour off as she reaches the top of the ridge, but overhead the sky is already fading, the bleached light of day giving way to blue and violet, the flat plain of the crater below marked with shadows. Wary of the loose rock underfoot she skids to a halt, Wu's anxiety about an injury in their last days on the planet coming back to her as she steadies herself in the low gravity.

Soon the wind will begin to rise, howling down from the highlands to the south, but for now it is quiet, the only sounds her breathing, the slow whirr and hiss of her suit. Glancing at her visor display she checks the feed from the habitat, then, with a flick of her eyes dismisses it, lifting her gaze to the darkening sky.

The stars come sooner here, their shapes and colours sharper through the thinner atmosphere. Yet it is still several minutes before the first begin to appear, their arrival heralded by the appearance of Phobos, its pale potato shape silvery in the last daylight. The first time she saw the tiny moon the speed of its passage across the sky seemed so alien; seeing it now she is struck by how familiar its swift orbit has become, the way this place has come to seem if not like home, then something close to it.

In her helmet the alert chimes, reminding her it is time to be heading back; she ignores it, unwilling to leave just yet. And then she sees it, a tiny disc of blue just cresting the hills to the east, the moment so sudden she feels her breath catch. Only just past full, she is pleased to see.

For a minute or two she stands, unmoving. This is the last time she will see this, the last time she will be here, and although she knows she should be happy the mission is over and they are returning home, the closer their departure has come the harder the thought of leaving has become. It is not that the thought of the launch makes her nervous, although it does; it is the knowledge that once they leave this place will be empty again, bereft of life, their presence here forgotten.

The alert chimes again, louder this time, more insistent; taking a final look out across the darkening plain, she turns away and begins to lope back down the hillside. Although she weighs less here than on Earth, she is still careful: even in low gravity a fall from here could break bones. At the bottom of the ridge she slows her pace, turns northward towards the habitat, its lights already bright against the dark, her helmet lamp picking out the ground ahead of her. Once, millions of years ago, this was a delta, these barren rocks submerged by warm water that flowed from the north to pool in the lowlands beyond. There was life as well: single-celled organisms feeding on the sunlight and the nutrients around them, beds of algae and pools filled with sulphurous water and stromatolites. Where they went nobody knows. All that is certain is that as the planet cooled the water disappeared, some leached back into the rocks and locked away as ice, some sublimed into space as the solar wind scoured the last vestiges of life and atmosphere from the rocks and dust.

As she reaches the perimeter, she sees Hartnett appear from behind one of the rovers.

'There you are,' he says, his voice clear in her helmet. 'We were just getting worried.'

She smiles, amused by his pretence they did not know where she was. Their training emphasised interpersonal strategies to allow them to live together out here. What it didn't mention was what they should do if they liked it here, if they wanted to stay.

'Still getting the site ready?' she asks and Hartnett chuckles.

'Triple-checking. You're going in?'

She nods.

'I'll see you in there,' he says.

Back inside she removes her helmet and strips off her suit, hanging them by the airlock. She can hear the others speaking in the command unit, discussing the launch, but rather than join them she turns left, into the passageway to the living quarters, not yet ready for company.

In her cubicle she crawls into the tube that has served as her bed for the past two years and activates her screen. Pushing aside the newsfeed she calls up her messages and begins flicking through them one by one. Most are routine – communications from colleagues back on Earth, notes from Mission Control – but near the end she comes across a message from Liwei. Tapping the screen she opens it, and a moment later her son's face appears.

As always her throat tightens at the sight of him. Because of the time lag, normal conversation is impossible. With her husband this has posed few problems, the two of them communicating by email in conversations that bounce carelessly back and forth. But with Liwei it has been more difficult: although his writing has improved in the last year or so, he still struggles to express himself effectively, meaning the only real way to communicate is like this, with recorded video messages.

This message was recorded several hours ago, early evening Beijing-time. Liwei is seated at his desk, the door behind him open to the living room. Although he must have been home for several hours, he is still dressed in his school uniform, his yellow neckerchief hanging loose. As the recording begins he hesitates, perhaps waiting to be sure the video is running. Then, with a grin, he begins to tell her about his day at school, about his lessons and what he has learned.

This is a ritual, of course, one they developed early on so he would find it easier to speak to her like this, but it is a good one because it reminds him of the value of education. When she was a girl in Tianjin her father made her do the same.

Today Liwei has won a ribbon in a maths competition, and as he holds it up she feels the old tenderness well up at the sight of his happiness and pride. Yet a moment later when he sets the ribbon aside and begins to tell her how proud he is of her now she is coming home, how proud all of China is, she feels her happiness slip away.

At first she thinks that it is simply because the words are so clearly not Liwei's but those of another: a teacher perhaps or someone on the newsfeeds. Her husband says having a mother who is so famous has been strange for Liwei. Yet it is not just about her being famous. Instead, it is the fact that every time she hears Liwei speak like this she finds herself wondering how well he actually remembers her, how much she is a person, a presence in his life rather than an idea, a disembodied face he watches each night. He was three when she left; he will be almost seven when she returns: years she will never regain, years in which he stopped being her child and became his father's, her absence severing some bond she knows will never be repaired.

None of this is unexpected: she understood the cost when she volunteered for the mission. Still, many had been surprised when she was selected and agreed to go, surprised that a mother would willingly choose to be separated from her child in this way.

At the time this had irritated her. After all, nobody asked the same questions about Reyes and Wu, both of who are fathers. Yet as she watches Liwei speak, she wonders whether those who questioned her decision weren't right in the end, whether it really is different for a mother.

There are options, of course. Before they left the crew all had eggs and sperm harvested as a precaution against radiation. At the time she had been reluctant, but her husband – perhaps anticipating a time when they might want another child to bring their family back together – had insisted, going so far as to accompany her to the clinic, sit beside her as she was strapped into the chair.

Whether he would do the same now she does not know; although his messages are as wry and friendly as ever, she sometimes detects a distance in them as well: a sense he has changed in their time apart, that he and Liwei have become a unit of their own, one she is no longer part of. There is no question he will be there waiting for her, but whether the bond they had will remain is less certain. Sometimes she imagines him next to her, trying to conjure his presence back into being, to remember his weight, his smell, the shape of his nape and back, but with each passing month it grows more difficult. Even her body feels different, less needy, more separate, as if she has grown away from her own biology.

Perhaps it is better this way anyway. All of them understand the world they are returning to has passed some kind of tipping point. In the time they have been away the changes have come with terrifying, brutal rapidity: heat waves and freezing winters arriving hard on the heels of each other, hurricanes and fires, floods and tornadoes destroying cities and towns. In the Arctic the last ice has finally disappeared and great gouts of methane have begun to burst upward from the warming seabed, in Malaysia and Brazil the forests are burning, in the oceans algal blooms spread like great green and red stains against the blue. Governments and the UN have programs in place to try and combat the changes but it is clear most believe it is already too late, that something irreversible has begun.

For the most part they try not to discuss it. Even when Reyes' sister went missing in Hurricane Foster, they did their best to avoid talking about it. It is not that it is too far away, or not quite. Instead, it is the knowledge that whatever it is they are doing here has become somehow irrelevant, a symbol of something already lost.

On her screen Liwei is saying goodbye, his words hurried and distracted, his attention already elsewhere. Watching him, she is struck again by how different he is from the child she remembers, how change marks us all.

This thought lingers as she directs her screen to begin recording, and in her brightest voice begins to tell Liwei about her trip to the ridge, about that last glimpse of Earth in the Martian sky, about the preparations for the launch, about how much she is looking forward to seeing him, about her hopes for his education. Reminding him of his promise to do better in English she tells him his father says he has been working hard. But nowhere does she say what she thinks, which is that leaving here saddens her, that she will miss this place, the work, that she knows in her heart this is the end of something, that their presence here will not be repeated, that they will be the last of their species to travel so far or see so much. That his life will be less than hers, and the future holds only loss.

And when she is done she says goodbye, tells him she loves him and she will speak to him soon, and then lying back she stares up at the ceiling, trying to imprint on her mind all she has seen, to remember this place, this time, so she will have it again once it is gone. Outside the wind is growing stronger, howling faster across the plain, the metal frame of the habitat shifting and moving against it with a sound like a ship at sea, moving on the tide.

III

As the shallows of the sea give way to the marshes, the shoal begins to divide, their bodies coiling and twisting away through the streams and channels and on, into the pools and spawning beds beyond. Only an hour ago they played together as they swam, their bodies coursing through the sun-dappled water of the weed fields; now they move restlessly, agitated, avoiding each other's sight as they give way to the call of the beds.

As always, it is the young who go first, their bodies filled with the speed and careless beauty of youth. For some it will be their first time, a thing desired and feared since they were old enough to understand the way their lifecycle circles back to this moment, the way they are bound not just to each other but to this place; for others, the shivering call will be more familiar.

Yet it is only as the last of them dart away that she realises this is her last time, that once she has spawned her exhausted body will die. How she knows she is not sure – they say it is a signal in the brain, a protein triggered by the scent of the beds themselves – all she knows is that as she sees the others disappear she feels a sudden stab of yearning, the feeling so strong she only just resists the impulse to sing to them not to go, not to leave her here.

This is grief, she thinks, or something like it. Yet almost as soon as the thought is there it is gone again, the feeling too, both receding as if on the edge of sleep, as if she is slipping outside herself. For a moment she tries to resist, not yet willing to let go, to lose herself, but then it is there, the scent, and she is moving in it, her body fluid, fast, moving in the stream as if in the quickening of mating as the call washes over her, the years falling away as she leaps and dives on, into the pool where she was born, the pool to which she has returned so many times, the pool where soon she shall die, her body finally depleted.

Between now and then, though, there is the spawning itself, that wildness and urgency, the spumes of eggs spilling out of her and clouding the shallow water of her natal pool. Impossible to describe, this yielding of the self to the body, to the hot quick pulse of the moment; impossible to forget as well. There are those who say this is when they are their truest selves, that it is in the ancestral streams that they remember what they once were, and although she has spent too long in the world to believe that she knows it is partly true, that there is something of themselves they have left behind as they have strived to shape the world to their ends.

When it is done she rises to the surface, her body weak, spent. Like all her kind she has contemplated this moment, wondered about its secrets, about whether she would fight. Yet now she is here she feels no fear, only sadness, as if all she was is already slipping away.

Where her body breaks the surface the air is hot, hotter even than the water. Overhead the Sun looms, huge and red, its light shimmering on the surface of the pool. Turning herself, she tries to take in its immensity, the way its heat surrounds her, envelops her.

Once her people called it Lifebringer, imagining it had birthed them, contrasting it to the moon swimming as quick and tiny as a hatchlet in the night-time sky, whose shape they believed guided their souls to the hatching grounds in the deeps of the sky. And in a way it was true, for it is the Sun that brought life to this planet, its heat awakening the seas from the rocks, triggering the chemical reactions that gave rise to life, to the schooling beauty of the seas and the lakes.

Yet what the Sun gave, so it will take. For it is old now, dying, and with each year it grows larger as it consumes itself.

Once they believed they might survive: that as it burned its fuel the Sun's hold on their red planet might lessen, allowing its orbit to expand. Yet already it is clear this was wrong, that the planet is growing hotter, that the oceans that give them life are drying up.

None of them know how long they have. A few years, a decade, maybe two. All they know is that one day soon the water will be gone, and one day after that the planet itself will be engulfed as well, consumed by the sun that once gave it life. It is something they all mourn, every day, the knowledge that this precious spark of life should be burned away, that everything they have built, everything they have made should die.

Yet as she feels her life ebbing away she finds herself wondering whether they are right to grieve. It is not the first time this has happened, after all. Once, billions of years ago, the planet bore life, microbial creatures that swam in lakes and rivers. In time they perished, dying as the planet grew colder so that for billions of years it was nothing but airless, icy desert. Back then there was life on the planet that lies sunward from them, the place some believe to have been their sister planet. Intelligence too, it seems, beings who built and dreamed and strived like them. Yet they too are gone, wiped away by the immensity of time.

There are other worlds, of course, other seas. The moons of the gas giants, or further out, where the planetoids and comets swing on their lifetimes-long orbits through distant space. And further away again, around distant stars there are other worlds as well, places so distant and strange as to be unimaginable. Some have spoken of sending ships to them, of adapting to life in different seas, yet she is not sure any of them truly believe it. After all, what would a life so diminished be worth? This world, these seas, they are what they are, these are the places they spawn and grow, these stars overhead are their own. What would they mean somewhere else? Could they return to the beds to spawn? What would their young be? No, she thinks now, better to pass on, to see the way time will cover them all. Below her the others are singing, the spawning done, the sound coming as if from far away, like a word or a name half-remembered on the edge of sleep.

Blur

Michelle Wright

Saminda's uncle regrets waiting for the morning light. He's sorry now and should have woken him earlier. And they should have got going sooner. But he'd heard the roads wouldn't be safe in the dark. And his wife thought they should let the boy try to get some rest. Saminda pulls his T-shirt down over his stomach and looks up at his uncle.

'I didn't sleep,' he says.

The Galle road is already crammed with traffic in both directions. Buses, ambulances and tuktuks lined up and patiently advancing, no horns, no weaving, as if in a funeral procession. His hands gripped tight on his uncle's shirt, his eyes blur and slip shut. The noise of the motorcycle is familiar but distant. It sounds just like his dad's.

Saminda pictures the four of them on it, coming back from the fish market with plastic bags snapping in the wind. His dad with his knotty hands clasping the handlebars, his little sister in front, her skinny thighs held tight in place, her ribs bouncing against the inside of his sinewy forearms, black eyes peering left and right. Saminda is wedged between his father and mother, his chest compressed against his father's curved spine, his mother behind him, her breasts soft and damp against his bony back. The wind snatches thin wisps of hair out of her long plait and whips them forward about his cheeks.

Once past Moratuwa, where the road turns back down towards

the coast, his uncle's motorbike slows and stops. He opens his eyes and it's like sleepwalking off an edge. Debris covers the road. Tall piles of it. Sections of roofs, splintered wooden planks, windows and doors popped out of their frames, looking stunned, asking, 'How did I get here?'

The air is still and humid, coating everything in a sticky gleam. And perched atop the piles: buses, cars, tuktuks, fishing boats. The boy and his uncle sit on the motorcycle and pick through the landscape in silence. Little by little, fragments of the recognisable emerge from the mass of charcoal grey and muddy brown. A whole coast of soil and sand churned up and thrown down.

He makes a note in his mind of what is still there: a red plastic bowl, a pink doll's head with pale orange hair, a silver framed wedding photograph, an unopened green and yellow packet of biscuits.

*

'Just two,' his auntie decreed as she handed him the green and yellow packet of Hawaiian Cookies and closed the pantry door.

'Thank you, Auntie,' called Saminda, already back in front of the television screen.

'*And that's another six. Two sixes in the one over.*' The commentator paused, as the camera jumped from the umpire's raised arms to the batsman's raised bat, to the defeated bowler. '*And Warne is not happy.*'

'Warne is not happy. Warne is not happy,' he imitated, slapping his bony knees and bouncing on the plastic-covered seat of the sofa.

He scanned the Pakistani players cards laid out on the coffee table in front of him, snatched up the image of Youhana, the new captain, and danced it around the edge of the table till it was face to face with Shane Warne's, taunting the bowler's ruddy, zinc-smeared cheeks. 'Murali is the King of Spin.'

'Saminda, what are you doing?' his aunt called from the kitchen.

'Watching the cricket, Auntie,' he replied, replacing the cards and sitting back down on the sofa.

'Who's winning?'

'It's a Test match, Auntie. Can't say who is winning.'

'Stupid game,' he heard her mumble from the kitchen, as she put away the breakfast dishes.

*

Soon after the tea break at the MCG, a news flash interrupted play. The reporter spoke of an earthquake near Indonesia. Early reports of a large wave hitting the coast of Sri Lanka. They called it a tsunami. He'd never heard this word. He called out to his auntie and she came and sat lightly beside him on the edge of the sofa.

'Are Mummy and Daddy safe?'

'Shhh! Listen, child!'

'Could it have hit our house?'

His aunt didn't respond. She just sat stiff and still, leaning towards the television screen, her mouth open, her lips pushed forward, as if inhaling the reporter's words. Her nephew turned and raised himself up on his knees, his head twisted towards her, watching her face for a sign. The plastic sofa cover squeaked and sighed as he shifted his weight from one knee to the other. Then, as if someone had yelled 'Action!', she closed her mouth, turned her head towards the hallway and screamed out. 'Raja! Come quickly!'

His uncle joined them and they all watched in silence. They sat and listened as reports started to come in from Trinco, then Batticaloa. There was news of a train overturned. On its way from Colombo to Galle. The same train they'd been going to take together the next morning. His uncle tried to call Saminda's parents. The phone system wasn't working. For an hour they waited for the newsreader to speak of Galle. Nothing. His uncle dialled his parents' number again, then again five minutes later, then again two minutes later, then over and over, until suddenly he stopped and put the phone down on the coffee table. He looked at it, then stared at Saminda, before slowly turning his face back to the television, his eyes suddenly deep in their sockets.

The television reporters talked of massive destruction all along the coast. Thousands dead. People washed kilometres inland. Sucked out to sea. And each time the reporter said the word *dead*, Saminda saw his auntie's left eyelid twitch.

By mid-afternoon his uncle had spoken to friends and neighbours. No trains or buses were getting through south along the coast. He called Saminda into the entrance hall and told him that they'd try to get back on his motorcycle. It'd be slow, but it should be possible on the inland roads. It was too late to leave that afternoon. It would be dark before they got very far. The roads wouldn't be safe. And his headlight wasn't working. Best to wait till the next morning. Saminda nodded. His auntie called him to come have something to eat in the kitchen. Walking through the lounge room, he glanced at the television screen.

'*Stumps*,' the commentator said. '*Stumps at the MCG.*'

*

When they reach the coast road, the rain begins. A constant light drizzle and before long pools in every hollow. His uncle tells him to close his eyes, but he sees them all the same. Bodies. Men and women, old and young – arms and legs splayed as though they're exclaiming, *What was that?* Eyes looking skyward asking, *What has happened here?*

And those who are still alive standing amid the debris – looking down. No one talking, or just in three- or four-word phrases, and to themselves, to the air.

'Look at that. All dead. No one left.'

Their skin is lighter, greyer than normal, overcast like the sky. Their eyes, when he sees them, are emptier, like they've pricked them with pins and let the water run out.

Concrete telephone poles lean into the wind like palm trees. Railway tracks twisted and continuing on their way above emptiness, the earth swept away from under them. The sounds of traffic, motorbikes, bicycles are dampened in the sodden soil. The birds are silent too. And all the dogs are gone.

Men sitting on debris, standing with their hands behind their backs, or arms crossed in front. Women with hands on hips, not in defiance, but to keep their shoulders up. To stop the sinking of their chests, holding off the gasping.

Small slivers of walls, right-angled corners with serrated edges. Already, on the remains of a wall, someone has put out an offering of food for the dogs and crows – the first handful of rice on a banana leaf.

The sea is what he notices most. So calm, hardly moving, watching. As if it had absentmindedly done its job, like it didn't have a choice. Had just come and then retreated, without even looking back. 'What do you want me to say?' it shrugged, like it had just tossed and rolled a piece of driftwood that was the town.

Leaning his forehead against his uncle's shoulder blade, Saminda keeps one eye closed and narrows the other. The world flickers through moist eyelashes like his grandfather's old super 8 films.

*

By late afternoon, they have reached Balapitiya and the bodies are starting to smell. Not overpowering yet, but sour, pungent, like a pot of buffalo curd left out too long in the sun. There are people stepping over debris, lifting their knees up high and gently placing their feet where it's safe, covering the bodies with cloths. White flags of mourning have started to appear, but also clear plastic or strips of red and white shopping bags.

He sees a Bo-tree draped heavy with large coloured flags. As they get closer, he sees they are not flags but pieces of clothing – sarongs, T-shirts, shorts, skirts, baby clothes. Around the tree and along the path to the temple, monks walk, heads down. At the base of the Buddha statue, a little girl sits cross-legged with a cut on her head. Damp blood, still red, strings a ruby necklace round her throat. She looks up at Saminda's face as the motorcycle rolls slowly by and the middle of her top lip forms a tiny *v*, just like his little sister's.

Near a hotel in Hikkaduwa he notices suitcases, plastic chairs, a pool umbrella like a javelin in the ground. Wrought-iron screens caught against trunks, woven through with fishing nets, newspapers and leaves. Further along, a woman's body is caught in the branches of a tree. Her long black plait wrapped like a noose around her neck. Children walk around silent, women drift with bundles on their heads, young girls with crying babies on their hips.

Before the light begins to dim, they continue on towards Galle. Going through the old Dutch gate to the fort, things seem almost normal. But as they emerge they see the cricket ground, completely flooded. In the centre, balancing awkwardly on the pitch are a red public bus and a battered yellow freight container. Water lies in stagnant pools, covering the grass with a brown sheen. Dead fish stare at the sky. They avoid the bus station, entombed in metal and wood and strewn with stranded bodies. They turn off along the beach road and weave their way through the turmoil at a walking pace.

Amongst the debris, they search for kilometre markers. It's difficult to know how far they've come otherwise. Saminda knows they must turn off at the 111-kilometre mark. One hundred and eleven. Like Youhana's score. When his uncle taps his knee and points to the marker, Saminda looks for the house of his best friend, Asanka. He looks for their food stall in front – the baskets of red rice and lentils, the heavy hanging stalks of bananas and clusters of yellow king coconuts, the bars of soap and packets of milk powder.

As his uncle slows to turn off down the road that leads to Saminda's house, he sees a single plank of wood still partly covered with the bright red handbills advertising mobile phones that Asanka's father had used as decoration when he rebuilt the stall just before Christmas. The monks had come down from the temple for the blessing. There is still a strip of the blue plastic bunting snagged on the broken piece of wood.

Entering the mangroves, the dirt path alongside the river becomes too slippery for the motorcycle, so they dismount and walk. As the river turns to face the coast, they first see the vehicles, then the shoes and clothes, and finally the bodies. Before the turn off to his parents' house, the surface of the water is no longer visible. Just metal and cloth and tangled hair and bloated skin. And a sour smell like overripe wood apple pulp.

When they arrive at the house, they understand at once. Pieces of furniture tumbled down to the paddy field. Strewn sandals and toys, cooking pots and carpets caught in window frames and bushes. A fragment of his father's radio balanced on the fence. His uncle says nothing. Just presses down on Saminda's shoulder, fixing him to the place he's in, and turns to enter the house.

Saminda waits without moving, eyeing his toes as they drill into the black sludge smothering the front porch. In pooled water by the edges of the concrete, a frayed shred of blue sky passes and unravels. His arms hang heavy by his sides with dread, and his tongue is swollen in his mouth. And still he stands and listens for a sign of life from inside the house, until the quiet starts to squeeze his chest and he has to get away. He runs up between the paddy fields, his feet skidding out from under him as he veers left and right around scattered objects. He crosses the main road, and heads up behind the temple and towards the school.

The water has reached only as high as the school's front gate. He runs up the steps to the junior secondary section and to the Grade 7 classroom. Placing his foot on the ledge of the windows, he hooks his fingers through the mesh grating and pulls himself up. With one hand he reaches up into the damp space on top of the window frame. His fingers skim over the splintered wood and stop as they touch the faintly curled edge of a card. He slides it off the edge of the wooden beam and brings it level with his eyes. He studies the image, the vivid green background and the white-shirted figure sweating in the bright sun. Murali doesn't look at him. He's leaning forward, eyes wild and glaring at the batsman, mouth wide open, his left forefinger pointing skyward. Saminda knows he's the best spin bowler ever. He knows he'll beat Warne's record once again. His dad says he'll do it next year, for sure. His dad says they'll go see him next time he plays in Galle. Saminda brings the card close to his face and smells the dust and damp. He squints until his eyes are focused on the sweating bowler's face, on his bulging eyes, and then he brings it closer still, until it fills his field of vision and the image becomes a blur.

Grief

David Brooks

We are early – have to be, to greet the mourners – and sitting on a bench beside the open coffin. A strict ritual. Knowledge passed from funeral to funeral, by those who have been to so many. There has been discussion as to whether her face should be lightly veiled, as it was when we entered and the lid was first removed, or uncovered. Aldo wants it uncovered, and it's at last his say. His mother. For some reason the funeral directors have made no attempt to disguise the wounds on her face and I can see now how large they are. But they are on her right side and we are seated on her left. Aldo touches her cheek tenderly – brushes it, rather, with the edge of his hand – then leans over, kisses her on the forehead. It is the first time I have ever seen him kiss her.

*

I am still thinking about the cat. A lingering image on the mind's retina. A dying glow. You look into the light – at some lit object – and then close your eyes, and the light, the shape of the object, is still there, blurred at the edges, its features lost; some force emanating from within. Except that in this case it was not light. Was, and was not. Is not. A tunnel vision. A vortex down which, since it happened, I am always falling yet never seeming nearer or farther away. A kind of vertigo. And the mountains today like great waves there on the horizon, about to engulf us.

*

The old lady died on the Tuesday. Sad, but no great surprise. I'd heard her from the rooms below, for six weeks or more, shouting, calling out names, lost in the corridors of herself. Long days of silence and then it would break out again. *She* would. I don't know what brought it on. The wind maybe. Or some weather inside her. Katia told me of her death almost matter-of-factly as I was talking with Igor on the balcony. There'd been a phone call in her study, and she came out. 'Nona just died,' she said, 'at the hospital a few minutes ago. That was my father. He's there.' And we went on with our day, tentatively, not knowing what else to do, waiting for something to arrive, to break.

*

A nausea, perhaps. The overwhelming weight of being. But also something more, surely. The heart was *wrenched*, as if something had pried it open. The opposite of nausea. Not closed in by things, but *offered* them, in their depth. Or drawn *by* them, *rushed into* them. As if one were being sucked out of oneself. A force. A kind of gravity. The cat at its centre, there in the boot-room.

*

At Alex's, while we talked at the table inside, our chairs angled towards the French doors so that we could see the view, the cats came, four, with a fifth somewhere off in the forest – dying, Jacqueline said. All of them were scrawny, under-nourished. Jacqueline fed them but they never fattened. Village cats. Worm-ridden probably. Katia always annoyed that Alex and Jacqueline didn't pay them more attention, offer more affection, *see* their condition. Katia rescued a white kitten from there two years ago, bonded with her instantly on the lawn, took her home. In twenty-four months she's become sleek, independent, strong. Bianca. At the window, late at night, while I read. Waiting for entrance. 'That one's Bianca's mother,' Jacqueline says, pointing out a gaunt, long-haired tabby, oldest of the four. Looking as if she might be dying too. 'No,' says Jacqueline, reading our minds,

'She has always looked like that.' So many cats in these villages. You'd think *they* were the inhabitants, not humans.

*

This late afternoon – this late afternoon and on into the evening – I have watched a mass of clouds gather in the north-east and darken to a deep bruise-purple, and felt the pressure mounting within them, electrical, torrential. Couldn't it be like that? The Outside? And now, just moments ago, seen the first lightning. A crack. A fissure in the sky.

*

Igor left, in any case, not knowing what to do. I waited for Aldo to return from the hospital, anticipating his grief. But when he came back he put the car away, went into the downstairs kitchen for a while, then came out and went down to the fields. Perhaps he was sobbing down there. I don't know. And as to what Katia was feeling, there are times I can't tell that either, especially when it comes to family. Her grandmother hated cats. And Katia had claimed to hate her grandmother for hating them.

*

You carry such things around with you. I was sitting on the terrace of that strange hotel a hundred kilometres away, a fortnight later. Who ever heard of a hotel room without a table, a chair? And so I'd come downstairs. It was quiet on the terrace, and shaded by the building, out of the sun. A broad, calm view of slopes covered with trellised vines, mountains capped with snow even at this late stage of summer. And in the vineyard just below the terrace a dirt track, leading off along the edge of the vines, turning at the end into a small wooded area, disappearing from sight. What is it about a track that makes one walk along it in one's mind, wonder what one would see? Grasshoppers, I thought suddenly, or a butterfly, a large bee on some thick clover beneath a vine-stock. And silence. There would be silence. That as soon as you listened to it would be full of busyness, the constant whispering and shuffling of things, the breathing that becomes almost a hum, a soft shrillness answering from within. Would the track reach the mountains, if I followed it? This dream, of all tracks merging, everything connecting, drawing you . . .

*

As the priest delivered the eulogy I was looking at the stones. The cracks in them, the spaces between, the broken places. Filled with crumbled mortar. Here and there droppings that Danaja's broom didn't catch. Of mice, not rats. Too small for rats. Evicted temporarily but watching from somewhere. Rafters, cracks in the walls. To come out and re-occupy when all was finished. This chapel not much used. Another year, two, before the next disturbance. Light filtering through dust motes. Tiredness in the priest's voice, or just a studied calm, as he went through the formulae, holding something at bay. That hugeness inside us, outside us.

*

She had fallen. I had been working at my desk and there'd been a commotion below, muted: I couldn't hear any sign of panic. A dragging of furniture, metal frame on tile, that can only have been her bed. Without the language I can't help much, think I am only in the way. And others were there in any case. And then, ten minutes later, Aldo, asking for Katia though he knew she wasn't here. And explained, although I only half-understood. Except that he needed to tell. I understood that. That she had fallen. Hurt herself. And went away, with a kind of shrug. His shrug. As much to the world as to me.

A few minutes later an ambulance arrived. I watched from the upstairs window as they brought her out. She looked unconscious, head back as if in mid-gasp, a wound on her cheek, another above her eye. Not much blood. Why do I think it thickens, in the elderly, almost reluctant to leave?

*

He had been there, Aldo, in the hospital, at her bedside. She'd complained of feeling sick, wanting to vomit, and he'd called for a nurse. By the time someone came she'd passed out and her eyes had rolled back. They had taken her away, and left him there waiting. Soon they returned and told him she had died. He told this to Katia that night, late, after I had gone to bed. They would not use the church for the funeral, nor the priest, not this one. No surprises there. They'd use the small chapel in the cemetery instead, and arrange for someone else to come. They'd have to spend the next day cleaning. The chapel stank of mice – or rats, who knew? Katia thought rats – and there were droppings everywhere. I offered to help, but no, she'd do it with Danaja. It was all arranged.

*

I don't remember when it was I saw the moth. On the light-fitting over the sink. There are moths here day and night during the summer, as there are anywhere when you leave the doors and windows open to catch the night air. Souls, people say. Psyche. This one of a bright green I've never seen on a moth before. Uniform, unvariegated, the colour of a grass-blade in late-summer sun. An after-image of day. But why? So that I would see it? Carry it into my sleep? As if it needed a ride somewhere, and I were psychopomp.

*

Katia is at loggerheads with the priest, a new appointee. Over an old transgression, on his part not hers. When they were at university together. A drunkard, and violent. She's had him banned from the house, by order of the bishop who's been inundated by calls to bring the previous priest back. His response to ban the previous priest from the parish entirely, so that the new one can get on with it. But now Nona is dead, and Katia's parents have bitten the bullet, gone to the bishop's house, caught him and his minions at breakfast. He'd have looked petty to refuse. A special dispensation. The previous priest allowed back, just this once.

*

Heavy rain the night before the funeral. Air clear in the morning, all the haze washed out. The far mountains outlined clear against the sky, mist like a white skin on the plain, peaks floating above it unanchored, cut adrift. I'd been worried that the grave had already been dug and would now be filled with water, but no, they must watch the weather. Came early in the morning and dug it then. Three men, who by the time the funeral had commenced had changed into suits. In the same small plot as her husband, dead forty-five years now. How would they do it? Dig until they find a trace of him and then place her on top? His coffin rotted now, surely. Gone. These things you don't think about until you need to. So many bodies in that small cemetery. And how will they manage with me? Not so hard I suppose. I will be ashes in a jar. Katia will hold me.

*

A thought crosses the mind. Or is it a vision, a glimpse? This of the moth – *as if I were with it* – in the garden somewhere, featherlight in the corners of darkness. Dreaming me, moving on.

*

A week after. The eighth-night Mass. Has she been waiting, for this final permission? Aldo is anxious that he not have to go alone, but the church is being painted; the first floor of the gallery next door is to be used instead. And Lucia, Katia's mother, is still on crutches after her operation and can't handle the stairs. He comes to ask Katia to go with him, knowing full well her fury with the church, and she too at first refuses – he has left it too late, the dinner is already on the table – but then unexpectedly relents. Leaves the meal half-eaten. She will be half an hour, no more.

I sit and watch the sunset. Half an hour, forty-five minutes, an hour. People are walking back from the Mass in first darkness. More people than I would have thought, but then Nona has been here a very long time. And then suddenly, from the courtyard,

Katia's voice calling, urgent. I go to the landing. She is holding something to her chest. A cat, she says, and it's dying, might be dead already, she can't tell. Bring water. Bring food. By the time I get down she has laid it on its right side on the floor of the boot-room. She rushes into the house to get a syringe, so that she can feed it the water drop by drop.

I watch it in the pool of yellow light, can see no movement. Long, thick hair, matted, gaunt, either very old or very ill. Both. It must weigh almost nothing but already the gravity has flattened it against the tiles. It. Him. Her. Such sad stillness. And then suddenly the right forepaw stretches, lunges almost, a spasm, and goes limp again. Within seconds Katia is back and tries to coax it to drink from the syringe, but the water simply runs out onto the floor. We place rags in the alcove at the side and she moves it there. There is no resistance in its body. It droops in her hands like something already far off. As we finish our dinner she tells me the story. That she'd seen the cat in the grass by the road, as she was walking to the Mass, sick, obviously dying, and straight afterwards had run back there, to find that it had moved to the other side. Robbie had called from his porch to say that it had been there for three days already, and the woman next door to him had been feeding it. She had checked next door, no one was there, so she had gathered it up and brought it home. When I express consternation that people have been walking past it for days and that no one has taken it to a vet, she tells me that I still don't know these people. For them it's just a cat. *It*, not *he*, not *she*.

*

It was later, just after ten, I think. I had been reading some dry philosophy, bored, skimming, looking for something. I suppose you could say my mind wandered, without in any way signalling that it was doing so. And there was a sudden tunnel, a *vision*. I was looking at the cat – although it was impossible, although I was at my desk and it was downstairs and across the courtyard, in the boot-room – as if through a portal, or port-*hole*, surrounded by darkness, in a pool of hot, rancid light. And had just realised what I was seeing – that it *was* the cat, so deep and so burdened with its dying – when the wave struck and whelmed over me and I was submerged in it, fighting for breath. Of anguish, a sadness beyond measure. And I was standing there, before Katia – there was nowhere else to go, the sobs breaking from me, despite all I could do to hold them.

When I slept at last it was to dream of a body discovered, a century after a shipwreck, frozen in Antarctic ice, and then of a bubble rising with unbearable slowness through a tar-like substance – a bubble that had been rising for millennia – at last reaching the surface, releasing its ancient, rotten air.

*

The mourners are filing by, grasping our hands as they pass. Condolences. With twenty minutes still to go before the priest arrives most of them are seated, in silence, thinking, waiting. A very pious man in a back row – Katia has pointed him out as the bishop's informer – takes out his beads and begins to say the rosary, and suddenly, as if a wave has swept over the room, the whole congregation of elderly women, elderly men, has joined him. Breaking from dry throats, scarcely more than a rasping at first, wind through dry grass, the prayer builds, pushing its way through voices almost too tired to stand, finding its passages, a bass drone slowly filling the space as water fills a jug, groaning up through the stones, an ancient poetry underneath, within, of grief and bewilderment, incomprehension, overlaid by the old rituals and recipes of containment, this chanting of the rosary, people burying their own dead again, any funeral a reawakening, reburying, re-grieving, mothers, fathers, daughters, brothers, friends, wives, husbands, again, in slow showers of earth, insubstantial, heavy as this shadow, out of the afternoon sunlight, her death mask almost beautiful in its rest, after the torment, waxen, pearl-grey, the fright and confusion become dignity, music moving through us in a kind of praise, making us instruments, wind, clay vessels, a kind of brooding bird, almost dove.

Frida Boyelski's Shiva

Abigail Ulman

Frida Boyelski had always wanted a daughter. Then she had a daughter and that daughter grew up into a young woman who said she was actually a young man.

'You mean to tell me, you're gay?' Frida asked.

'No,' Ruthie said. 'I'm telling you I'm trans. Did you read the book I gave you?'

'When do I have time to read books?' Frida asked. 'I have a gay daughter to deal with now.'

'Just read it. It'll help you understand.' Ruthie was standing next to the kitchen door, a backpack strap slung over her shoulder.

'Where are you off to?'

'Leah's place. I'm gonna stay there for a bit, just while it's school holidays.'

'Does Leah know about this?'

'Yeah. She's been really supportive.'

'What about Jack? Does he know? How does he feel about his girlfriend – feeling this way?'

'He knows. He's known for ages. He's happy for me.'

'Is he doing this trans thing now, too?'

'It's not something I'm doing. It's something I am.'

'Is Jack that thing, too?'

'No. Jack's cis.'

'What—?'

'Mum,' Ruthie cut in. 'I have to go.'

'Please don't go yet.' Frida had the strange feeling that if she let Ruthie leave now, she might not be exactly the same person when she came back. She followed her daughter out to the garage and watched her get on her bike. 'Why do you want to be someone you're not? What's wrong with who you are?'

'This *is* who I am,' Ruthie said, her feet already on both pedals. 'Just please read the book.'

Frida Boyelski didn't want to read the book. She knew that when she started reading the book, Ruthie would be a girl – *her* little girl – and by the time she'd read through the whole thing, turning the pages through chapters like 'The Politics of Renaming' and 'Mastectomy and What It Means', her daughter would have slowly and irrevocably turned into a person she didn't know, had never known; certainly she would no longer be the person Frida had given birth to sixteen years ago.

Frida hadn't immigrated to Australia and learnt English at the age of twenty-six so she could read a book like that. She had moved here so she could meet a man, have a daughter, and give that daughter the opportunities she herself never had. Frida left the book where it sat on the coffee table, and she called in sick to the nursing home for the first time in the twelve years she'd been working there.

'Are you okay?' asked Zelda at the front desk.

'My daughter's – leaving,' Frida said. 'She's gone. Things will never be the same.'

'It's Margaret's birthday,' Zelda said. 'She left a piece of pear strudel in your pigeonhole. What should I do with it?'

'You can eat it,' Frida told her.

'No, no, I'm gluten free this whole month,' Zelda said. 'I'll leave it in the fridge for you. It's from Chaim's Bakery. They put so much glaze on it, it'll probably outlive us all.'

Frida hung up and made another phone call, this time to the *Jewish Observer*. 'Hello,' she told the girl who answered, 'I'd like to put a message in the Bereavements section. Can you help?'

When that week's edition of the *Jewish Observer* landed on

doorsteps all over Frida's neighbourhood, it contained Frida's message. *This is to announce that Ruthie Boyelski, daughter of Frida Boyelski, will soon no longer be a girl. Frida will be sitting shiva for her daughter at her home address for the next week. Visitors welcome.*

Frida Boyelski remembered watching her father sit shiva decades ago, when his own father had died. She covered all the mirrors in the house with bedsheets as he had done, because vanity was supposed to be eschewed in periods of mourning. Frida knew you were supposed to create a small tear in a piece of clothing to communicate your suffering. She cut a gash into the collar of her work shirt. Her father had spent the seven days of shiva sitting on a low chair. Frida considered trying to bend her achy knees onto a cushion and sit there, cross-legged, the way Ruthie sat when she and Leah did yoga in her bedroom sometimes. But then she remembered Ruthie's old playset, with its tiny chair and matching play-table, on which countless teddy bear tea parties had been enacted when Ruthie was a child.

Frida found the furniture under a tarp in the garage. Ruthie's old dollhouse was there, too, its tiny windows laced over with spiderwebs, and there was Ruthie's old bike, with its pale pink frame and the hot pink streamers sprouting from the handlebars. Frida pictured Ruthie's seven-year-old face scrunched up at the sight of the bike on her birthday morning. 'I told you,' she'd cried to Frida, 'I want a BMX racer.' Frida had other memories, too – a frown over a fairy princess birthday cake, screaming fights about pinafores purchased for Passover, and a thirteen-year-old Ruthie perched on a stool in front of the bathroom mirror, scissors in one hand, a loose lock of hair in the other. Frida took the small chair, pulled the tarp back over the other objects, and went inside.

On the first day of Frida Boyelski's shiva, the rabbi came. He gave Frida a butter cake that his wife had baked, and he read a prayer from a small book. Then he asked Frida how she was feeling.

'I've been better, Rabbi,' Frida said. 'I always wanted a daughter. And then I got one.'

'The time you spent with your daughter isn't gone,' the rabbi said. 'You'll have that forever.'

'But it was too short, Rabbi,' Frida said. 'I thought I would have a daughter till I died. I thought she would get pregnant, and give me grandchildren.'

'Life isn't what we expect it to be,' the rabbi said, half a piece of his wife's butter cake in his mouth. 'But it's a blessing in all its forms, nonetheless. Most bereaved parents have lost their children to illness or an accident. At least your child is still with us.'

'Do you have children, Rabbi?' Frida asked him.

The rabbi looked surprised by the question. 'Yes,' he said, 'I have three daughters and two sons.'

'Uh huh,' Frida said. 'Enjoy your children, Rabbi. And thanks for coming.'

The rabbi started to say something else, but Frida fixed him with what Ruthie liked to call her *Don't-even stare*, so he wiped his mouth, muttered the customary wish for Frida to live a long life, and saw himself out, a crumpled paper napkin in his hand.

On the second day of Frida Boyelski's shiva, Cousin Shulie came to see her. 'Ooh,' Shulie said, 'where did you get that side table? Are those new pants? Do you want to see photos of my Danielle? She's captain of the trampolining team and she played one of the leads in the school's production of "Beauty and The Beauty". They decided the beast character was too negative for the kids. Last year poor Robbie Simons was traumatised because they cast him as a Nazi in *The Sound of Music*.'

Cousin Shulie perched on the edge of the coffee table, which, given the size of her behind and the rickety legs of the table, seemed to Frida an ill-considered seating choice. Before Frida could say so, though, Shulie started to weep.

'Why are you crying?' Frida asked her. 'You still have *your* daughter.'

'I'm crying because it's my fault,' Cousin Shulie said. 'We've always been competitive, the two of us, since we were little. And

I was jealous of you and Ruthie. You were so close. She looked up to you. My Danielle has been rolling her eyes at me since the moment she first opened them. I was so envious, I used to wish horrible things on you. I wished you unhappy, I wished you to lose everything you have, I wished Ruthie to leave you. And now it's happening. It's my fault. All my fault!'

'Shulie.' Frida rolled her eyes. 'Get up, go home. It's not your fault.'

'I prayed to God,' Shulie said. 'More than once.'

'You think God can bear listening to you and your screeching?' Frida asked. 'God blocks your voice out just like the rest of us do. Go home to your family. Take some butter cake for Danielle.'

On the third day of Frida Boyelski's shiva, Danielle came. She sat in Ruthie's favourite armchair and bowed her head. 'It's my fault,' she murmured, so quietly Frida could only just hear her. 'When we were kids, Ruthie and I spent every weekend out in my cubby house. We'd play "Mothers and Fathers" and I always insisted that I get to be the mother. I'm a year older and I bullied her into it. Ruthie had no choice.'

'That's not why this happened,' Frida said. 'I don't know much, but that much I know.'

Danielle squinted at her through the jagged ends of her fringe. 'Every weekend, Auntie,' she said. 'For years on end, I made her play the boy.'

'Have you ever known Ruthie to do anything she didn't want to do?' Frida asked. 'She probably wanted to play the boy. That's why she let you be the girl. Maybe she was secretly getting her way all along.'

On the fourth day of Frida Boyelski's shiva, the women from work came: Margaret, Shanie, Johanna and Zelda. They brought crackers, smoked salmon, tzatziki and capers, and told Frida all the gossip she'd been missing at the nursing home while they ate the crackers, smoked salmon, tzatziki and capers.

Johanna stayed on after the others left. She was originally from South Africa and had spent her twenties living in Bordeaux, and this made her famously open-minded amongst the staff at work.

'What's the big deal?' she asked, lighting a menthol cigarette. 'Boy, girl, *il est tout de même.*'

'What would you do if your daughter told you she was no longer a girl?' asked Frida.

'I don't have a daughter.' Johanna blew a small smoke ring through another, larger smoke ring. That was true. Johanna famously had a chihuahua called Giuseppe that she loved dearly, and a husband called Olivier who she was crazy about, *après tout ce temps.*

'What if Olivier came home suddenly and said he was a woman?' Frida asked her.

'Honestly?' said Johanna, tapping ash onto the edge of one of Frida's good plates. 'I'd be shocked. And uncomfortable and angry and miserable. But I think eventually I'd see it as just the next big adventure of my life.'

'It's the next big adventure of my life.' Frida tried that out on her ex-husband when he came to see her on the fifth day of shiva. But she was avoiding eye contact as she said it, and she knew Ivan didn't buy it for a second. He was sitting on the couch, cracking his knuckles and staring at the artwork on the wall as though he'd never seen it before, as though he hadn't helped pick it out himself.

'This is your fault, you know?' he told Frida. 'You should have started seeing other people after the divorce. Instead, Ruthie was forced to become the man of the house.'

'Bullshit,' Frida said. 'You went away and had your new wife and your new kids, and you didn't visit. How could she feel like Daddy's special little girl if Daddy wasn't around?'

'Maybe it's because you let her stay up late on school nights watching *Grey's Anatomy* when she was too young for it,' Ivan said. 'Kids need structure.'

'Maybe it's that time you smacked her bottom when she swore at you,' Frida spat back. 'You're the one who taught her to swear in the first place. What did you expect?'

'I'm not the one who let her eat all that fast food. You know that stuff is full of hormones.'

The argument went on and on, circling back through all the parental wrongdoings that had occurred during Ruthie's short but apparently eventful life, until finally they returned to the very moment of Ruthie's conception.

'It's because we did it sideways,' Frida said. 'What kind of man insists on doing it sideways on his honeymoon?'

'It's because you insisted on listening to that terrible music every time we made love.'

'Bing Crosby,' Frida said, 'is a genius.'

'Bing Crosby, Bing Crosby.' Ivan waved his hands in the air. 'Why didn't you marry Bing Crosby if he's such a genius?'

'I wish I had,' Frida said. 'Bing Crosby wouldn't want to do it sideways on his honeymoon.'

'I had to do it sideways!' Ivan leaned forward and shouted. 'What other way could we do it without making a racket or rolling right off that tiny bed they gave us?'

Frida Boyelski fell silent. She stared over at Ivan Boyelski, and he stared right back. The daylight was waning behind the living room curtains, and they sat together, both of them thinking back to their honeymoon: the narrow bed, the moon spying on them through the skylight, the last few moments that their new family had been two instead of three. 'We were so young,' Frida said.

'Yes,' Ivan said, 'and now it's Ruthie's time to be young.'

'Go home to your family, Ivanchik,' Frida told him, 'and take some butter cake for the children.'

On the sixth day, it rained, and no one visited Frida. She sat on the low chair all morning, but the cold was making her fingers stiff, and her achy knees ached even more than usual. She got up and turned on the heater. She made herself a cup of tea and chewed down the last piece of butter cake. She went around the house, turning lights on and turning them off again, feeling like she was looking for something or like there was something she was supposed to do, even though this was her shiva week, and she had nothing else planned.

She ended up at Ruthie's bedroom door. She pushed it open and stood there, looking at the unmade bed and the posters taped to the wall, saying *Occupy Glenhuntly! 4pm Sunday* and *This is What a Feminist Looks Like.* Rain trickled down the window and rain shadows trickled down the walls, making it seem like the whole world was crying tears onto Ruthie's little-girl desk, the little-girl bed, and the little-girl wallpaper covered in flowers that Frida had picked out years ago, because it had seemed like a good idea at the time – like immigrating, like getting married, like staying in this house for years after all of that was over.

On the seventh and final day of Frida Boyelski's shiva, a boy came to visit. He was a teen boy, with short, feathery hair, and holes in his ears where earrings used to be; he was wearing jeans and a baggy blue jumper and he had a backpack slung over his shoulder. He came and sat cross-legged in front of Frida on the living room floor. If he noticed the book sitting unopened and unread on the coffee table, he didn't mention it.

'Hello,' Frida said.

'Hello,' said the boy.

'What's your name?' Frida asked him.

'Rafael,' the boy said. 'Rafael Boyelski.'

'Can I call you Ruthie?' Frida asked the boy.

'No,' the boy said.

'Are you still going to call me Mum?' Frida asked him.

'Yes,' the boy said. 'Unless you want to be called something else?'

'No,' Frida said. 'Mum is good.'

'Okay,' the boy said, 'Mum.'

'Can I still brush your hair sometimes?' Frida asked him.

'No,' he said.

'Will we still go shopping together?'

'Maybe. But I'm not wearing a dress ever again.'

'Even on Passover?'

'Especially on Passover.'

'And, if you don't mind my asking, do you still have all your – parts?'

'Yes,' the boy said. 'For now. But soon I want to start taking testosterone.'

'And, if you don't mind my asking, will you tell me when you do that? I won't try to stop you. I'd just like to know.'

'Okay,' the boy said, 'I will.'

Frida Boyelski had always wanted a daughter. Then she had a daughter and that daughter turned out to be a son. And now it was six o'clock and her son was standing up and saying he was hungry, and when Frida suggested that they make dinner and eat together, he yawned and stretched and said, 'Okay, sounds good.'

Frida marvelled at the sight of him, Rafael – his skinny legs and sturdy posture, the easy way he exposed his lower belly as he stretched his body upwards, the grace with which he leaned over and reached his hand towards her. His fingers were slender and strong, and he gripped Frida's arm and held on tight as she struggled, and then managed, to rise to her feet.

Publication Details

James Bradley's 'Martian Triptych' appeared in *Dreaming in the Dark*, edited by Jack Dann (Subterranean Press, 2016).

David Brooks' 'Grief' appeared in his collection *Napoleon's Roads* (UQP, 2016).

Brian Castro's 'Love, Actually' appeared in *Review of Australian Fiction* (vol. 18, no. 5, June 2016).

Gregory Day's 'Moth Sea Fog' appeared in *The Big Issue* (August 2016).

Tegan Bennett Daylight's 'Animals of the Savannah' appeared in *The Big Issue* (August 2016).

Jennifer Down's 'Alpine Road' appeared in *Overland* (no. 221, Summer 2015).

Elizabeth Harrower's 'A Few Days in the Country' appeared in her collection *A Few Days in the Country & Other Stories* (Text Publishing, 2016).

Julie Koh's 'The Fat Girl in History' appeared in *The Sleepers Almanac X* (Sleepers Publishing, 2015), and in her collection *Portable Curiosities* (UQP, 2016).

Jack Latimore's 'Where Waters Meet' appeared in *Overland* (no. 222, Autumn 2016).

Nasrin Mahoutchi's 'Standing in the Cold' appeared in *Southerly* (vol. 75, no. 2, 2015).

Fiona McFarlane's 'Good News for Modern Man' appeared in her collection *The High Places* (Penguin Random House, 2016). Copyright © Fiona McFarlane 2015. Reproduced by permission of Penguin Random House Australia Pty Ltd.

Michael McGirr's 'A Review of *Over There* by Stanislaus Nguyen' appeared in *Meanjin* (Winter 2016).

Elizabeth Tan's 'Coca-Cola Birds Sing Sweetest in the Morning' appeared in *Overland* (no. 222, Autumn 2016).

Abigail Ulman's 'Frida Boyelski's Shiva' appeared in *Frankie Magazine* (August 2015).

Ellen van Neerven's 'Blueglass' appeared in *The Canary Press* (Issue 8, 2015).

Michelle Wright's 'Blur' appeared in her collection *Fine* (Allen & Unwin, 2016).

Notes on Contributors

The Editor

The *Australian* newspaper has described **Charlotte Wood** as 'one of our most original and provocative writers'. She is the author of five novels and two books of non-fiction. Her latest novel, *The Natural Way of Things*, won the 2016 Stella Prize and the 2016 Indie Book of the Year, and was shortlisted for the Queensland Literary Award and the Miles Franklin, among others. It is also being released in the UK, North America and throughout Europe. Her latest book is *The Writer's Room*, a selection of long-form interviews with established Australian authors.

The Authors

Georgia Blain has published novels for adults and young adults, essays, short stories and a memoir. Her first novel was the bestselling *Closed for Winter*, which was made into a feature film. She has been shortlisted for numerous awards, including the NSW and SA Premiers' Literary Awards, and the Nita B. Kibble Award for her memoir *Births Deaths Marriages*. Georgia's most recent works include *The Secret Lives of Men*, *Too Close to Home* and the YA novel *Darkwater*. In 2016, in addition to *Between a Wolf and a Dog*, Georgia also published the YA novel *Special* (Penguin Random House Australia). She lives in Sydney, where she works full-time as a writer.

James Bradley is a novelist and critic. His books include the novels *Wrack, The Deep Field, The Resurrectionist* and most recently *Clade*, which was nominated for the NSW Premier's Award for Fiction, the Victorian Premier's Award for Fiction, the WA Premier's Book Award for Fiction, the ALS Gold Medal and the Aurealis Award for Best Science Fiction Novel.

David Brooks, co-editor of *Southerly* and Honorary Associate Professor at the University of Sydney, is the 2015/16 Australia Council Fellow in fiction. His recent publications include *Napoleon's Roads* (stories; UQP, 2016), *Open House* (poetry; UQP, 2015) and *Derrida's Breakfast* (essays on poetry, philosophy and the animal; Brandl & Schlesinger, 2016).

Brian Castro is the author of ten novels, including the multi-award-winning *Double-Wolf* and *Shanghai Dancing*. He has also published a volume of essays. His latest novel, *Blindness & Rage*, will be published by Giramondo in 2017. He is chair of Creative Writing at the University of Adelaide.

Gregory Day is a writer, musician, poet and literary critic. His work has won the prestigious Australian Literature Society Gold Medal and the Elizabeth Jolley Short Story Prize. His most recent novel is *Archipelago of Souls* (Picador, 2015). He lives on the south-west coast of Victoria, Australia.

Tegan Bennett Daylight is a fiction writer, teacher and critic. She is the author of three novels and a collection of short stories, *Six Bedrooms*, which was shortlisted for the 2016 Stella Award, the ALS Gold Medal and the Steele Rudd Award. She lives in the Blue Mountains with her husband and two children.

Jennifer Down is a writer, editor and translator. Her debut novel, *Our Magic Hour*, is available through Text Publishing. *Convalescence*, a short story collection, will be published in 2017.

Elizabeth Harrower is the author of the novels *Down in the City, The Long Prospect, The Catherine Wheel* and *The Watch Tower* – all of which have been republished as Text Classics – and *In Certain*

Circles, which was published in 2014 and shortlisted for the Prime Minister's Literary Award for Fiction in 2015. Elizabeth lives in Sydney.

Julie Koh (許瑩玲) has written two short story collections: *Capital Misfits* and *Portable Curiosities.* Stories from both have appeared in *The Best Australian Stories* (2014 and 2015) and *Best Australian Comedy Writing 2016. Portable Curiosities* has been shortlisted for this year's Readings Prize for New Australian Fiction and the QLA Steele Rudd Award. Julie is the editor of *BooksActually's Gold Standard 2016.* 'The Fat Girl in History' is dedicated to Gary Lo.

Jack Latimore is an Indigenous writer residing in Melbourne. His fiction has previously appeared in *Overland* and the anthology *GeekMook.*

Nasrin Mahoutchi writes in Farsi (Persian) and English. Her short stories have been published in anthologies such as *HEAT, Southerly* and *Meanjin.* Some of her works have been broadcast on ABC Radio, Radio Eye and Persian Radio. She has received funding from the Australia Council for the Arts. She has finished her DCA at the University of Western Sydney.

Fiona McFarlane is the author of *The Night Guest,* which was shortlisted for the Miles Franklin Literary Award and the Guardian First Book Award, and *The High Places*, a collection of stories. Her stories have been published in the *New Yorker, Southerly* and *Zoetrope: All-Story.* She lives in Sydney.

Michael McGirr is the author of *Things You Get for Free* and *The Lost Art of Sleep.* His book *Bypass: The Story of a Road* has been a popular Year 12 English text in Victoria. He has reviewed over 900 books for the *Age* and the *Sydney Morning Herald.* He is currently dean of faith at St Kevin's College in Melbourne.

Paddy O'Reilly is the author of three novels and two collections of short stories. Her novels and stories have won and been shortlisted for a number of major awards, and been published, anthologised and broadcast in Australia, the UK and the USA.

Kate Ryan writes fiction and non-fiction. Her work has appeared in publications including *New Australian Writing 2, The Sleepers Almanac, Kill Your Darlings, Griffith Review* and *TEXT.* Her children's picture books have been published by Penguin and Lothian. Kate's story 'Sunday Nights' was shortlisted for the 2015 Josephine Ulrick Award. She has a PhD in Creative Writing from La Trobe University (2013), and in 2015 her essay 'Psychotherapy for Normal People' won the Writers' Prize in the Melbourne Prize for Literature. She is working on an adult novel.

Trevor Shearston has published a story collection and seven novels. The last, *Game*, was longlisted for the Miles Franklin, and shortlisted for the Christina Stead and Colin Roderick awards. He lives in Katoomba.

Elizabeth Tan is a Perth writer who recently completed her Creative Writing PhD at Curtin University. 'Coca-Cola Birds Sing Sweetest in the Morning' is an excerpt from Elizabeth's debut novel, *Rubik*, which will be published by Brio in 2017.

Abigail Ulman is a writer from Melbourne. She is the recipient of a Wallace Stegner Fellowship from Stanford University and was named a 2016 Best Young Novelist by the *Sydney Morning Herald.* Her debut story collection, *Hot Little Hands*, was recently published in Australia and abroad.

Ellen van Neerven is an award-winning writer of Mununjali and Dutch heritage. Her first book, *Heat and Light* (UQP, 2014), was the recipient of the David Unaipon Award, the Dobbie Literary Award, and the NSW Premier's Literary Award for Indigenous Writing. *Comfort Food* (UPQ, 2016) is her latest release.

Michelle Wright's short stories have won awards including the *Age*, Alan Marshall and Grace Marion Wilson. Her short story collection, *Fine*, was shortlisted for the Victorian Premier's Award for an Unpublished Manuscript in 2015 and published by Allen & Unwin in 2016. Her first novel will be published in 2017.